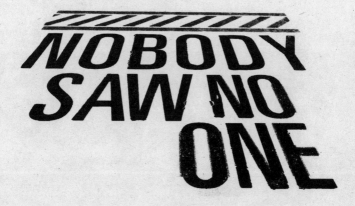

Other books by this author:

Blood Donors

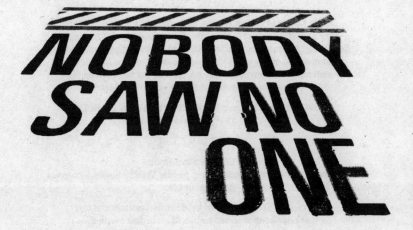

STEVE TASANE

**WALKER
BOOKS**

First published in Great Britain 2015 by Walker Books Ltd
87 Vauxhall Walk, London SE11 5HJ

2 4 6 8 10 9 7 5 3 1

Text © 2015 Steve Tasane
Cover image of male figure reflected in puddle © 2015 Karina Simonsen /
Arcangel Images

This book has been typeset in Cambria

Printed and bound in Great Britain by Clays Ltd, St Ives plc

British Library Cataloguing in Publication Data:
a catalogue record for this book is
available from the British Library

ISBN 978-1-4063-5076-0

www.walker.co.uk

For Rosie, my beautiful muse,
soul sister and fiercest critic

1. HOT DOGS

This tale ain't about me, Citizen Digit, even though I'm a walking story myself. Why d'you think everybody calls the Digit a master storyteller? Because I'm the Complete Works, is why.

Listen up to the Mystery of Alfi Spar – a saga of lost identity, crime and cold bloody murder, thrilling to the earhole.

I'm stage centre of this tale, naturellemente, so – twist my arm and break my legs – I'll begin at the beginning, with me assistificating *ComputerWorld* Oxford Street with their security measures.

In other's words, Citizen Digit is out on a shoplifting expedition.

What's the best bit about liberating goodies from shops, you may ask? It's the joy of removing the impossible. Like the Magician and his Vanishing Ladyfriend, Citizen Digit can make things disappear at the drop of a hat.

Imagine something so big you can hardly lift it, never mind shoplift it; something so masstastic you wouldn't be able to get it out the shop without an in-store Sherlock holding the door open for you like you was the Queen of Windsor herself huffing and pufficating with a – yes indeedly – a freshly shoplifted flat-screen TV.

Picture it: said flat-screen TV covering all of Citizen Digit's handsomeness, up higher than his head, all screen, zero face. One pair of legs beneath, eight sticky fingers clutching the edges. I'm a proper forklift.

Not possible I hear your mumblifications. *No one can steal a TV without getting spotted.*

Ah, but the trick ain't not getting spotted. The trick is not getting *noticed*. Skulk around looking all shifty-kneed and the Sherlocks will be onto you straight away. Pick up the TV and walk straight out with it, nobody'll bat an eyeball.

The best bit ain't even when In-store Sherlock opens the door for you on account of seeing you in such struggles, and you say *Thanks very muchly.*

What the Digit loves most comes two seconds later, when the door swings shut behind you. The first steps along the pavement. The whole world is the empty space behind your back. That heart-stomping moment with no hand grabbing your shoulder. No *Oi!* from behind. Just one big black hole that could swallow you up.

Two more steps. Three steps.

Four steps, and the Digit has gone supernova.

If it wasn't for the fact that getting caught Sucks with a capital *S*, I'd take a big bow for a mid-pavement ovation. The whole of Oxford Street ought to rattle their jewels, point their phones and post the Master Thief's gorgeous fizzog all over YouTube. But in this instance, that would defeat the purpose. Gotta make do with blending in, walking away with a brand-new flat screen. Surfing the heart-stomp. Wotta buzz.

On this particular incidence, the nanosecond our story begins, Citizen Digit ought to be lifting lightweight. iPads is what the Digit prefers. iPads is just as valuable as flat screen TVs, only your arms don't ache.

But Virus ordered a flat screen at the last momento. Virus is what you'd call my *Line Manager*. He's immediately superior. Says we need a flat screen or two to pull the punters in. "It's visually big, my poppet," says old Virus. "Little iPads don't catch the punter's eye. We'll wire it up, stand it in the middle of the display. It'll look magnificent."

Yeah, but the Digit's breaking into sweatiness from the labour. That ain't cool. The Sherlocks can sniff sweat. *Notice* you.

Still, no such thing as a perfect crime. And I'm outta there before they can sniff twice. Thank you *ComputerWorld*, I do believe my duty is done.

This is when I run into Alfi Spar.

I acquainted Alfi when I was in Care. Tenderness House Secure Unit they called it, like it was a hotel for nervous peeps with sensitive skin. Alfi was one of the WhyPees.

For your inf: *WhyPees = YPs = Young People = kids.* Kids like me and Alfi who aren't able to be cared for by normal Groans – that's grown-ups – because of our Behavioural Difficulties.

Alfi Spar had worse Difficulties than any other WhyPee in the world. Alfi is a Born Loser. He's a squealer also, and a whingebag. How he actually became a best friend of sorts is a mystery because Citizen Digit is particularly particular about his bruvs.

I'm too soft, that's my trouble. Citizen Softness, that's me.

I'm toughing myself up as from now. Ain't even going to mention Tenderness House no more. I'll tell you why: the point-dot of a second the truth comes out of the Citizen's mouth, the Authoritariacs label it a lie. It's a CryWolf22 situation, ain't it? Citizen Digit is a proven thief and rascallion. Therefore if he speechifies anything, it is automatically a lie. So I ain't going to say nothing more about it. The world is going to have to find out the truth about Tenderness House Secure Unit by some other means. Forget I mentioned it.

Alfi's the one obsessed with making mentions of things. Squealer-Boy's issue is that he makes Accusations with Malice. It's a good job nobody's ever given him a whistle 'cos he'd never stop blowing it. Any time he thinks the Groans have broken any rules, he makes an official complaint to the SS – that's Social Services, yeah? Always harpifying about lousy carers he's had over the years. He's like CryWolf222222. You wouldn't believe the kind of accusations he's made:

Theft, corruption, drug-dealing.

And other stuff we daren't accuse them of. Stuff that's true but seems too untrue to be true, and therefore cannot be happening.

So you make your exit, don't you? Shift yourself to a different reality. That way it ain't happening no more.

Looks like Alfi Spar finally wised up too.

Which is how come prodigal shoplifter Citizen Digit is achieving the unheard impossible of lifting a flatscreen TV in barefaced daylight, and Alfi's sitting there on his flattened cardboard box, *Homeless & Hungry* sign, hat on the pavement with 20p in it, a busker with nothing to busk. Everybody can see him, all shiverish on that soggy cardboard, scratched and bruised and sorry for himself. It's just that nobody cares, is all.

Alfi Spar was always sussless. Here he is, straight outta nowheresville, messing up my tidy life. *Again.*

Boomf!

The flat screen shatters into a trillion pieces as it hits the pavement. Seven years' bad luck.

Now everybody's staring at us.

"Oi! You!" In-store Sherlock comes bouncing out the shop, all purple-face and sweat-stink.

"Leg it!" I'm instructing Alfi, who's demolishing precious seconds gathering up his begging hat that ain't even worth the 20p nesting in it.

"Byron?" He blurts out my name. My Not-Name. Always a blabber, Alfi Spar.

"Run, Squealer-Boy!" I'm tugging him up by his chicken-wing arm.

I hate getting spotted. It's utterly ruinatious.

On the other hand, I *love* leading the Sherlocks a merry dance.

So I tighten my grip on Alfi Spar's wishbone and shuffle my tush to the Oxford Street Boogie. Triple-time, for your inf. *Beep beep* pedestrianistas, here we come!

I'm frozen on this pavement, even on top of a flattened box and wrapped in this blanket I found. I stink too. Honking. Got to get a dog, to snuggle up to, keep me warm.

In an hour and a half all I've had is 20p in me hat. Can't no one read? Homeless & Hungry. *Can't no one see us? I'm getting nasty looks, so I know they can. But I've been trod on enough times. No sorries. Everyone rushing to the next shop. I should be shopping. I should have an iPad. I should have a dog. A hot dog.*

It's me first time in this city.

The only other city I been to is Bradford, the nearest big place to the village where I lived six months wi' me foster family, the Barrowcloughs. I thought Bradford were big, big as you could get. But London is a hundred Bradfords all crammed up. It's no surprise I'm starved. No one eats in London. London eats you.

What's that make me, then?

A crumb.

Scran. I've had none since yesterday – a hot dog that turned me stomach. I had to do an emergency poo in some bushes in a park. A bloke in uniform spotted us, chased us off. You're never invisible when you're trying to poo.

Could anyone do a poo and stay invisible?

Yeah. Byron could do a poo in the middle of Oxford Street and make it so no one 'ud see.

Byron were one of the Tenderness YPs. A master-thief. A bad 'un. A magician. He could make things disappear with a click of his fingers. But Tenderness House en't Hogwarts. It "caters for the well-being and emotional development of young people from disadvantaged backgrounds".

Only a muppet 'ud cop that.

Tenderness crams up all the most criminal kids from everywhere, lads and lasses, so they can all teach each other their tricks – lock-picking, car-jacking, bag-snatching, you name it. If you ever need a grade-A tutor to run a workshop on credit card scams, just visit Tenderness House.

Course, I en't no crim. Not Alfi Spar. It in't nicking, picking things outta bins. People've had enough to eat, is all.

I think I stink. **Pooh!** *Yeah, I defo stink. I had to scarper before wiping, din't I, when I were squatting in the bushes. Folk look round – what's that pong? Looking for dog poo on their shoes. But it en't dog poo. It's me, Alfi Spar, homeless and hungry on the streets of London.*

The day I arrived, a lorry driver dropped us off. He had

ham sarnies. He must o' known I were starving, 'cos I were slobbering like a dog. He wanted us to move away from me window seat, sit in the middle seat, next to him, begging for scraps.

Four hours I'd stood on that hard shoulder, trying to thumb a lift. Loads o' cars beeped at us or had passengers staring out the window, laughing at us freezing in the road. Then Mr Trucker saw us and stopped, helped us up into his cab. He kept swivelling his eyes off the road and patting me leg.

"How old are yer?" he said.

"Sixteen," I lied.

I'm fourteen really, but Byron taught us that. "Whatever age you're at," he'd say, "always say sixteen. Even when you're nineteen. Sixteen is the appropriated age. 'Specially when you're fourteen. Stay wise, yeah?"

Byron's a year older than us, but you'd think he were grown-up, the way he goes on.

I reached London and scrounged half a sarnie, wi' the trucker patting me knee any excuse he had, even though I were proper skanking. Everyone always goes on about me nice smile. It's me fortune, they reckon. Half a sarnie, leastways.

I were beginning to get freaked out, wondered whether I'd have to jump out. This weren't exactly the point of fleeing from Tenderness, were it?

What were Byron's fabulous advice back then?

Smack 'em in the goolies and run.

That's more or less what he did, Byron, in't it?

Me an' all. I followed his example.

It were a relief when the truck hit Central London.

Relief for about thirty seconds, that is. Central London, with a million people trampling, crushing, pushing and tutting, swallowing you up.

Just as mad as everybody made out it is.

I found some card and borrowed a pen to make a sign, cupped me hands, raised me eyes. Looked for a friendly face, but all I saw was legs. Hours of them.

So I hung out by bins. If you pull the grub out quick enough, it's hardly touched the rotten stuff at the bottom. It's winter too, so stuff won't go off soon as it's dumped. You could call it dining out.

Pizza slices. Bags o' chips. Noodles. All sorts of scraps. I did half an afternoon round one bin. It really in't nicking. But a copper give us dirty looks, started strolling over, so I were out of there.

If they catch us, they'll send us back. And if I end up back at Tenderness, I'm a dead lad. Governor Newton'll get his hands on us.

Call me Norman *he used to say. So t'other kids used to call him Call-Me Norman. But not to his face.*

Never mess with Norman. Never.

I'm sticking wi' begging. Begging's all right, even if no one gives you owt. It makes you … not exactly invisible – just not worth bothering with.

I will eat. I will. I'll get another hot dog, a fresh 'un.

I'm going to get a proper dog too, with thick fur like a woolly blanket and hot doggie breath like the hand-driers in public loos. A hot tongue, to lick me face clean.

I'm going to get a little hairy terrier, like the dog in The Wizard of Oz. I'll fight the monkeys. Kill the witches. I'm going to— "Byron?"

He clatters over the top of us. Summat massive shatters all over the pavement and I duck me head under me arms. A flat-screen TV? Really? Two hundred miles from Tenderness House and the most insane of all the YPs bumps into us on Oxford Street, with a security bloke right after him, shaking his fist. Just great.

He starts pulling us up.

Should I go with him?

No. Yes.

Yes, I should. No, don't.

The security guy pulls us an' all. They grab an arm each. I'm torn. How come I always get seen by people I don't want seeing us?

Byron were the only mate I had at Tenderness. At least, when he weren't looking out for Number One.

I twist me wrist free of the security guy's sweaty grip, and before me brain knows it, me legs are running again, alongside me so-called friend.

Byron catches me eye as we run, winks at us.

I wish he wun't do that. Whenever he does that winking business, it means a bad moment is going to take a sharp turn for the worse.

2. LEG IT

Back in my pre-Digit days, Byron was always Genius Number One at Chase-Me. Me and my sisters, Tricia and Dee, playing all afternoon long, round the car park behind Sainsbury's. Sun beating on the tarmac. Tacky heat, drippy summer smell. Hiding under parked cars. Breathing petrol fumes. Blissfulness.

So Sweatpant Sherlock's got no chance keeping the pace with Citizen Digit. I can zig and zag round his shiny boots till I'm seventy-nine years old. They'll call me Zimmer-Frame Bolt.

But the trouble with running down the muddle of Oxford Street is every Sherlock in the vicinity is pulling out his beating-stick and handycuffs and yelling descriptives in his phoney to all the other Sherlocks. Next thing, every Sherlock around is carrying the Citizen's description and it's not tolerable.

I refuse to be ID'd.

In actuality, I orchestrate the perfect plan. Each day, the Digit decks himself out in finest high-street threads. One day, I'll be H&M'd up, the next, American

Apparelled. Day after, Burtoned to the max. Always changing the look; always keeping it smart. Citizen Digit travels incogneatly – unlike them foolish kids in hoodies, thinking they can pull the polyester over their eyes so nobody's going to see their faces. What happens instead is every hoodligan in the vicinity gets snapped on CCTV, the camera zooms in, not on their pimples, but their feet, their *trainer* types. Identifies them by logo. They're lurching round with their bottoms hanging out their low-strung strides, so the Sherlocks can match the trainer type to the colour of their UnderKleins. Not only do they get ID'd but when they try and run for it their strides fall round their ankles and they trip up over their undone laces. Losers.

But the Good Citizen? See me on CCTV any time of the day, but don't notice me. I'm dressed in my Marks & Sparks best, from my sensible shirt to my goody-two-shoes.

All my threads liberated fresh from the shop floor, of course.

And on this brisk and sunny winter morn, as we flashdance down Oxford Street, how are me and the Squealer kitted up? Citizen Didge: smartness and casuality; Squealer-Boy: crimful and grot-hoodied.

'Cept now he can't see where he's blundering on account of his hoodie blocking out all his view. Alfi Spar's feet are chicken-dancing in aimless panic. The Sherlocks are snatching and grabbing behind us. I ain't even got the flat screen that kicked off this tedious Chase-Me business. When I get back to Operations empty-handed Virus will give me proper verbal meanies. He hates it when his boys don't bring home a decent day's liberatings.

On the other hand, I'll be bringing him Alfi Spar. A New Boy's gotta be worth six flat screens at least. Virus is going to adore Alfi Spar, because Alfi's got the face of an angel. A WhyPee with a VDU as innocent-looking as Alfi Spar's is worth many a penny to an entrepreneur like old Virus.

All the Digit's got to do is make sure he gets there in one piece.

A Sherlock snatches at Alfi's hoodie, almost gets a grip on him. It's up to Super-Didge to rescue the innocent. I dive between them, stop dead, curl into a ball. Fat Sherlock topples right over the top, goes sliding across Oxford Street gravement, unpeeling most of his cheek.

Alfi's standing there, jaw wide open like he dislocated his brain. I swear, he puts out a hand, offering to help the stupid Sherlock back to his feet.

I tug Alfi's hood back up, grab him by his waistband and chuck the both of us onto the deck of a passing bus. Off we speed. Clean getaway.

Three seconds later, Alfi's holding out his palm, offering up his 20 tragic p. He gives me that old pathetic look of his, and says, "Do you reckon this'll do for the fare?"

I'm despairing.

*

A ticket inspector gets on and I hold up me hand to check the ticket price, but he blanks us. It's Byron, in't it? He has this way of not being noticed. And I'm ignored too, on account o' sitting next to him. Like I've caught his invisibility.

But I'll be the one who cops it if anyone points us out.

Never ever stand next to Byron when he's up to his tricks. It'll be you gets fingered for it, every time. Just like he dragged us into all that business at Tenderness. I notice he han't even mentioned Tenderness. Does it even bother him, what might have happened to us after he went flying off? That week after he left were the rottenest o' me life.

I don't even like him. He's trouble. Come to London *he* says, everything's all right in London.

"Look, I en't comfy wi' this. I'm going to get off."

I try sliding past him, but he drapes his arm round me shoulder, squeezes. "Alfi. Dude-boy. You made it, didn't you? All this way. You must have a special Citizen Digit radar. Fateful, don't you think?"

Uh-oh. Me and Fate have never got on wi' each other. Otherwise I wun't have ended up in Tenderness in the first place. I'd still be wi' me lovely foster family, the Barrowcloughs.

I pull away, but Byron tightens his grip and gives us his goofy smile. "You looked pretty frost-bottomed sitting all Johnny No Mates on the pavement back there. How about you let me take you somewhere warm, get some hot potaters down your neck?"

"Look, Byron—"

"Citizen."

"Citizen. You were dead right about what were happening at Tenderness. But I en't mad on getting mixed up wi' no illegal stuff."

He throws us his look of mock surprise. "I've never been so insulted in all my life, upon my life."

That en't true. Byron dun't go round calling hisself Citizen Digit for his IT skills. His fingers are so sticky he can sneak keys from jailers, tills from counters – he could probably nick the toilet paper from the Houses of Parliament wi' no one noticing. He's dead proud of it. Allus covers his tracks too. He's been fingered for countless crimes, but only convicted of one. He always comes out wi' the same line. Upon his life.

"Yes, indeedly. I'm engaged in legitimate busyness these days. It's a proper shop, trust me. Up Seven Sisters. Trading licence, V-A-T, the whole caboodle. Sincerity itself."

"No way," I say. "You're not even old enough to have a proper job."

"Correctimundo!" He claps his hands together like the deal is sealed. "That's why the Citizen don't get no wages, yeah? He just helps out. Gets a soft bed. A warm bed. And hot nosh every day. Hot nosh, Alfi-Boy."

Hot nosh. I'm even more starving now that I've scarpered half the length of Oxford Street. Has any human ever been as hungry as me at this point in time? And knackered. I'm proper knackered.

"Course," he carries on, "if you really aren't interested, you can jump off the bus right now, go find that bit of cardboard you call a mattress and forget you ever bumped into your old crewmate the Citizen." He folds his arms.

Last night, I slept in a skip. Had to find a place where I wun't be seen. If the cops find you and you're underage, they take you in, that's what I heard. They take you in, then take you back. Back to Tenderness.

I slept in a wheelie bin for a few nights once, before I struck lucky wi' the Barrowcloughs. It en't bad. But someone told me about a dosser who slept in a wheelie bin that got picked up by a crusher. Two seconds later he was pulp. So I stopped that.

Last night's skip were empty, a canvas tied over the top so no one 'ud fill it wi' their own junk. If you know enough about knots, you can loosen 'em and squeeze in. I picked up a pile o' free newspapers to line the bottom, cover the muck, and you wun't believe, it were actually fairly comfy. After a while, a couple o' men climbed in next to us. I were freaked, 'cos they might be a couple of ... what was it Citizen Digit called 'em? Jim'llfixits. I lay there, trying to look tough, like I could kick 'em in the goolies. No one said owt. We all just nodded at each other, and they wormed down into their sleeping bags. They were just after warmth, same as me. To be honest, once I got used to the idea, the more the merrier. Body heat, en't it?

It were cold enough, though. Stinking an' all.

Citizen   Whatever-He's-Calling-Himself-These-Days

interrupts me thinking. "Look, Alfi, I ain't even bothered with you that much. You cramp my stylishness. Let's quit while we're behind, yeah? Why not hop off at this next stop? Give the Citizen's regards to the old dosspots, yeah?"

But what if he were right the first time? Maybe I were meant to bump into him. This could be me turning point.

Hot nosh. I am so hungry.

Go for it, Alfi.

"You sure it's legit?"

"Crime doesn't pay, bruv, does it? Ain't that what you always said? I'm wisdom itself these days. Citizen Digit's flying straight as an arrow. I'll show you the shop, if you like? Get my manager to serve you some hot grubbings."

"All right." I shrug.

He raises his hand, clenched, and we bump fists.

Hot grub.

I've a bad feeling about this.

Then he says, dead casual, like he's asking about the weather or summat, "You still got that evidence?"

I can hardly bring meself to think about it. I don't answer.

"From Tenderness?" he goes on. "Is it safe?"

I close me eyes. "It's safe," I say.

I wish I'd never even seen it. Wun't be here now if I hadn't, would I?

We hop off two stops before Operations. Virus insists upon it, in case of any Sherlocks on our tails.

"Lead them a merry dance, my little soldier," he'd say. "They like a dance, our boys in blue. Always give them what they want."

Alfi Spar almost blows away in the wind when his feet hit the street. He was always the skinniest WhyPee at Tenderness. Ain't he only gone and achieved the impossible? Made himself skinnier.

He goes all feak and weeble and reaches out to take my hand like a toddler-boy. I'm tolerating it, for the sake of keeping him standing. At Tenderness, this kind of thing would get us a gonad-kicking, but not here. That's the beauty of Seven Sisters, you get all types. See African boys walking down the street hand in hand, it's just cul-turality, ain't it? See hairy old winos who smell of poo-poo, with their bottom hanging out of their pants, quot-ing *Star Wars*, nobody going to blink twice. This is North London. Vietnamese, Jamaican, student, Muslim, Jew, Cockney, gangsta, pigeon-eater – anything goes. That's why Virus runs his operations here. It's what drew the Citizen here in the firstness.

You ever want to disappear? Get yourself a one-way ticket to Seven Sisters.

Course, on his ownsome, a peanut brain like Alfi Spar ain't going to last five and a half minutes. He's got no idea what's a whatness. In actual factness, I must be a peanut brain myself, bringing the boy back here. I've been safe here, under the radar. Supposing Governor Newton – Call-Me Norman – is on his tail? If Alfi brings

Call-Me to our door, Citizen Digit is headed for the cemetery. But what am I going to do – leave Alfi to the vultures and wolves that prowl the streets looking for poor-boy pickings just like him? Without Citizen Digit watching his back, Alfi Spar is dead meat.

We reach the shop. *Cash Counters*. Its bright yellow sign is the only bit of sunniness along this stretch of road. Virus has one of his henchies clean the sign and sparkle the windows each morning. "Let the punters see what we've got," he says, "right through into the shop. Dazzle them, Citizen, dazzle them before they even know they're looking."

I tighten my grip on Alfi's hand, paste a grin across my VDU, and we step inside.

3. CASH COUNTERS

Unbelievable.

It is a real business, a proper shop wi' shop assistants wearing matching yellow shirts with a Cash Counters *logo and nametags and all. Customers browsing what's on offer.*

All kinds of electrical stuff, laptops, mobile phones, digital cameras.

Byron won't let go o' me hand. Them light fingers of his have a cage fighter's grip.

He drags us further in, points at the wall, at a sign:

Cash Counters cashes cheques and gives loans at affordable rates.

They buy things as well as sell 'em, but only from people wi' proof of ID and address.

And look:

Cash Counters is a member of the Consumer Finance Association and is regulated by the Office of Fair Trading.

And there's more signs all over the walls o' the shop. Cash Counters is the First Choice for a Fair Deal.

Another sign on the wall says SMILE, YOU'RE ON TV.

I smile. And Byron loosens his grip on me hand.

We wander through towards the back. The shop assistants are watching us from the corners o' their eyes. I spot Byron making eye contact with 'em, but none of 'em greets us or even shows that they've seen us. But the customers all stare, probably 'cos I brought me pong in with us. I'd love a bath. A hot bath, after some hot food. Oh, this is all right. Defo the thing to do.

Citizen Digit dun't say a word, but when he gets to the bank counter at the back, he nods at the bloke behind the glass, who bends down and clicks a button. Then the Citizen pushes at the big door next to it, and we're through into the storeroom. Surely we en't allowed? I step back, certain a Tenderness Care Assistant is going to dash out and yank me arm up behind me back, make me shoulder pop, march me off to a room with a door that locks. Then everything carries on right where it left off...

"Chill," Byron whispers.

The bloke behind the counter steps out and smiles at him. Byron smiles back.

"Found us a new recruit?" the bloke says.

Byron shrugs. "Up to Virus, ain't it?"

"Go on up."

We make our way over piled-up boxes, gear that must be worth a bomb. I try not to brush against 'em 'cos me hoodie is so grimy. Byron – sorry, Citizen Digit – is kitted out in shiny new clothes. I've seen them shoes he's wearing, through shop windows. They cost a packet. I look at his smart top with serious envy. I look like a dosser. Me heart

*jumps up against me chest. I'm feeling faint – again? – and
I stick out a hand so I don't lose balance.*

*But Byron has his arms under me pits, guiding us up
the stairs, over soft carpet. A lad with his hoodie pulled
down low so you can't see his face is skulking at the top.*

Byron says, "Oi! Dictiv—"

*"Helpin' hand with the fresh meat?" A voice comes
from under the hood. Next thing, his hands are all over us.
He en't bearing me weight at all. He's tickling us, all over,
light like a feather.*

"Knock it off—" says Byron.

*"He's needin' help stayin' upright. True?" The tickler
cuts Byron short.*

*"Too right. Practise your dipping another time. Meet
Predictiv Tex," Byron mutters to us. "So called—"*

*"'Cos he states it straight. So?" His voice is weedy, but
his tone is all Rough Kid. "Instant messagin'. No wasteman
Digit time." I can't understand what he's going on about. He
tugs at me arms, rotten breath in me face. He's all shadow,
determined I don't see his features.*

*There's a door at the top. I can hardly lift me eyelids.
I'm done in. Byron kicks at it, a musical rhythm, his hands
not free to knock. The door swings open and we tumble in.*

*"Play nice," says Predictiv Tex, slamming the door
behind us.*

*"Well, well." I hear a voice, all lah-di-dah, like a Senior
Case Worker. "Citizen Digit himself. And what luxury items
have you brought back home this time?"*

"A friend. He's malnutritious, ain't he?" Digit drops us into a big, soft sofa.

"Is he indeed?" says the voice, all treacly. "Then he's come to the right place."

I look up, see a white face, soft and smooth like an advert for soap, wi' smiling, pearly teeth. Big green eyes, twinkling down, like a cat's. A hand reaches towards us, whiffing of air freshener, fingernails clipped, neat.

He's wearing a suit. And a tie!

Byron has set us up. He's Social Services, in't he? The shop is a front for the SS!

The hand hovers in front of us.

I look to Byron. How could he? But he's nodding at us, dead keen.

He expects me to shake it. Don't I know better than that?

"Hello, little soldier." The tip o' this bloke's tongue flicks against his lips, looking for a fly to catch. "My name is Virus. Delighted to make your acquaintance."

Suddenly he don't look like the SS no more.

To be brutally truthful, Alfi looks like he's going to poop his panties, which going by the smell of him will be the second time in twenty-four hours. Virus hates getting his hands dirty. I most definitely should have left Squealer-Boy where I found him.

But then Virus goes on to say the magic words. "The Citizen informs me you're feeling a tad peckish. What say I have one of my boys cook you a Full English? I gather that's what you young people have a taste for."

He sees me dribbling too, like I'm Captain of the Salivation Army, and says, "And you, Digit, and you." He leans in. "You've done well," he whispers, for my ears only.

Have I though? Alfi's fixing me with his fiercest stare. "It dun't matter what – I won't go back to Tenderness. I won't let 'em take us."

So that's his beef and gravy. He thinks Virus is an Authoritariac, on account of the sharpness of his suit. He's learned over the years to distrust any Groan in a suit. It's understandable really.

"Virus ain't like that." I offer reassurance. Last thing I need is Alfi getting in a flap and blabbing about everything. "He's like us. Only big. Don't be fooled by the stylishness of his threads, Virus is—"

"Virus is a believer in free enterprise." The Great Manager cuts over the top of me. "He believes that if you have fine things to offer, then the world has fine things to offer back. And you look like the kind of young man who has plenty to offer." He sits on the sofa next to Alfi, not too close, so as not to brush against his grimes. "What's your name, young fellow?"

Alfi throws me a disconcertified look. He's recollecting all my watchful words about never naming names, certainly never naming your own name. It's as bad as handing yourself in. It's why we use falsies – me, Virus, my good companion Predictiv Tex, all the rest of us. You give them your name, you're signing yourself over.

Put it this way. Rev up your Search Engine and tap in the words *Citizen Digit*. What's going to flash up at you? Nothing about my good self, that's for sure. Because Citizen Digit don't have no online presence, does he? Therefore, no visibility. On the other hand, tap in the words *Byron* .... (hah-ha! Didn't think I was going to give myself away that easily, did you?) and you'll get my whole Horrible History. Byron's history, leastways. All fed into hard drives and weaved round the World Wide Web by Authoritariacs everywhere. Once you're online, they've collared you.

Which is why Citizen Digit is officially offline.

So why Alfi Spar is looking to me to guide him in his answer is beyond me. Even so, I endeavour a favour – *another* one – by not saying *Don't tell him it's Alfi Spar!* Insteadily, I give him a hint. "Go on, new boy, show some mannerisms. Give the gentleman a name."

Behind his eyes, I can picture Alfi's peanut brain cracking open its shell in an effort to *think.*

I think he's thinking of Full English: egg, bacon, beans, sausage, et cetera, et cet.

He stretches out his arm and shakes Virus by the hand. "My name is Alfi Spar," he says.

Sucker.

For a millisec, Virus's eyes widen a little, as if he's surprised. Then he gives a little clap. "Charming," he smiles. He wipes his fingers clean with a tissue and clicks his fingers. "Predictiv! Your presence, please."

In strolls Tex.

Wherever you are, whatever your doings, Tex is always just the other side of the door.

"Mr Dictiv," says Virus, "have a word with Bones, and—"

"Mass fry-up for the crew, yo?" says Predictiv Tex. "I'm on it."

Virus fixes his gaze on Alfi, like he's trying to read him. Which ain't hard, 'cos if Alfi Spar was a book he'd be *Nursery Rhymes For Numpties*. Put it this way: his thoughts come in LARGE PRINT, don't they? Virus can see Alfi's starvatious and zausted, which is exactly how he likes it.

"While we're waiting for the food, young man," he suggests, "how about a hot bath and some clean clothes?"

Smart. Virus knows Tex will have had his fiddly fingers in and out of Alfi's pockets, rummaging for tiddlebits. But Virus wants a closer look. Alfi's already surrendered his name, free of charge; let's see what else he has on offer.

Alfi's directed to our luxury bathroom and dumps his toxicated threads in a pile outside the door. It's the Digit himself who's instructed to retrieve them, which ain't nice, on account of Squealer-Boy's old flakey poo, and who knows what. These fingers ain't for dipping into that kind of dirt.

"Get Tex to do it," I say.

Mistakenly stated, ain't it? Virus's fizzog twists and cracks like that flat screen did when I bumped into Alfi Spar. He jabs his Smartphone up at my cheek before I have time to back off, and he zaps me.

It catches me unawares. Lightning streaks across my cheekbone and knocks me to the floor. I'm spotting stars.

"I do apologize." Virus's lips sneer at me through the dazzlespots. My cheek is still burning. He fidgets with his phone, switching off its power. "Perhaps I didn't make myself clear."

No one knows how he's done it, but Virus has added a special app to his smartphone, that gives a nasty surprise. A Zap App. He wipes the phone clean with his hankychief, cleaning off the Digit sweat.

He's clear all right. The Digit ain't had a zap from old Virus for quite a while now. The Good Citizen was forgetting himself. Answering back, like he was an equal, when he's still only blessed with skinny kid muscles.

I stroke my fingers against my smarting cheek, back away.

"Digit," Virus says. He produces a clean tissue, dabs it over his frown lines, magicking back his smile. "Come here."

Smarting. Smarter now.

"Here, son."

The Digit inches back towards where Virus is lounged on the sofa, all stately, like the Lady of the

Manor. He pats the cushion next to him. "Sit."

I do as I'm told. The zapper was set on low voltage. I've seen him once zap a drunken fist-swinger with enough juice to BBQ his flesh. It's Virus's specially constructed gizmo. A micro-cattle prod, to keep his boys docile. Citizen Digit has just enjoyed a warning zap.

I heed it.

He puts his arm round my shoulder and eases me towards him. He knows the Digit's impeccable hygiene ain't going to get no crumbles on his holy suit. He strokes my head, soft. Sighs.

"I wish you wouldn't make me do that," he whispers in my ear. "You're the most talented of them all, Didge, you know that. You've done an excellent job with the new boy. Keep to the path you're on, and you'll do well in life. Very well."

I'm biting my lip. The shock's made my eyes moist. I grit my teeth at him.

He reaches inside his jacket pocket, slides out his smart leather wallet. Produces a twenty.

The Digit knows enough not to snatch at it. Virus holds it in front of my face for a few seconds, crisp and clean, like it's been spat straight out of a cash machine, Queen Elizabeth's fizzog twinkling out at me. He tucks it into my pocket, pats my head again.

"Go through his rags," he repeats, full of kindliness this time. "Bring me what's in them, then chuck them in the incinerator. And glue yourself to young Alfi Spar.

Tight as you can. Do it well, Didgy-Boy, and you'll see quite a few more of these."

He pats the note nestling in my jacket pocket. Smiles gently, strokes his thumb lightly against my still-sizzling cheek, letting me know to be on my way.

Citizen Digit does as he's told.

Even the Barrowcloughs never had a bathroom as smart as this. The bath is so big that when I stretched out I could almost swim the backstroke. It's got a big brick of purple soap that smells like rich ladies. A fluffy white rug under me feet.

"Can I help you, sir?" I ask meself in the mirror. "Can I interest you in today's special deal?"

I smell the fry-up that's been cooking while I had me bath. The smell of Life. Life as it's meant to be.

This bathroom is actually bigger than the Relaxation Room at Tenderness House.

Call-Me Norman forces you to relax at Tenderness.

Not that anyone 'ud ever believe it. And I tried to make them. Believe me, I tried.

So I ran. Ran here! I'm a Cash Counter *now. Me and Citizen Digit. "Might I recommend our Payday Loan, sir? It's a deal I think you may find rather attractive?"*

I shampoo me hair. Scrub me fingernails. "Could I help you with that, madam?" Fresh undies. "No, please, madam, there's no need to tip – Mr Virus looks after us here, exceedingly well indeed."

I put on me grey trousers and a yellow Cash Counters *polo-shirt.*

Dead smart.

I'm off to eat now. I'm off to eat and then I'm off to sleep like a king.

Then I'm off to work.

Then I'm off to eat again.

Just watch us.

Eat, work and sleep. Then eat again.

Life.

4. GOOD GRACE

Alfi Spar is hoovertastic! He—

"Disappears items swifter than you do, ain't it, Didge?" Predictiv Tex speaks for us all. Six of us boys, gathered round Virus's dining table. Virus at the head, as is his right. We're all ever so slightly gobsmashed at the way little Alfi is suckering up sausages like a Dyson.

Poor little Alfi-kins. If anyone was a born sucker it's him. Literally.

All the WhyPees at Tenderness knew about Alfi being a born sucker. He brought it on himself, always showing off the scrap of paper he reckoned was a Birthday Certificate. Without a shadow it wound the other WhyPees up. Having a mum of your own is a delicate point in any residential unit.

The Digit fished that scrap out of Alfi's secret pocket, while Alfi was drowning his fleas in the soapsuds.

When I talk about *scrap* of paper, that is exactly what I mean. It ain't no actual Birthday Certificate. Alfi's mum had scrawled *This little boy is called Alfi.* Then she'd pinned it to his baby blanket just before waving her last goodbye to the human planet.

Most other WhyPees reckoned Alfi's ma died before she even managed to finish spelling his name, and he should have been named *Alfie*. But the Citizen's got keener peepers, ain't he? Alfi's mum wanted no mistake about it. No way had she meant to write *Alfie*, on account of her putting a full stop to it after the *i*, and then giving it an underlining truth – <u>Alfi</u>.

Everyone at Tenderness knew about his mum's mortal coil uncurling ten minutes after birthing Alfi in a shop doorway.

As if that wasn't sad enough, he wasn't even blessed with a second name. Nobody knew who Baby Spar's da was – least of all Alfi's ma. According to some of the more ignoramus WhyPees, not only was Alfi's ma too thick to spell her own baby's name, she was also a Sex Labourer.

As if they'd know. It used to drive Alfi absonutly loopy, and who can blame him?

But it was the *other* rumour that always pushed him over the ledge. The one about how he came by his conveniently local second name.

Tenderness rumour-mongrels had it that Alfi's mum was an Illegal, over from Eastern Europe, toiling for a gang from someplace like Letsbeavinya. No passport, no name, first or second, to speak of. So what were peeps expected to give little Alfi for a second name? The law says we all got to have a second name.

I know says some Bright Spark. *We ought to name him after where he was found.*

Oh yeah agrees his mate, Light Bulb. *Well, where was he found then?*

Doorway of a supermarket, wasn't it?

Better call him Alfi Spar.

Ha ha ha. Not.

Told you, the boy was a loser before he was even a day old. You gotta feel sorry for him, yeah?

Nevertheless and allthemore, while Alfi was drowning his fleas, the Digit dipped into his pockets and dug out that scrap of paper.

And as for the Tenderness evidence that I'd deposited into his safe-keeping? Not there. I guess Alfi Spar has a brain cell or two after all.

Let's just hope Call-Me Norman never gets his smokey-stained fingers on it – or us. Believe me, a low-watt zap from Virus once in a blue moose is leisurelike compared to what Call-Me Norman will do if he catches us.

Actually, the Digit hated taking Alfi's Birthday Certificate. Alfi ain't got nothing much to start with. Mother-memory means everything to those of us who have nothing. I wished I could have held it in safety for him, but I had to hand it over to Mr Electric Eel, didn't I?

So now Alfi Spar is hoovering up Virus's bacon and eggs, and Virus has Alfi's Birthday Certificate. *Cash Counters* would consider that a *fair and just* exchange. That Birthday Certificate is Alfi's personal *precious,* ain't it, and there shouldn't be any real reason why Virus would want to keep it, besides his magpie tendencies.

Except that bit of paper is Alfi Spar's very identity.

And that's one of Virus's recreationals, ain't it – stealing peeps' identities.

I give it two minutes from Alfi's last gulp of grubbings before he says to the Great Manager, "Oh, Mr Virus, sir, I wonder if I might possibly please retrieve an item of personal value from my mucky old pockets, sir?"

And Mr Virus Sir is going to go, "Oh, I'm so sorry, dear Alf, I'm afraid we burned all your old clothings on account of them being nuclear toxical."

And then Alfi Spar – as the Good Citizen has seen for himself with first-eye experience – will lose all sense of reasonability. In fact, I reckon Alfi is going to go a little Ape Poo.

And Virus is still fidgeting with his Smartphone's Zap App. He always has it to hand when he's in the company of his henchboys.

The Digit's trying to shovel the last of his sausages down, before it all goes Armageddish.

Food, glorious food. Me stomach's gone to heaven. Mr Virus seems even kinder than Mr and Mrs Barrowclough.

I wonder if he's fostering all them other lads? Maybe he'll foster me. Or adopt me!

I bet he could. He runs his own business – Cash Counters is almost a bank in a way. So Mr Virus must be almost as respectable as a bank manager. He'd be sure to score highly on a Suitability Questionnaire. He must be used to filling in them kind o' forms. There's six of us lads sitting round stuffing our faces. A couple of 'em look younger than me. We've got big shiny plates like a posh restaurant, and proper napkins an 'all. Look at these knives and forks. Matching. Never seen owt like it. Not even the Barrowcloughs had matching cutlery.

Mrs Barrowclough – "Call me Jenny," she said, but not in a creepy Call-Me Norman way – taught us how to make apple crumble and trifle. She spent half her life in that kitchen, said it were good for us to learn to cook, 'cos it were a life skill that 'ud allus come in handy. I'd allus be helping her out. Mr Barrowclough – Doug – said that I were turning into a proper Jamie Oliver. He had his own business, making furniture, and he used to make miniature carvings for me and t'other lad they fostered. He tried teaching us how to do carvings ourselves, but I cudn't get the hang of it. I learned to make a killer soufflé though, and he helped us design me own cookery book, 'cos he were good at calligraphy. He said it were – what? A related skill *to woodcarving, and between the three of us – me, him and Jenny – we'd make a cookery book that 'ud make us famous, in our village at least.*

T'other lad used to get right narky when we worked on that cookery book. We never did finish it.

Then at Tenderness, there were nowt nice like that going on. Only the bad stuff.

So, yeah, this'll do. Cash Counters'll *do us, even if Mr Virus in't no Jenny. The trick is to not get sent back to Tenderness. Maybe if I could convince Mr Virus about the truth at Tenderness House he could speak to the authorities on our behalf. Get Tenderness House shut down and Governor Newton sacked – or maybe even arrested! What a result that'd be.*

I'm just about to ask Mr Virus what happened to me old clothes when there's a buzzing on the wall. An intercom. All the lads freeze wi' their forks half way to their mouths.

That lad called Predictiv Tex – funny names they've all got – drops his knife and shoots a look at Mr Virus. "What if it's the—"

Mr Virus picks up his Smartphone and points it at Tex. "What if some of us have over-extended vocabularies?" He looks narked. He wipes his mouth with his napkin and nods at Byron. "See who it is."

But Byron's frozen to his seat.

Mr Virus waggles the phone, like a teacher making a point. "I said see who it is."

Byron gets up, dead nervous, and Mr Virus is gesticulating at the two younger lads. "Get those boxes up to the top office. Then stay there. Lock the door behind you. iTunes." He looks at another boy. iTunes must be his name. "Take their plates. They were never here."

Everyone moves dead fast. Mr Virus shifts his attention to me. Looks like he's thinking, but I can't tell what.

"It's all right," Byron shouts from the entry-phone. "It's Grace. Everything's rinky-dink."

Rinky-dink.

But is it? Everyone looks like at Tenderness when one o' the big lads has a bag o' dope out on the table and somebody rushes in and yells Call-Me Norman's coming!

But there en't no contraband here. Just egg and bacon. What's the panic?

"Ahhh, Grace." Mr Virus closes his eyes, and relaxes. "Grace," he repeats. "Digit – buzz her up. Boys!" he calls out. "Back to your seats. It's only Grace, honouring us with a visit."

Mr Virus looks at me and smiles. "Alfi," he says, "you're in luck tonight. Grace is a dear friend of ours. It'll be a pleasure for you to meet her."

All dead peculiar. Half a mo later, there's a knock on the door. The same funny rhythm Byron used.

"Tex." Mr Virus clicks his fingers and Predictiv Tex leaps up and unlatches the door.

There's this girl standing there. She's tall and thin – but shapely too, like the dummies you see in the window displays of lasses' clothes shops. She's got eyelashes long as shoelaces and earrings big as Hula Hoops. Big glossy smile an' all, all under a big hat wi' feathers in it. She whips it off and shakes her head, so her hair's flying everywhere – thick long locks. The most amazing hair ever.

"Grace," Mr Virus smiles. "Do come in. You've missed dinner, I'm afraid."

"Ain't 'ungry, am I?" She steps in, unbuttoning a long black leather coat. "All right boys? Safe?"

En't I seen her before somewhere?

Everyone starts jabbering at the same time. Grace *this and* Grace *that. Leaping from their seats, offering her bits o' sausage.*

Mr Virus lifts his hand. He holds it still in the air. Dead still. Looks like he's getting a headache.

"Oi!" *Citizen Digit snaps. Everyone shuts it, sits back down. Mr Virus casts his eyes across the table at us, making sure we're all quiet and still, then he nods at Grace.*

She grins back at him. "Yer tribe's growin' more critical every day. 'Ow many nephews you actually got, Vi?"

Mr Virus gestures to one o' the boys, who straight away stands, so Grace can take his seat. Grace gives the boy her coat to take. She's wearing a pink jumpsuit and when she sits down her perfume floats over us. She smells like the soap in Mr Virus's bathroom. Like flowers.

"Grace," *says Mr Virus,* "meet Alfi Spar. He's Cash Counters' latest employee. Alfi?"

He looks at me. Grace looks at me. They're all looking at me.

Don't muck it up.

"Hello, miss," *I say, sounding like a Year Three girl. Feel me cheeks going all red. Tex and the others start sniggering.*

"You can call me Grace, sweetheart." *She beams at me.* "Whole postcode does." *She shakes me hand. Me whole face is bright red now. She turns back to Mr Virus.*

"'E's a darlin' this one, ain't he?"

"Well," says Mr Virus, "a friend of the Citizen's is a friend of ours."

"Ain't it," she says. "Wot's 'is talent, then?"

Mr Virus sort o' twinkles at me. "His face, Grace. Just look at that face. Did you ever see such an honest angel face in your life?"

She nods quietly, biting her lower lip like she's thinking it over. "You wouldn't suss it, then," she says, "that 'e's a little finger-dipper."

What? *It's Byron who's always nicking stuff, not me.*

She grabs me arm and reaches up inside the sleeve o' me Cash Counters *shirt. Her nails tickle. I squirm away.*

"Sensitive, ain't yer?" *She pulls her hand out, holding a gold cigarette lighter.* "Mus' be the cool metal against yer skin."

How'd that get there?

"Yo!" *yells iTunes.* "My lighter! You gettin' crashed, New Boy!"

He comes charging at us like he's going to bash us up, but Grace steps between us and somehow gets iTune's hands in hers and dances him away from us. "What's your beef, iTunes? Yer lighter's still in your pocket, like for ever."

iTunes reaches into his pocket and brings out the gold lighter. He laughs.

Neat. How did she make it disappear *and then* reappear? *She's a* magician.

"Where's your brains?" Citizen Digit says to iTunes, putting a hand round his shoulder, and giving him a friendly pat. "You know Grace's tricksies well enough by now."

iTunes grins at Citizen Digit and goes back to his seat.

"Digit," says Mr Virus, "give iTunes his lighter back."

Grace pulls open the Digit's jacket and wags her finger at him, like he's a naughty boy. He looks all shame-faced – though I can tell he's just playing – and puts his hand in his pocket and bring out the gold lighter. "Apologetics, iTunes." He shrugs.

"iTunes!" Mr Virus snaps his fingers. "You need to sharpen your wits. A blind man could have seen that one coming."

I can't help but laugh.

"Good times?" Grace ruffles me hair and it feels like she's sprinkling stardust on me head.

Mr Virus gives a long, loud sigh, like he's playing a character in Eastenders. "Digit." He shakes his head. "You're a little slow tonight also."

Citizen Digit pats his pockets. Looks like he's missing summat of his own! "What a liberty!" he laughs, turning towards Grace.

"Uh-huh." She holds up her palm. "Young Alfi needs that crinkle much more than you."

What? Me?

Oh. There's twenty quid sticking out me pocket.

I'm rich!

"Betcha can't pull the same stunt with me, Angel-Face," Grace taunts us. She turns round and wiggles her bottom at us. There's a wallet sticking out her back pocket. "Come and 'ave a go – if you think you're soft enough."

I dunno what happens, really. We're all dancing around playing Pick the Pocket, dipping our fingers in and out, having a proper tickle, falling about in hysterics. Even Mr Virus is joining in.

I en't much cop at it, get me fingers slapped a couple o' times. But twice I manage to get a hanky from Mr Virus wi'out him noticing, and once from Grace. Unless she's letting us win deliberate? And I manage to smuggle a slice o' bacon down Tex's sock. He never predicted that, did he? I snatch a plastic crocodile from one o' the younger lads and run round the table, and under it, and over the top of a chair and he still can't catch us – until Byron jumps on me head and flicks cold baked beans down me ear.

After a while, I start to conk out. I'm flat on me back while everyone's still mucking about. Me eyes need a bit of a rest. Next thing, Byron is leaning over us and he's waving the twenty in front o' me. But ... that's impossible! I stuffed it deep inside me trouser pockets.

"It's mine by rights," he says, with a smile, "but you know what? The Digit don't have much need of money. He has all he needs – donated by generous friends. You have it, Alfi-Boy. I reckon you need it." He tucks it into me breast pocket. "Come on, Angel-Face, Virus has got beddybyes all set up for you." He tugs us up. He's right. I'm shattered.

I throw me arm round his shoulder, pretending I'm too tired to lift meself. He struggles to hold us up, giggling at me big fake yawns.

Grace appears, gives him a hand lifting me. She whispers in his ear, private-like, but I catch it. "So," she says, "another one of yours, Didge?"

"It must be you, Grace," says Digit, "you're magnetic, ain't you, to us Tender Boys."

Tender Boys.

I'm between 'em, wi' me arms round their shoulders, pretending to sleepwalk up to me room. I'm only half pretending, en't I? Grace pulls back the duvet, while the Citizen takes off me shoes and lifts me legs up onto the bed. Dead comfy.

Grace leans down, all smiley-eyed. "Alfi," she whispers, "I got sumfink for yer. I think yer might 'ave misplaced it."

Me birth certificate. She must o' fished it out o' me old clothes. How did she know?

She fixes us a look, like no one's ever given us before, like she can see right inside us. "Seems your mum must have bookmarked you as her Favourite Number One."

I dunno what to say. No one's ever said owt like that to us before. She pushes me birth certificate into me palm and squeezes me fingers around the folds.

"Keep it safe," she says. "It's proof of yourself."

It's who I am.

Grace knows. She looks into me eyes. Sees me.

"Don't let no one delete it."

Her and the Digit share a look, like they know summat, and both their eyes flick back at the other room, towards Mr Virus, just for a second, like they've played the best trick o' the night – on him.

She turns round, skipping back, hair bouncing. She turns her head, gives us one last look. "Pleasant dreams ... Alfi Spar."

5. MAN AND DOG

Alfi Spar suffers from a humour haemorrhage. He ain't even ticklish. How Grace has managed to get Grumbly Guts giggling along with the rest of us is proof she's a proper Mary Pop-in.

Trisha and Dee used to tickle my feet, when I was still Byron. Even though they always watched out for me, 'cos they were older, they'd still tease. As a matter of actual fact, they'd tickle my feet with *feathers*. Trish would hold me down while Dee unlaced my footies, unrolled my socks, and then they tortured me. Other times, we'd play Garden Gorilla and I'd chase them up the tree and wouldn't let them down. Before Mum dropped out of the picture and Dad moved in down the pub.

After me and Grace put Angel-Face Spar to bed for the night – sleepybyes, soon as his head hit the pillow – Virus got down to serious busyness, fidgeting with his gadgets, trying to figure out what online accounts he can hack at. He ain't called Virus for nothing. All the shoplifting is just for daily spends. Hacking is his real investiness. He sets up his swotboys at their laptops to begin their nightshift, while me and Tex set about licking clean whatever's left of the grubbings. Our job is to bring the gear in. We avoid the tedious shiftwork: cracking access codes, guessing passwords, so Virus can spread his technoworms.

Grace is sitting there, agitated. It's catching. Virus is agitated too. And Tex. We've all caught agitateditis. There's only one individ who spreads illwill as rapidly as this, and the Citizen knows full well who that is.

After a while, there's a hammering. It's the coded rhythm, as banged by a mob of toddlers on a sugar high.

"Jackson," says Grace, getting up.

She unbolts the door and it crashes wide open, smashing against the wall, almost giving her a faceful.

He never enters a room quietlike.

Jackson Banks stromps in, a boy with a limp on one side of him, a dog with a torn ear on the other. JB gives a slow glance round the room, like he's looking for someone to play with. He's got the thumb of one hand hooked into the pocket of his strides, casualitylike, but the ring fingers of his right hand are clenched tight. He's got four rings, glistening, twenty-four-carat diamond knuckle-dusters.

His boy is called Crow, a sore-faced, skinny kid with a jutting, sulky lip. He's got a scar running down his face, and it ain't no fancy one like Harry Potter's, just an ugly scribble. The dog, Obnob, is of the permanently shifty variety, his ragged ear all torn, like he lost a bit of it in a fight.

Word of advice: never put your hand down to give him a stroke.

Jackson wraps an arm round Grace's waist and pulls her into him for lipsmacks. In his other hand he's got his gym bag, bulging with loot.

"Intercom system's bust," he grins. Bust, as in smashed to smithers. Anything Jackson Banks lays his fingers on seems to disintegrate.

"I do wish you wouldn't do that, Jackson," says Virus.

"If I can, the Sherlocks can." Like that settles the matter. His nostrils twitch in the direction of the table, where Tex is mopping up the last of the egg with a slice of bacon. "Meat." Jackson appropriates a smile.

Jackson Banks is one of those peeps who's got a shark of a smile. It's like his gnashers are the real him, his lips are just clothing, like a jacket for teeth.

"I'm sorry, Jackson, you're a little too late. Twenty minutes ago we had a feastful." Virus shrugs sorrylike.

Obnob snarls, leaps onto a chair, then right up onto the table, shoving his maw into Tex's plate.

"Oi!" Tex makes a grab at the plate and the dog bites his hand. He continues snarfing, growling and gobbling stimulatiously.

Tex's hand drips red fingerjuice on the tabletop and Virus *tsks*. "Does it have to? Its claws are scratching the finish."

Jackson laughs, like it's the funniest thing since armpit farts. He flings his arm across the table, clearing it of dog and plate with one swipe. The plate shatters on the floor. As Jackson chuckles, Obnob rolls back onto his feet, gives a dirty, big bark and lunges for Jackson's boot, clanging his canines against the steel toecaps.

"Crow." Jackson addresses his boy. The dog instantly drops his grip and scurtles towards a corner. The Digit's seen this before. Crow reaches a hand down his track-suit bottoms – the limping side – and produces a crow-bar almost the length and width of his own leg, and hands it to Jackson.

For your inf, this is why he's known as Crow and why he appears to have a limp. He carries that crowbar everywhere. It's Banks's main housebreaking tool, so he wants it close by, but not too close, in case the Sherlocks take an interest.

Jackson Banks hurls the crowbar at his dog, which ducks behind a chair just in time, where he sits and griz-zles. Jackson applauds. "Who's a clever boy?" he clucks. "Who's a good boy?"

Then he shifts his gaze back to Crow. "Fetch it then."

Crow scurries across the room to place the danger-ous weapon back in its righteous place. He limps back to Jackson's side. "Good boy." JB pats him on the head.

Sufficient to say, Citizen Digit always avoids making himself a playmate of Mr Jackson Banks.

Banks is the only one of Virus's acquaintances who don't bother with no pseudo-name. Everybody knows Jackson Banks. He parades himself round in broad daylight regular as the 29 bus. He don't need no invisibility. Who's going to grass him up? Who'd dare? Jackson's a regular Gym Bunny, got muscles on his nipples. Looks like one of those peeps who tows tractors with a bit of string hooked through his lower lip. Addicted to steroids, cortisone and human growth hormone, is Jackson Banks. The Lance Armstrong of burglars. He actually injects testosterone, and worst of it is, he injects his dog as well. They share the same needle. The Digit's seen it.

"Goodies." Jackson picks up the gym bag and deposits its innards all across the table, like Bad Santa. Virus grimaces as a pile of iPads, iPods, laptops and phonies make fresh scratches on his polish. Jackson tosses the empty bag aside. He likes gym bags, on account of their consistency. They look the same empty as they do stuffed. Handy, if you're a housebreaker.

"How much?" he asks Virus.

Virus is squinting and tut-tutting over the stash, making mumblings about *outdated* this and *old-school* that and *prehistoric* thingy and *redundant* whosits, writing down figures on a scrap of paper. All the while, Jackson is chuckling away to himself, like he's remembering one of his own jokes. Grace is smiling along with him, dutiful girlfriend, like he's R-Patz instead of the Wolfman's uglier brother. Finally, Virus totes it all up and hands Jackson the paper.

Jackson looks at it, snorts, scrunches it up, then eats it. When he's done, he burps and looks round the room like he's expecting applause. Then he smiles back at Virus and repeats, "How much?"

Virus mutters in reply. Ain't a satisfactory answer. Jackson snarls.

"J," says Grace, softlike. He glares at her, like she's spoken out of turn, his humour all gone. She looks away.

"Aaah..." Virus attempts a smile. "You're in a playful mood tonight, Mr Banks, but I can assure you this figure is more than fair. Most of these items are so outdated as to be practically worthless. I'll get hardly anything for them in the shop."

"Ain't the items, Fairy Cakes – it's wot's in 'em."

Banks is right. Selling these electronic toys is a mere sideshow. Virus specializes in sucking them dry of their data. His icepick mind can hack into anything. If you're misfortunate enough to have one of your gadgets fall into his whiter-than-whites, you'll find an email sent to all your friends saying you're stranded in Strandenovia with a lost wallet and need hundreds of dosh put into an emergency bank account pronto. Et cetera, et cet. He'll suck your gizmo dry like a cyber-vampire, then sell the empty plastic shell on the shop floor.

It's tidiness itself.

But that ain't even the beginning of it for old V. What gives him the deepest shivers of delight is mental torture and blackmail. The Digit has seen it in action, ain't he? Seen Virus at work on one of his hacked accounts, and had the privilege of being talked through the process.

Which goes like this: just suppose yourself to be – for one half a mo – a mappily harried Groan, with a well-respected job – schoolteacher maybe – and lovely kids – Olivia and Jeremy, say – but you've got a few dirty little habits. Unsavioury websites you like to visit now and again. Supposing one of your FB "friends" sends you a message, about how they know all about it, and wouldn't it be a shame if your wife was to find out, or your kiddlies, or your boss, or all your other FB friends. But don't worry, that'll never happen ... and maybe you could do this "friend" a small favour, a weekly financial outgoing that needs addressing....

It's a Privacy Tax, ain't it? A hi-tech Protection Racket. Virus gets the regular weekly payment, but – and this is his real job satisfaction – also the knowledge that said respectable Pillow of Society is quaking in their boots at the fear of being uncovered as the perverated individ they really are.

Nothing gives Mr Virus more delight than to twist the twisted.

The *Cash Counters* buying and selling trade is just a front. Even so, Virus hates parting with his hard-earned. He wants to haggle some more. "Banks by name, banks by nature," he smiles. But when JB matches his smile with his own sharkful, he adds, "All right, all right – add another fifty."

"Hundred."

"Fifty, and I'm swizzling myself."

"Swizzle. Swizzle. Like it. I like it. Let's play Swizzle." Banks waggles his fingers, like *Swizzle* is something fingers do to other body parts.

Virus offers up a small laugh. "Old friends," he chuckles gratingly. "As we've been acquaintances such a long and lustrous time, let's agree on sixty."

"Seventy. Or I get me crowbar and we'll have a game of Bishbash. Posh dinin' furniture an' all."

The Great Manager gives a small clap. "Well, then, I think we have ourselves a deal."

Banks holds out his hand, fingers all a-flap for the cash.

"Ah, now, dear Jackson, you know as well as I do that *Cash Counters* empties its coffers at closing time. *No Cash Is Kept on the Premises Overnight*, yes?"

Jackson Banks snaps his teeth together, *snippety snap*. "Listen, Fairy Cakes, I want money."

The Digit has seen these exchanges before. JB always wants cash. Virus never wants to part with it. Jackson threatens Virus while pretending he ain't. And Virus hands over the cash.

"Jackson..." Virus squeaks.

"Crinkle," Jackson says. "Thick roll of crinkle." He waggles his tongue in Virus's general direction. "Please," he whispers, making his tone all high-pitched like a girl's. "Pretty please?"

Virus croaks and reaches inside his pocket. Course, he could always zap JB, couldn't he? But he wouldn't dare.

Even at maximum voltage, Jackson could snap Virus's neck in a millisec. So Virus fumbles with his wallet and hands over a wad of notes. "There's half there," he says. "That's all there is. You'll have to come over for the rest tomorrow."

Jackson winks at Virus, all conspiratorial. "We know otherwise, don't we, V? All about your special savings account, hey?"

"Don't know what you mean," Virus says, in a grump.

Mr Banks lets it drop. He smiles his fangful smile and pockets the cash. "Grace'll come tomorrow. Don't disappoint."

Virus looks like he don't know which is offended most, his scratched tabletop or his wallet.

And what is Citizen Digit doing during all this, you may well ask? I'm sitting quiet, ain't I? In the shadows. If Jackson Banks don't notice me, then Jackson Banks can't share with me none of his playfulness.

Don't be seen. Don't get heard. That's the way to Digit.

I reckon that's why Crow ain't big on the chattables – if he keeps quiet enough, Jackson might forget he's there altogether. Invisible-ize himself like the Good Citizen.

Crow belongs to Jackson, see. He's got all the authenticates, documents and unsurance cover on the kid, so it's all legit. The Digit don't know where JB got the docs. I reckon Virus hacked a few files and inputted the data. Like I say, once your story's on the interweb, it's God's honour. So if Jackson and Crow ever get stopped in the street by the Sherlocks, online references confirm it all: Jackson Banks is Crow's Foster Dad. Can you like it? The Digit never heard anything so ridic in his life.

JB uses the poor sap to squeeze through spaces too tiny for most burglars. And what the Digit does know, is that that's how Crow got his scar – trying to squeeze through a smashed-in window that still had a shard of glass wedged in the frame. Ouch.

Jackson gives Grace a celebratory slap on the booty. "Come on, Gracie. The night is young. So are we." She spares me a parting smile as he slides her towards the door. Leastways, her mouth is smiling. Her eyes are somewhere else all together. She catches my look, and her mouth goes into cheery overdo. She is not right, and it's the one thing Digit can't figure out – why's she with Banks?

Crow-Boy limps along by his side, as ever. "Obnob," Banks mutters, and the dog comes scurrying from his hiding place, sniffer slung low to the ground. He bares his fangs at me as he passes.

Banks doesn't bother closing the door behind him.

"Always a pleasure doing business with you!" Virus calls, sliding the bolt shut, before capsizing into a chair and wiping his sweaty brow vehemously with a wad of tissues.

6. UP AND AT 'EM

Best kip I've had in years. Now I'm set for the day. Always rise early. Get a head start on all the other lot. Advantage: Spar.

First up I put on me Cash Counters *uniform, before having a look around. It's a titchy room, not much more space than for this little bed and bedside table. Me room at the Barrowclough's were much bigger, and had a window overlooking the garden. There ain't no window here, but it is clean and it don't smell. Not that the Barrowclough's smelled – well, it did smell, o' fresh air and cooking. After the cooped-up pongs o' the residential unit, the Barrowclough's were heaven.*

Here, there's not more than the whiff o' disinfectant. I reckon Mr Virus likes to keep it nice for us all.

This room could be all right. I could pin up some posters, put a rug down over the lino. Maybe paint over the white walls – bright blue, or a mix! A different colour for each wall. Planets and stars on the ceiling.

A room. My room.

I open the door soft-like, so it won't creak and wake t'others. At Tenderness House I were always up and at 'em well before Byron and the rest were awake. They'd get narky if I woke 'em too early. But I like dawn. I like the sun coming up, greeting the day.

Also, you get first dibs at any grub.

There's a latch on the outside o' the door.

Why din't I notice that last night?

I were shattered, weren't I?

I guess Mr Virus used it as storage before converting it into a bedroom for his lads.

I mean, even if there's three floors, including the shop floor, and the dining room is huge, and the bathroom posh like a hotel, there's still, what, seven of us kipping here, including Mr Virus. Maybe more, who knows? So you'd reckon the rooms 'ud have to be quite small. I don't mind. It's me own room. I wonder if Mr Virus'll let us keep a dog. A small dog. He could sleep under me bed.

I'll ask him later.

I creep downstairs, see what grub's in the fridge. At Tenderness you made do wi' what you were given, when you were given it. But I bet Mr Virus says all for one and one for all.

I slide noiseless into the dining room and then I freeze. He's at the table. Like me, Mr Virus is rise and shine, up and at 'em, work to be done. He's got his back to me, poring over his computer.

So I stand there. I lean against the wall, soaking it all up. The first light o' the sun is beaming over Mr Virus's shoulders. He's sitting straight, good posture like grown-ups allus drum into you so you don't grow crooked. He's got

*a clean white shirt on, ironed an' all. It wun't be surprising
to see he's wearing a tie.*

Feel smart, be smart, *that's what Mr Barrowclough
allus reckoned.*

*But I don't want to think about Mr Barrowclough. It
makes us sad. Today is a new day.*

*Then Mr Virus stands up and goes over to the wall,
where there's a picture hanging. He lifts the picture off,
and there's a metal square against the wall. He fiddles wi'
it, and it opens up, like a cupboard. It must be a safe. He
stands there, staring into it, and brings out a big metal
box, about the size of a shoebox, which he starts caressing,
like it's a pet cat or summat.*

*"You don't deserve it," he says, to hisself, I suppose.
"You can't be worth any of this, when you're so ... bad." I
wonder what he's going on about. "You're no better than
the naughtiest of the boys. Don't be a disappointment."*

*But he dun't turn round. It en't me he's slagging. He
puts the box back into the hole in the wall and stands
there, staring at it. Starts tusking at himself. He puts his
phone to his cheek, like he's listening to a message, sighs,
and shrieks. He falls sideways, like he's been zapped.*

Is it a migraine? They come out o' nowhere.

*He straightens himself. "See if you can't set a better
example in future," he says. To himself.*

I go over and tap his shoulder.

*He slams his safe shut and spins round, his phone
gripped in his hand like it's a knife.*

It ain't Mr Virus. I step back.

Composure.

It is *Mr Virus.*

"Alfi," he says. *He reaches forward and touches me cheek wi' the phone. I feel the cool casing against me skin.*

Me heart is thumping. I don't know what to say. He used the phone to hurt himself.

"Alf." *He smiles, putting the phone down.* "You gave me a shock. I didn't know boys of your age rose at such an hour. I thought you must be a burglar, forced your way in."

"I'm sorry."

I am sorry. *Don't I allus find a way to mess things up? I've only been at* Cash Counters *five minutes.*

"I thought you were hurt," *I say.*

"Hurt?" *He puts his hand to his cheek.* "I ... no. No, I just startle easily. Were you standing there long?"

"I suppose you were busy at your work. I'm really sorry." *I need to let him know.*

"It's all right." *He repeats,* "Were you there long?"

"No. I – I were just watching you work, was all."

He gives us a smile. "Learn anything?"

"You put on a clean shirt," *I say, more brightly. Change the subject, Alfi.*

"You're a very observant young man," *he says.* "You'll go a long way, I'm sure."

I gesture at me uniform. "I'm all ready."

He shakes his head, kindly. "Oh, dear me, no. I'm sorry,

my sweet. We just gave you those clothes because the ones you were wearing weren't really ... hygienic. No, no, you couldn't possibly work on the shop floor. You're too young. It's against the law. Why, imagine the trouble we'd all get into. Don't worry, my boy, we'll find ways for you to be useful. You'll pay your way. But you're our guest for now. I'd like you to enjoy yourself, relax. Today, for instance, you're just going to hang around, have some fun with Citizen Digit. He can show you how things are, give you a tour of the local area. He's your pal, isn't he?"

"Yes," I say. I suppose he is.

"What a laugh we all had last night!"

"Yes," I say.

"Are you good at secrets?" he says.

"Only if they don't hurt anyone."

"Ahh, Alfi," he says. "You're wise all right. Honest too. Well, look, what you just saw behind that picture there, that's my little secret, isn't it? And it's a good secret, because it doesn't hurt anybody. It's just my personal items. Sentimental things, you know. And if anybody were to know about them, well, it would hurt me, wouldn't it? That's why it's a good secret for you to keep. Am I right?"

"Yes, Mr Virus," I say.

He puts a hand on me shoulder and smiles. "You're a good boy. We'll find ways to keep you busy. We'll have plenty of errands for you."

Fair enough. I used to run errands for Mr and Mrs Barrowclough. I just need a chance to prove meself again.

Get in wi' good grown-ups, make it stick.

He peers at us, dead close. "Alfi Spar you say your name is?"

I nod at him.

"Interesting," he said. "And how would that be spelled exactly?"

So I tell him. "S – P – A – R."

"No, no," he says. "Not Spar. Alfi. How do you spell Alfi?"

Funny question. But I tell him, about the missing E an' all. He seems pleased.

"Well, Alfi, why don't you pop into the kitchen? Make yourself some tea and toast. I'll finish off here and then I'll come and join you."

I walk past a side room on the way to the kitchen, and see three lads, around my age. I din't see 'em last night. They're all sitting hunched over computers. Playing games, I suppose, or on Facebook. It's only seven in the morning though. They must be even earlier risers than me.

But no one gets up early as me. It's definitely a bit funny.

I make some toast and sit at the kitchen table for a while, thinking about how hard it is, getting things right. Perhaps Mr Virus dun't have enough space for us here, and might want to send us somewhere else. I look round at the kitchen, with its shiny surfaces and pots and pans all sparkling clean and stacked tidily on shelves. Everything spick and span.

I'm no fool though, am I? If Citizen Digit loves this place so much, it can't be completely legit, can it? But it is a proper shop, with all the official documents and that. Some of the gear's bound to be knock-off. I bet Mr Virus dun't approve. You can tell he tries to run a straight ship. I bet he has his hands full trying to keep troublemakers like that Predictiv Tex on the straight and narrow. I've met enough lads like Tex in me time. I en't no mug. But it's got to be better than the streets. And it's defo better than Tenderness House.

I have six slices of toast, dripping wi' jam. Din't realize how hungry I still was. I try to make sure I don't make any sticky mess. I put away the jam jar and rinse the knife clean straight away.

Then I hear a voice and I turn around. Mr Virus is standing in the hallway, sending them lads away from their computer games, off upstairs. In his white shirt, he looks a bit like a doctor, in a hospital. He comes in and sits across from us, giving us his deepest gaze. Then he slides his hand across the breakfast top.

"A little gift," he says.

I don't like little gifts. They remind me o' Tenderness. You never get owt for nowt.

Can you believe it? It's a proper smartphone. I reckon it's the same one we were playing with last night, when he had us try and take it from his pocket without him seeing us. Looks like it's got an app for everything. Music and games an' all. I don't dare touch it.

"Go on," he nods. "It's yours."

But, remember – it were a Smartphone got me in trouble at the Barrowclough's. The other lad who lived there – Jacob, who they'd already adopted – he planted it in me coat pocket, din't he? They'd given it him for his birthday, and he told 'em it had gone missing. Kept on and on about it, until I had to empty all me pockets, and there it was. And next to it were a hundred quid that he'd taken from Mr Barrowclough's wallet.

When Mr Barrowclough – Doug – saw his wad o' money and Jacob's Smartphone, he sort o' slumped, like the life had slid out of him. He gave me one look: stern, disappointed. Like I were a stray dog taken in despite everyone's warnings, and I'd bitten his hand when he bent down to stroke us. I'll allus remember that look. He turned away from us, wun't meet me eyes any more, not even when Social Services came and took us away.

He called the police an' all. He told Mrs Barrowclough he wun't have us in their house a moment longer. He and Mrs Barrowclough – Jenny – had had trouble before and he wun't stand for it again. Jenny kept looking at us, and looking at Mr Barrowclough, and at Jacob (trying to act dead innocent) like she just cudn't make sense of it. How could I do all that baking with her, and make the cookbook an' all, and then just nick from 'em? Like they meant nowt to us. How could I?

I hated seeing Jenny looking like that. It would have been better if she'd refused to look at us, like Doug.

I cudn't stand it. "It's him!" I jabbed me finger at t'other lad. "Jacob stole your money! And he planted the phone in me pocket. Jacob's the bad 'un!"

Cudn't they see?

Doug held the palm of his hand up at me face to cut us off. He were disgusted.

T'other lad proper framed us.

So not only din't I get adopted, but they stopped fostering us too. Sent us back into Care.

I saw Jacob sniggering as the SS took me away. I should o' smashed his stupid face in when I had the chance. I knew Doug and Jenny 'ud be stuck with him for allus now. The Barrowcloughs deserved better than that.

One day, I'll find a way to let 'em know the truth.

But then it got worse. Because I'd been thieving, they din't take us back into the usual children's home. It were Tenderness House for me; the beginning of everything bad.

Yeah, I remember.

Mr Virus is still staring at me, but no way am I picking up that phone.

Search for Alfi Spar on the database – any database, they all cross-reference, don't they – and it'll say he has, what's the phrase? A tendency to steal. It'll say Has a history of theft.

I en't taking it. I'm shaking me head.

Mr Virus sighs. "It's not a gift," he says. "It's to go with your uniform. All Cash Counters employees have one, so we can keep in touch. If you're required for duty, young Alfi, we need to know that you are ... obtainable."

Is it a good idea? I en't sure. It'll be handy though. Go on then, take it. No. Wait.

"Thanks," I say. "Shall I take it when it's time for me to start work?"

He's chuckling at me. "No, no, no." He shakes his head. "That's the whole point, isn't it? When we need you to begin, that's when we need to contact you. Meanwhile, it's yours." He pushes it at us. "It's got games. Movies too. Are you turning it down?" He frowns.

Bad manners. I've upset him. I pick it up and shove it in me pocket. "Thanks," I say. "It's great. Thanks."

"That's my poppet," he says. Pats me hand. "You and I are going to get on marvellously." Then he leans in close and says, "Where did you say you were living before you came down to London?"

"I din't," I say. He waits for me to say more, but I en't such a numpty, am I? Not any more. So I say nowt.

"Wherever you've come from," he says, after a bit, "you did right to come here, to Cash Counters. We'll treat you well, you know that, don't you? The Digit would have told you that, wouldn't he?"

I nod, but I'm still saying nowt. Mr Virus seems all right with that. "Good," he says. Then he yells, "Tex!"

Suddenly, Tex appears alongside us. Was he there all along? "Threads for the youth?" says Tex.

"Threads for the youth," Mr Virus mimics him. "Let's get young Alfi out of this uniform, see if we can't get him *done up as trendily as you and the Citizen, hey?"*

"Yo, boy," Tex says, like the lads at Tenderness, trying to come on all tough. "Let's play."

7. DISASTROPHY

So here we is, Citizen Digit, the Textually Predictiv, and young Alfi Spar, formation-strutting along Seven Sisters Road. Alfi's pleased as vodka punch, 'cos he's tarted out in the Citizen's finest threads. "What's yours is ours," Virus reminded me before I handed over my Topman combo. Only Alfi don't look like much of a Top Man on account of the threads being too big for him. He's a sheep in wolf's clothing. The Digit always gets a perfect fit, 'cos I try them on in the shop, don't I? Leave 'em on, then walk out.

"I like the *Cash Counters* uniform," Alfi says to me, "but your stuff's dead smart, Byron."

"Citizen."

"Yeah, Citizen." I can see his braincogs whirring. He says, "What about an AKA for me?"

"Already got one, ain't you?"

Squealer-Boy.

Tex interjex: "Threads."

"Threads?" Alfi likes it, I can tell. What he doesn't even realize, is that the only reason he's anywhere near the Citizen's threads is because Virus ain't going to have him parading round wearing a *Cash Counters* advert. Any trubs, and that'd lead the Sherlocks straight to HQ.

But Virus has banned any operations this sunny day. He's made it clear there's to be no risk of trubs. The Citizen is under strictest structions to keep his digits out of the local establishments. Virus reckons young Alfi ain't ready. Too right. I'm not convincible he ever will be. Obsessed with honesty is young Alfi. Thinks he's Peter Parkey Spidey-Man, without any of the Spidey-Sense.

Can't think what use Virus'll get out of him. He's less use than an iMac without a hard drive.

But Alfi's doubly chuffed, showing off all the Apps on his Smartphone. He can't leave it alone. Penny ain't plummeted yet, that a Dumbphone is what he's actually carrying round. He'll work it out eventually.

"Hey, Byron—" he says.

"Citizen."

"Citizen." He's desperate to get it right. He turns to Tex. "Predictiv," he says, "Citizen – how about you put me number in your phones. *Threads*. Threads's number. And I can put yours in mine, *favourites*."

"We ain't got no phoneys," I tell him.

He puzzles it. "Wh—"

"Some fool pinched 'em." Tex predicts his question. "Yeah, dem got taxed, ain't it."

Tex thinks that's funny. The Digit ranks it semi-smirkable.

In fact, Alfi's got his phoney so he's never out of Virus's range. Not just callable or textable, but *traceable* too. Virus has a GPS embedded in it. Wherever Alfi Spar goes, the Great Manager knows. Though why Virus has such an interest in Alfi is beyond my imaginings. I'm of the personal opinion that he's a liability. Virus should have figured this pronto – what's happened to his famous brains?

Additionally, Alfi's phoney's got no numbers in it, has it? Alfi ain't twigged yet that *Cash Counters* don't even have no phoney number. Alfi-Boy can't twig anything unless the whole branch comes down and bonks him on the bonce. You should have seen his face when he found one of the nightshift kids sleeping in his bed.

"I thought I were going to have a room o' me own," he whinged.

"Space, isn't it?" I explained.

"So those lads were playing computer games all through the night?" he asked, boggle-eyed. "Then they sleep in our beds during the day?"

"Something like that." He needs to wake up and smell the doggie-doo.

Now Alfi looks at me deadly serious. "What about Facebook, Didge? You could be me first Face—"

"We ain't on Facebook," says Tex.

Alfi rolls his puppy-dog eyes in my direction.

"Forget about it, Blabber-Boy." Alfi is so tragic, he don't even have no Facebook friends.

We're strolling our bones up towards Finsbury Park, to show *Threads* the sights. Village simpleton, ain't he? He's agog at the prolickeration of food shops and what-not, from Turkish supermarks to Afro barbershops, the Shish Shack to Nag's Head Market – where you can pick up chilli peppers hot enough to melt your eyeballs. To be Uncle Frank, the Digit never dips his fingers into any of these places anyway. They're just local stores and stalls, run by local Groans. All a bit downmarket. The talent is better utilized a couple of bus rides away – up Highgate or down Upper Street.

Even so, Predictiv Tex can't help himself from popping into Tesco Local, to see if he can't liberate some snackeroos. He gives me a look that says it all, and dives in without saying a word. Boy's gotta do what a boy's gotta do…

At the same time, me and Alfi realize this is a chance to update ourselves as to where we're at. Delicate, but crucial. Alfi-Boy turns to me and says, "Tell me, really, Byron, is Mr Virus on the straight and narrow?"

"Course he is," I fib with one hundred per cent integrity. "Anyway, Alfi, surely even a goody-two-boots like you had to liberate an item or two to get all the way from Tenderness to Londinium?"

"No!" He looks offended to the max.

"What are you?" says me, equally offended. "Are you just dumb, or super dumb?"

"I'm smart! I'm just honest. Don't you get it? It's

because they reckoned I were a thief that I got chucked out o' the Barrowcloughs'. I wun't have ended up in Tenderness otherwise. You wun't've either, if you din't have to pinch everything you fixed your eyes on."

Enough nonsense. I ask what's been on my mind all along. I lean in close and whisper, "So what happened at Tenderness after I left? With Call-Me and the others?" I try and make myself sound all nonshalonse, like I don't really give a monkey's tuppence.

"I left 'em a message, din't I?" he says, all sly.

"What? You mean you texted them?"

"No. I wrote it in big letters on the wall. That I was off to tell the world all about 'em."

"Yeah, yeah," says me. "What really happened?"

He looks at me straight as a lace. "Big letters," he says, dead proud, "on my room wall. Thought I'd let them be the worried ones for a change."

"*What?* Alfi, that's not nesser-celery wisdom itself." My eyes can't believe what my ears are hearing. If it wasn't Alfi Spar I was talking to, I'd assume he was being sarky.

He looks at me looking at him looking at me. "Wun't that the plan?"

All of a sud, my pacifistic fingers want to take up strangulation. I shove 'em deep into my pockets. I need more answers yet.

"What about the evidence then?" This being the billion-dollar question. "You still got it?"

"I gave it to me Senior Case Worker."

"*You what?* Alfi, that's not..." But I'm too jaw-dropped to finish the sentence. I'm utterly disgrunted. "Well, we've got no evidence then, have we? It's pointless."

Senior Case Worker, my stinky finger. He might as well have given it to Help The Aged. My heart is sinking as my head digests this disastrophy.

But he bounces up and down like he's just busting with good news. "That's just it, see. I went to the library, didn't I? And it so happens that I—"

He stops, abrupt. Tex has bounded out of Tesco, reaching into his jacket and bringing packs of sandwiches out from his armpit. "Mission accomplished!"

Alfi's peepers pop wide open. "Oooh! Second breakfast! I'm starved. Thanks."

That boy would eat his own shoes if you smeared them with ketchup. That's the end of this conversation. It's just as well; this discussion ain't for nobody else's ears, in particular a Parrot-Face like Tex.

Alfi swore to me the evidence was safe. I put myself at great personal liberties for him at Tenderness House, and stuck out my limbs for him here in London. How's he respond? He irresponds, is what. I've had it. Citizen Digit has got better things to do than babysit the brainless.

What if he brings Call-Me Norman to our door? We ain't even got the evidence now.

Maybe it'd be better to drop him, like pickled chilli from a kebab. He got out of Tenderness; he's safe and sound. Isn't that enoughski? Isn't the Citizen's job done? I got a tidy situation going on here with Virus – why let Blabber-Boy mess it up?

It makes my brain go all bomb-like; like there's a lit fuse sizzling through my earhole. And when my brain starts burning, my fingertips start twitching. Virus made me General Well-to-Do today in my role as Keeper-Out-of-Trouble for Alfi-Boy. But maybe it's time for some insubordination. Alfi Spar needs to get real to the street. And if he don't like it – well, he can always skulk off back to the cow pasture.

Predictiv Tex is catching my eye. He's thinking what I'm thinking, as ever. We'll let our fingers do the talking. When all else fails, get dipping. I've never known a situation not be improved by a little pickypock.

Yes, yes, and yes indeedly. My twitchy fingers are telling me true: it's pinch o'clock.

8. THE QUICK ONE-TWO

It goes like so: you match the walking flow of your target, and when the crowd is thick and slow – particularly at road crossings, of which our lovely Seven Sisters has many, you gently unzip the target's backpack, inch by inch. Everyone's bunched up tight, so no one can see, and if the target feels it, well we're all pushing and a-shovelling anyway. Take your time. Idealistically, it's a three-man job. When it's time for the dip, Man Number One is the diversion: *'Scuse me would you happen to have the time? Oh, thank you so. And you wouldn't happen to have a light, would you? And do you know is this the right way to the tubeway? Et cet, et cet.* During this time, Humpty Bumpty Man Number Two does a small shoulder collision with the target. *Whoof!* Quick as a flash, his hand's in and out of the target's bag. Got the wallet. On a perfect day, this is immediately slipped to Man Number Three, who strolls straight off in a different direction, powered by total invisibility. That way, if the target twigs his wallet's been lifted, he immediately suspects Visible Man

One, or Visible Man Two. But Men One and Two don't have no lifted goods on them, do they?

Sorry, mate, don't know what you're talking about.

Foolproof.

We'd never plunder the local shops (Tesco Local ain't local, by any meanness), but the mass of Groans milling around include the occasional wealthbag. Types dripping so much gold they don't twig if their backpack is suddenly a couple of kilograms lighter.

Tex has spotted one, ain't he? You can tell rich pickings from the shoe type up to the hair stylistics. Quality shows, and the Citizen knows.

Course, today Alfi Spar is our Invisible Man Three, and he's away in Spar-La Land, fully engaged watching the street's carnival of oddballs. He'd hardly notice the quick one-two, so well rehearsed by the Tex and the Didge that we could do it with our eyes blacked out. But this target is too irresistible. Dictiv gives me the look that says he reckons we can carry this one with just Men One and Two.

A bit of a laugh, ain't it?

What could possibly go catastrophic?

Alfi's got his beak stuck in a stallful of papaya. I reckon he thinks he's landed on Mars – all he's ever known is the village post office. He reckons eggplant is a bush where chickens get hatched. So, while he's sniffing at the veggies we make our move.

Our target's a youngish Groan, done up to the

nineties in Gangsta gear, but he ain't no Gangsta Boy. The Citizen can tell by his dweebling shuffle and his soft white neck like the Royal Fumbly's. His iPod's got those big earphones like earmuffs. His fingers look like a doll's. Poshboy.

I'm Visible Man One, the diversion. Tex has already got the zip to the backpack caringly half opened, and he gives the signal: a flick of the right ear (not the target's ear – *obviously* – 'cos that'd be a bit of a giveaway) and I move in.

I give him a little shove, don't I? Get my elbow in his ribs, like I lost my balance. "Sorry, mate." Put up my grubs, show it was all accidental, no army intended, et cet.

Out the cornea of my eye, I see the Dictiv make his move. His street talk may be more Dr Doolittle than Dr. Dre, but he has a surgeon's delicacy when it comes to operations. His fingers slide in. One slip and it's guts for garterdom. Out they come, slow and easy, with Poshboy's wallet magnetized to the tips.

"Tex, no!" Alfi Spar decides to pay attention at zackly the wrong moment.

Two things happen stimulatiously: Poshboy turns around, and Tex tosses the wallet to Alfi, which he catches.

"My wallet!" wails Poshboy. "Thieves! Police!"

Suddenly we are all MAXIMALLY VISIBLE in all the WRONG ways.

Time for Citizen Digit to do his disappearing act.

Of course, Squealer-Boy just stands there like a great big Day-Glo MELON.

I should o' known. Byron'll never change. And Predictiv Tex is in on it too!

I hold out the wallet so the bloke can have it back.

But before he can take it, somebody from behind grabs me wrist.

"Got him! Call the police!"

"What? No!"

I look round for Byron, but he's gone. Tex has gone too. How'd they do that?

Whoever's grabbed us is twisting their other hand round me jacket collar, swearing at us.

A couple more seconds and I'll be caught. Come on, Alfi – act!

I wiggle free and take off up the street.

"There he goes!"

A couple o' cops on t'other side o' the road stare in our direction. Moving in, in that slow and decisive way they have, holding their palms up to stop the lines o' traffic, to get at us. Everyone is staring like I'm suddenly the centre o' the universe. A zillion hands are grabbing at us as I dodge and dive.

"Over there!" Fingers point me out. It's as well that I've allus been fast on me feet. I duck round a corner. No one took any notice of us begging in Oxford Street, when I were

crying for attention. Now I cudn't be more visible if I were made o' neon.

Dun't matter; I can outrun all of 'em. I spot an alley, which might as well have a big sign up above it with "hiding place" painted on it. That'll be where the Digit's disappeared hisself, in among the wheelie bins.

"Didge?"

He in't here.

"Tex?"

Nor him.

I could hide in one o' the bins, cudn't I?

Out o' the shadows, Citizen Digit leaps up at us, grabbing us by the jacket and giving us a proper shake around.

"What you up to?" I hiss.

"This is a rubbish hiding place," he says. "You need to vanish, Alfi! Vanish!"

Like he wants rid o' me.

He lets go, spins round, and he's gone. Just like that.

If it's so rubbish, how come he were hiding here? He's right though. Three of 'em come round the corner. "Here!" they yell, and I'm scarpering off up t'other end.

"I think he's got a knife!" someone shouts.

I en't! The only thing I've got is that bloke's wallet in me hand.

Oh.

One o' the cops grabs a hold o' the hem o' me jacket. I zigzag back round him, twisting, and tear away.

"I see him!" It's t'other cop, blocking me path.

I sprint. Too fast to catch, en't I? Coppers only have two speeds: slow and steady.

I'm back on Seven Sisters. Zipping past legs. Hands. Buggies.

Where's Byron? Where is he? And what direction is Cash Counters? Now's not the time to get lost.

I'm dashing over the traffic. Lines of buses and cabs roar along the road, all trying to run us down. Beeping. Honking.

"Over there!"

"Thief!"

I'm running. Hiding. Hide. Hide.

Faster.

I spot 'em. Citizen Digit is sitting at a bus stop, wi' Predictiv Tex. What are they up to? Waiting for a bus? Why aren't they scarpering?

They're visible for anybody to see. They've got their arms crossed and their legs stuck out, chatting to each other like they own the place. An old lady is sat next to them with her shopping trolley.

Oh, yeah, I get it: visibly invisible. That old trick.

Fair enough. I stop in front of 'em, huffing, puffing.

But Predictiv Tex is shaking his head at us. Subtle-like, but defo shaking his head. The Digit won't even catch me eye.

"What...?" I say.

And the old lady looks at us like I'm scum. She tightens her grip on her trolley, like she reckons I'm after snatching it off her. She looks like Jenny, me foster mum. I stand and gawp at her. She looks just like Jenny looked, on that rotten day. She jabs a finger at me. "Here he is!"

I glare at the Digit. He looks back at me and shrugs. Tex is looking at his iPod. They ignore me. The Jenny lady looks at Digit, shakes her head, sadly. He shakes his head back, sadly. Then the Jenny lady, Digit and Tex, all three of 'em stare at me, all three shaking their heads. Sadly.

See? He's just a lad called Byron, with another lad, waiting for a bus. Citizen Digit and Predictiv Tex have vanished off the face o' the earth.

It's a superpower I don't have. Never did have it, did I?

Superfool Spar. That's why he wants rid of us, the Digit, in't it?

"Stop! Thief!" The two cops have spotted me. I puff, pant and run. Keep on running. Running works. Running always works.

Everyone is staring and trying to trip me. All of Seven Sisters Road is after me, in their bright shirts and bandanas and tunics and bling and hijabs. "Thief!" They're jabbing their fingers at me. "Thief!"

Thief.

Not again. It en't fair.

I look behind me. Byron and Tex are stepping onto a bus. They let the Jenny lady climb on first.

One o' the cops is almost at me.

So? Leap. Zig. Zag.

I'm doing me best, but somebody trips me. Up I go, up in the air, like I got flying power...

...down I come. No power at all. Hello, concrete. The pavement hammers up and smacks us in the fa—

Oucherooni! That didn't go quite as planned.

We nab the back seats on the top deck and watch as a mob gathers round Alfi's knocked-out oddbod.

That boy couldn't disappear if you gave him a one-way ticket to Narnia and shoved him in a wardrobe.

"'E's enough showoff, ain't 'e?" says Tex. "An' 'e's wearin' your threads. You can kiss them off, Didge."

The Citizen can live with that. Topman. I've cat-walked more stylish. But I'm not too conf how Virus'll react to us letting New Boy get long-armed on his very first day. This is carelessness itself. Least my fingers got the chance to frisk him clean in that alley. If he can keep his squealer-slot shut, he can at least pretend that he isn't anybody.

Of course, if he *does* blab that he's Alfi Spar, they'll drag him back to Tenderness House. Call-Me Norman will be waiting for him. He'll be wanting to know what's happened to the evidence the Digit gathered on Alfi's behalf. The evidence that Squealer-Boy gave to his Senior Case Worker.

So what happens to a whistleblower who's lost his whistle?

In Call-Me Norman's case, the Digit guesses it will involve stitching together Alfi's squealer-slot, throttling his windpipe and punctuating his lungs.

Once they get Alfi back to Tenderness, he's carcass.

But before they make him carcass, they'll make him blab. Shouldn't be hard, as blabbing is his hobby. He'll lead them all back to Seven Sisters Road. Back to Virus.

And to me.

That means I'm carcass too.

I come round in the back seat of a police car. Handcuffed. Thanks a lot, Digit. Me head hurts like I've been hit with a concrete block. Oh, yeah. I have been.

I wun't mind, but I never even did owt. It were that Tex lad. How come I allus get blamed?

It hurts so much, it makes me eyes water. Through the tears, I can see a policeman peering at me forehead. "He'll live," he says, like I just bashed me elbow against a cupboard. I need a hospital, a nurse to rub on some anti-bump cream. But that en't going to happen – it'll be the cells for me, and then—

No. Don't even think it. Don't tell 'em owt, and maybe they'll let you go. Whatever you do, don't tell 'em –

"What's your name, son?"

– your name.

Uhh, wake up Alfi. If they find out who you are, they'll send you back.

Think. Think!

Ah-hah! I know. I say, "Threads..."

"What?" The copper leans in.

"He said his name's Fred," says the other voice.

86

"All right," says the mouth filling me vision, "You've just given your head a bit of a knock, Fred. Can you tell us how old you are?"

Remember the Digit. Always tell 'em sixteen, whatever. Works for him, dun't it? So I say it.

"You must be older than me then," says the copper who's driving. "'Cos I must have been born yesterday."

Oh. Ha ha.

And the other copper says, all doubtful, "Any ID?"

No ID, no idea, as the Digit 'ud say.

Oh no. There's me birth certificate. I shoved it in me jeans pocket before leaving Cash Counters. It's got me name on it in big letters. I move me hand to feel for it, like a muppet.

"Let's have a look then," says the copper, and he digs his big copper hands in. Comes out empty. Me birth certificate is gone.

Gone?

Byron! He must o' took it when he bumped into us in the alley, to give us a chance to keep me name to meself.

More likely to give hisself a chance. That'll be why Tex threw the nicked wallet for me to catch. So's I'd become a thief like them. And a liar.

Then the copper is going through me other pockets and he finds the phone. I'd forgotten about that. "This yours?" he says. I say nowt. He starts pushing the buttons, frowning at the screen. Turns to his mate. "Empty," he says. "Not a thing on it. No numbers. No history. No last call." He looks back at me. "This brand new then, is it, Fred?"

I don't get it. How come it dun't have Mr Virus's Cash Counters number in it? Me head hurts. Throbbing.

Mr Virus. Hah. I suppose Cash Counters is just the same old story.

That's it, in't it? They want us to give up Alfi Spar, be a little Freddy Pickpocket like them. Well I won't. I won't do it. I'm Alfi Spar, and I en't no thief, nor no liar.

Then I hear the cop in the front, on his radio. "Yeah. Attempted robbery, Seven Sisters Road. Young pickpocket. Bringing him in."

The copper next to us smiles, dead sarcastic. "Looks like you're nicked, young Fred. I don't know. You young 'uns must enjoy being locked away."

So that's it. I'm a thief again.

9. TENDERNESS ITSELF

Imagine the horrors that must have been scrawled all over Alfi's fizzog when he first arrived at Tenderness House. The Good Citizen was used to the place by then, having advantaged his self of its leisure activities since six months previous.

Tenderness House is a Secure Unit. Locks and keys and windows that won't open – windon'ts. Rules and regularities, rewards and sanctions. For WhyPees that have fallen off the Googlemap and don't know the way back. Protecting society from us, and protecting us from ourselves.

The Unit is run by a private enterprise corporation called Reliance Plus. They're in charge of a dozen other Houses around the UK. The more of us young hoodligans crammed into these places, the bigger the profit for Reliance Plus. Crime does pay.

The Good Citizen himself was an expert at dodging these places. Since I lost Trisha and Dee and Dad, I'd gone through a right royal succession of foster families and care homes. Lovely families, some of 'em, but substitutes alwaystheless; substandard subletting sorrowgates, ain't no denying it. Poor tragic Byron – no matter how hard he tried to please, to fit himself in, smile and play and help with the chores, those Mr and Mrs Sorrowgates always had the well-thumbed Byron File nestling on their kneecaps: Sherlock statements, hospital notes, psychiatricks' reports. That clipping from the *Daily Mirror*. Byron could never avoid seeing himself, his sisters and Dad in the *Mirror*. And neither could the Sorrowgates.

Famous, yeah? Once seen, never forgotten.

At first, Byron was mad at his mum. Certainly, Dad's drinking was out of hand before Mum upped and left us. Even at boy Byron's toddling age, dear Dad managed to out-toddle me, staggering back from his sessions with the booze. Instead of building blocks, little Byron had empty cans of lager to build up and bulldoze down.

So how could Mum leave me and Tri and Dee to that? How come she never took us with her? Why'd she leave us – with him?

Uhh. What Byron put up with depresses the Good Citizen even now. Dad got worse and worse, until that final day when he got truly, deeply, Famously Drunk.

Even then, Mum never came back.

The Digit's got her to thank for teaching him the original great disappearing trick.

So Citizen Digit shoved Byron's tragic head right down the toilet bowl. Drownded him right out. Danced

90

out of the loo with springs on his heels and quips on his lips. With a song and a dance, and a laugh and a joke for all the Misters and Misses. *Don't look at the Byron File, ignore the* Mirror – *watch the Good Citizen dance!*

All them psychiatricks wanted me to talk about it. The carers, the fosters too. I preferred to dance to a merrier tune, tell fairer fairy tales. So I taught myself gobbledegook off the gogglebox. I learned to speak Trotterese, from repeated viewing of *Only Fools and Horses*, the language of *Loadsamoney* and *Dad's Army*. Spending hours glued to TV Gold, soaking up the oldies' shows – *Morecombe and Wise* and *Happy Days* and *The Two Ronnies,* et cet, et cet.

Once you've learned how to wear all those masks, it's a doddle to pick up other things. Pilfer voices first, then learn to pinch other bits and bobs. One bit and one bob at a time. Mask up and become the master thief.

You can get away with blue murder if you've got an honest fizzognomy. I did too. Well, not murder, but pilferation. Citizen Digit's tricky fingers danced their dexterous dance, his marvellous mask and magical powers putting clear water between him and Byron's Tragic Life Story. After all, who wants to play the Victim all the time? Citizen Digit saves the day, over and over again.

"Oh, little Byron," they'd whimper, "you must be so sad. What can we do for you?"

Lock that saddo in the cupboard – out leaps Super-Didge. "What can *I* do for *you*?"

Here's a scarf I picked up from Peacocks. Suits *you*, Mrs Foster-Lady.

Here's a chess set I came across in Smiths. I know you love a game, Mr Daddio.

Here's a kettle. Fast-boil. Just for you, Sharon-Mum.

Try this hat, Uncle Eric. A friend got it for me from BHS.

Oh, look! China pigs. Please don't thank me. It was nothing.

But they never wanted any of it, did they? They wanted to rip off the Citizen's mask and find Byron and his tragedy and grievousness.

But Byron was well hidden, so the foster fams passed by, then the care homes. And Digit never got caught, he was too criminally masterful, except for that *once*, and that's when Tenderness and Reliance Plus PLC and Call-Me Norman hit the house party and it all went upsie-downsie.

Byron's file with his sisters and dad, one Secure Unit, one locked room, one bleached and sterile bed, one boy's head filled with memories of a different life.

Calm down, Didge.

Stick to the story for the good peeps. This is Alfi's story, not Byron's.

Tell it. One word at a time.

All me life, I'd been in kids' homes or foster families o' one sort or another. It weren't too bad. The kids' homes you'd make a few mates and the staff were almost allus all right. But soon as you'd make one friend they'd get farmed out to a foster family, or you'd get farmed out yourself. You'd allus be the New Kid, allus finding your feet, or sticking your foot in it. Never be nowhere long enough to have any stuff of your own. No pets o' course – most o' the foster families din't have pets 'cos some lads and lasses are freaked out by dogs. Or are cruel to cats. Or allergic to hamsters. Or whatever. Pets don't like having to meet new kids all the time either, so serious foster families 'ud just avoid the problem. So, no pet dogs. How come I were never permanently fostered, like Social Services allus promised us? A Kid Is For Life, Not Just For Christmas. I reckon there were too much wrong wi' me. Once, I maybe even gave a foster mum cancer. They said she were the finest picture of health, and she'd fostered other kids before and had nowt wrong. The foster dad reckoned she'd hugged us too often, that I sent her soft in the head. When she got diagnosed he reckoned she must o' got it from me 'cos I had summat bad radiating through us like a ... exactly: like a cancer. 'Cos me own mum died, and that. I dunno about that, 'cos my mum died from giving birth to me, which I suppose were my fault, defo. But that's not summat you can pass on to other mums, is it? Din't really matter, 'cos once me foster mum went into hospital, the dad said he cudn't cope wi' me as well as wi' visiting her, and I had to go.

I had one foster family were dead nice to us. I thought

I'd struck gold at last. They were always giving us sweets and presents and hugging us and it were perfect. Then the police and the SS came and took us away again. I were asked loads o' questions about how they used to hug us, and whether or not I always slept in me own bed. When I settled in the care home after that, one of the carers told us I'd had a lucky escape, how one o' their previous kids had made a complaint.

Another family – after a few months, they found themselves pregnant, and it turned out they'd rather have a new baby o' their own, not an old second-hand one like me.

Other ones were just rotten. One lot I were with actually used to sell bags o' cannabis – from their own kitchen – and when I let the SS know about it there were all Hell let loose. Another lot were claiming for foster kids that din't actually exist. I had to go to court and be a witness.

I'd allus live me life by the book – the rule book – and I'd allus let them in charge know about it if rules were getting broken – even if it were them in charge who were breaking the rules.

They say you can't do right for doing wrong, but wi' me it were more: you can't do right for doing right.

It en't as easy as you'd think, finding a family for yourself.

The family before the Barrowcloughs, I were determined to get right. I tried to help out with all the housework and shopping and stuff, and I'd make sure I'd always be right there for 'em. Wherever they went I made sure I

*were right beside 'em. Hung as close as I could. They said I
drove 'em mad. They cudn't cope wi' me. Clingy, they said.
They wanted a boy who were more independent.*

*I tried to be independent wi' the Barrowcloughs, but
after t'other lad set us up as a thief, they told us I were
allus distant and untrustworthy. All that baking cakes and
biscuits were just me trying to hoodwink 'em.*

*It weren't fair. All me life I've done right by folk, never
nicked or nowt, and I allus do as I'm asked, and what happens? I get logged down as a thief.*

Me!

*So: a Secure Unit it is. I looked it up in a dictionary
before I got there. Secure. It means Safe.*

The Good Citizen had always managed to avoid Secure
Units – by not getting caught. But I'd earwigged the
rumours. They weren't no palaces, for sure. And
Tenderness House was no exception.

During the drive there, my guardiman handed me
this list of rules:

1. No mobiles, iPods or other small electronic
    equipment allowed.
2. No TVs or radios in rooms, unless earned as an
    allocated privilege.
3. No alcohol, tobacco or illegal drugs.
4. No chocolate allowed, as chocolate is a
    stimulant.

5. No sweets, snacks or other food types allowed in from outside.
6. No swearing.
7. No spitting.
8. No fighting.
9. No jewellery (rings, necklaces, bracelets, ear-rings).
10. No inappropriate clothing ("inappropriate" as defined by on-duty Carers)
11. No hugging or any other physical interaction.
12. No borrowing or lending.
13. No guests in rooms after 9 p.m.
14. Lights out by 10 p.m.
15. No leaving the premises, unless accompanied by allocated Carers.
16. Daily shower compulsory.
17. School lessons compulsory.
18. Physical fitness lessons compulsory.
19. Weekly psychiatric assessment compulsory.
20. All Carers' instructions must be followed without question.
21. Windows will NOT open. Any attempt to force windows will result in sanctions.
22. Any breach of the above rules will result in sanctions. Sanctions to be decided by Carers and not open to appeal.

I looked at the guardiman and said, "All this must be

harsh for you guys. But what about us guests – any rules we should know about?"

He laughed till his helmet fell off. Not.

We were buzzed through the securigates. The Citizen pondered the high fences and wondered if they taught pole-vaulting in Fizzical Fitness.

Call-Me Norman liked to meet'n'greet all the new WhyPees personally, so we'd all know what's a whatness straight away. The guardiman scruff-walked me straight from the police van to Call-Me's office.

If only the WhyPees' rooms were equal to the Governor's we'd have been in the lap of lux. He had big windys that were opened wide, letting in the sun and not quite excavating the cigarette smoke which (I sussed later) clung to Call-Me Norman wherever he went. He had a big leather chair with panels on the arms, probably doubling as electric cigarette lighters – or a switch to electrify the perimeter fence. Speakers on the wall crackled out classical music. Mindless violins. And through an open door behind him I could see a big comfy sofa in front of a Widescreen TV. His own private lounge.

The guardiman plonked me centre-stage in front of the Governor's desk and stood to attention.

Governor Norman Newton was one ugly bug, made all the more so by a fizzog-ful of hair, not unlike rolling tobacco. The hairs were scattered unevenly across his bonce, like he'd previously gone bald but been given a bad tobacco transplant. Pubey brown hairs were sticking out of his ears and chin and cheeks, and pro-truding like spiders' legs out of both nostrils. He looked like if you stuck a lighter under it, he could have smoked his own nose. He was munching biscuits, Bourbons, but didn't offer me any. To my deepest relief.

Insteadily, he looked me up and down, like he was thinking of making a purchase of me. He said, "Byron *Blank Space*," (still not giving it away, am I?) "I'm the Governor here. Governor Newton. But you can call me Norman. There's no reason why you shouldn't get on well at Tenderness House. It's tough here, but fair. Any issues you have, you just come straight to me and I'll sort things. You've read the guidelines? In a minute I'll have one of the staff show you to your quarters, give you the tour and so forth. But first, if you wouldn't mind giving me your signature here."

He thrust forward a sheet of paper crammed with big words in tiny print. It was covered in spit-soggy Bourbon crumbs.

"What is it?" says I.

"It's our Agreement," he smiled, dribbling more crumbs into his chin fluff. "Our contract. It just means: you be good to us, and we be good to you."

"Hmmm." I looked him in his hairily scary face. "I'll have to have my legal representatives go over it first."

"Barry."

Barry?

Next thing I know, my arm is wrenched right up my

back, so my shoulder feels like it's going to pop its clogs. I'm screeching – can't help it – and tears are dribbling out of my peepers.

"Byron," he says, all sad. "I think you became slightly over-excited for a moment, in need of mild restraint."

Barry yanked my arm even higher. I screeched louder, like a littl'un.

"Barry is our Head Carer. He is using one of the legally authorized forms of restraint. Applied when any of our young people are in need of calming down. Please, Byron, calm down."

He dug out another biscuit and munched away while Barry yanked my arm higher still.

Welcome to Tenderness.

Governor Newton – Norman – insisted I share some of his chocolate biscuits, and I thought I should, even though I could see they were covered wi' crumbs from the ones he were already munching.

While I forced the biscuit down he stared at us, all quiet, with a funny smile on his face, like he were imagining us, sort of elsewhere.

Apart from his general creepiness, I thought Tenderness House might not be so bad.

Me room weren't too nice though. It were all stuffy 'cos the heat were switched up too high, but you cudn't open the window. And it had a peephole in the door, so the Carers could spy on you while you were in bed. First night I were there I saw movement through the peephole. Someone were watching us ... for ages.

The next day when I were getting to know the place, I saw cameras up on most o' the corridors, so they could see what everyone were up to. Which were mostly skulking about looking bored. There wun't no TV in me room, but Tenderness had a common room with a big TV, so I went there. It were there I first met the Digit – Byron, as was – and he gi' me the rundown o' the place. Then one o' the Carers – Barry – yelled at us 'cos we were sitting too close to each other and that were against the Agreement. Byron went and sat away from us 'cos he din't want to get sanctions, and that were OK. But after a while Barry left the room and this big lad came in, called Sniper. Plonked hisself next to us and put his arm round us, and when I tried to pull away he put his hand round me neck and squeezed it so it hurt. So I thought I'd better stay where I was. Then he put his other hand in me pocket and started rummaging round. Byron sat and watched, but din't say owt. I had nowt in me pockets apart from a snotty tissue – I'd had enough sense to keep me personal stuff locked in me room.

"Stuff this," said Sniper, "I'm off to watch telly."

"What's he mean?" I said to Byron. "The telly's right in front of us."

Byron were quiet for a moment, then he explained that some o' the lads and lasses did jobs for Call-Me Norman, and got rewarded wi' their own TVs and stuff.

"What sort o' jobs?" I said.

"Nothing for you to worry about," he said. But he looked at us in a funny way, like he knew summat really bad, which I were gonna have to find out about meself. Which reminded me o' the way Call-Me Norman looked at us, and I wished I were back wi' the Barrowcloughs.

To be truthfully brutal, Alfi Spar was easy to dislike.

First up, he was rubbish at pretty much everything, but because he was so pathetically quote-sweet-look-ing-endquote, most of the girls at Tenderness House would be all cooey-cooey over him. The WhyPettes were always trying to help him out and do him favour-ables. Like he had a host of big sisters tending his every need, which went down a storm with all us other boys. I mean, I didn't have – Byron didn't have – Tri and Dee hanging with me any more, did I? Some of the WhyPees were keen as custody to make some of those WhyPettes their own luvverly girlfriends, so when they saw them drooling over a little squitz like Alfi Spar it sent them into deepest jealousies.

Second up, none of us were angels, were we? Do the crime, serve the time, yeah? The Good Citizen was sin-cerely miffed with himself for having got caught with his fingertips where they oughtn't be, so only had him-self to blame. But rather than gnash my fangs at them that caught me, tried me, and locked me up, I was busy planning an escape of great spectacularity. The rest of the WhyPees kept their heads down and made the best of their time. But Squealer-Face was all *I'm an innocent man! I shouldn't be here! Why have they put me in amongst thieves and hooligans? I'm better than this!* Boy knew exactly how to come last in a Popularity Conquest.

Third up: as if that wasn't quite enough to make everybody hate him (apart from the pretty WhyPettes), he had his Birthday Tificate.

We'd all gone through our fair share of mothers. By the time you end up at a place like Tenderness House, you've somehow managed to misplace your birth mum – through consequence of death, drugs, beatings, crime or mental sickness – and a handful of foster mums too.

So there's Alfi shoving his Birthday Tificate under everyone's noseholes going on and on about how much she must have loved him and how she gave him his name and what a special name it was and she must have done it during her last breath, et cet et cet et cet. And he was sadness itself, really, because he never actually knew his mum. At least I'd got to spend time with mine, for a few years at least. A lot of us had. Didn't stop him droning on about it though, did it?

He was pathetic. I felt sorry for him.

But, fourth up: he got given his own TV after only a couple of weeks. He hadn't even been asked to provide any favourables to Call-Me Norman, which made all those that did green with it. And also a tad suspish.

See, Citizen Digit had been getting an idea or two about how comes Sniper and some of the other WhyPees and Pettes got rewards like TVs and whatnot, while the rest of us didn't. Rumours were abounding.

Staff never took their peepers off Alfi Spar – he had that sort of face. It seemed like the Groans were watching, and waiting. For what, we'd know soon enough. And the Digit would know, 'cos the Good Citizen knew all.

Sniper, for your inf, had evening duties at Call-Me's twice that first week and looked all the uglier for it. You could tell he wasn't overmooned about it. Sniper was doing all the duty; Alfi Spar was getting all the reward.

You hardly had to be Brain of Britney to figure that Alfi was being prepared for something special, and Sniper couldn't stand for it. Thought he was the special one, didn't he? You could tell by the clench of his fists every time Alfi's angel face was in the vicinity that Sniper wanted to bash the holiness out of it. Alfi required a bit of uglification.

Even by Tenderness standards Sniper was viperous. All WhyPees feared him. Hated him too, mainly because he'd pinch things out of spite. It's not like he wanted the stuff for himself. If you was writing a letter and you got distracted, you'd turn round and find someone had pinched your pen. If you was having a shower, you'd get out and your towel was gone. Going to play football? Laces swiped from your boots.

You'd find the pen, floating in the soup cauldron at lunchtime. You'd find your towel in the sports changing room, covered in mud off of somebody's boots. You'd find your laces cut into one-inch strips, stored in a tub of marg in the kitchen area.

Who the culprit? Swiper Sniper every single time.

Oh, that boy was the Devil Incarcerate. He thought it was hilarious. He was like a naughty five year old, in a fifteen-year-old psychopath's body. Jackson Banks reminded me of him – a lost boy rummaging round in an old lag's headcase.

I ain't claiming I myself am Sainted, but just to be front-up: the Digit never ever pinched from other WhyPees, only from Groans and PLCs. I got principalities, ain't I?

And Sniper would deny every single accusation until he was a blue-faced Smurf. Ain't nothing you could do to make him fess up.

In partnership, this was due to his handiness with his fists. Sniper thought nothing of pounding the oomph out of those littler than him.

So, one day, Alfi Spar's Birthday Certificate went walkies and we all of us got the shock of our lunchtimes. Tadpole Alfi marched right up to Sniper the Viper and demanded, "Give it back."

Did I mention that Alfi Spar is as stringy as a piece of string?

"Ain't got it," Sniper sneered. Alfi hadn't even said what *it* was. "Anyway, even if I *did* have it, what would you do about it?"

Alfi's eyes literally changed shade, from grey-blue,

to a righteous bright blue. "I'll tell!" he said. He was shaking with indignancy.

Everybody laughed. We couldn't help it. Stupid Squealer.

Sniper actually snorted.

He towered over Mumsy-Boy by a good ruler's worth. But you know what they say about height not being the long and tall of it? Alfi's heart was bigger than Sniper's any day.

But Sniper doesn't see that, does he? He gets that sneery, snidey-faced look when there's going to be unpleasantries.

He sticks his chin out at Alfi Spar. "Don't know why you're so vexed, Spar. You leave your jacket lying around, means I'm entitled to go poking round in it." (That's Sniper's kind of insane logistics and in Tenderness, it was true.) "Means I took it legitimate, don't it? It's you who's the illegitimate one, ain't you, Spar?"

You should have seen Alfi Spar's fizzog. He had that look he always gets when anyone disses his dear dead mum. First time I ever seen it, and impressive too. Like he wants to strangulate your windpipes. Sniper was right though; Alfi's middle name's Bastardo.

"Shut up," Alfi says.

But Sniper snipes on. "Hey, Alfi, ain't it true your *whore of a mother* dropped you in the doorway of Lidl, and you should really be called Alfi Lidl?"

Alfi says nothing to this.

All the other WhyPees are watching keenly. It was about time Alfi Spar learned his place.

"Good job your mum didn't snuff it outside of an Aldi. Imagine that. You'd be called Alfi Aldi. Harsh."

Quack quack. Time to get ducking.

Alfi snaps. He grabs a chair and demolishes it against Sniper's leg.

Despite his hugeness, Sniper's instantly grounded. He reaches up to try and get his sledgehammer hands round Alfi's throat, but Alfi smacks him back down with what's left of the chair. *Carackajack* – the wood splinters zackly like Sniper's shinbone.

Alfi's hand darts through Sniper's pockets and in two seconds flat he has his precious scrap of paper back in his grubbies.

Then Barry comes charging in and you think he's going to bend Alfi into a position of restraint. But, no, we all sit jaw-dropped as Barry grabs a hold of Sniper's collar and drags him away in the direction of the Relaxation Room. The Relaxation Room is where they lock you when you need to seriously relax.

None of us breathes a word. Then there's the sharp tang of stale tobacco. I look round and I see Call-Me Norman standing in the doorway, with his arms folded, staring at Alfi Spar as if there's nobody else in the room.

Alfi's blushing, either from the exertion of biffing Sniper, or embarrassments. His blond mop's all ruffled from the scuffle. Call-Me's got a greedy glint in his eye like he's anticipating a whole pack of Bourbons.

Alfi Spar smiles feebly back at him like a dumb donkey.

The rest of us don't know where to look. It's deeply disconcerting. Call-Me keeps on beaming all licky-licky at Alfi, and Alfi's going redder and redder.

We can all tell. Call-Me loves that blush.

"Spar," he says, "come to my office."

Off his box or not, the Digit knows it's time for Alfi Spar to do some wisening up.

10. ANGEL TEARS

Next day, the Governor gave us an iPod – all o' me own. I was dead suspicious at first, after what happened wi' the Barrowcloughs and the mobile phone, and I cudn't understand why the Governor 'ud be giving us gifts, specially since we weren't even supposed to have iPods.

He said, "It's a reward for good behaviour."

But I han't been a good lad, had I? Everybody knew that Sniper were one o' Call-Me Norman's favourites, so how come I were getting rewarded for bashing him up?

"For maintaining order," he went on. He reached out and stroked me chin between his finger and thumb, dead creepy. His fingers were yellow, from his smoking. Then he took me hand, placed the iPod in me palm and folded me fingers over it. His hand were twice the size o' mine. It were like me fingers had been swallowed up by his fist.

He dismissed us and I went straight off to the washroom and scrubbed meself.

So I'm sitting in the Social Room later on, listening to the iPod, blocking out all the stupidity o' the place, when another fight broke out. You cudn't get away from it. Least this time it had nowt to do wi' me. Two lasses, scrapping over some lad. So I turned up me volume and turned me back on it.

I see the Head Carer Barry come rushing out of his side office wi' a face like thunder. He looked dead mad, but I'd seen the way he liked manhandling the YPs. He were well up for it.

As the scrapping in the Social Room got bigger, I happened to look towards Barry's office, and there were Byron. All of a sudden, like. It were as if he just magicked hisself there. He were poking around Barry's desk, which meant he were going to get sanctioned. I dunno why – he wun't o' done the same for us – but I went in to warn him.

"Byron!" I hissed.

"Citizen Digit," he corrected us.

"What are you doing?"

He chuckled. "I been waiting for this moment," he said. He had Barry's laptop open and were going into the private files. I cudn't believe it.

"Byron!" I hissed again, but he weren't taking no notice. So I said, "What are you up to?"

"It's everyone's files, ain't it? I'm looking for someone. For when I get out. Someone who can help."

"They're letting you out?" This were news to me.

He gave a snort. "Yeah," he said, "they got bored with me and said I could go. Here she is," he said. I looked at the screen and there were a picture of a girl, the type of picture they take of you when you first arrive at Tenderness.

The Usual Suspect.

"She's nice," I said. I looked at the date. It were taken about five years back.

"She's in London now," he went on. "Some of the WhyPettes reckon if you can find her, she'll help look after you."

"How do you mean?"

"When I escape."

"What!"

"She knows places where you can stay. Safe places."

And he's printing out her picture on the office printer. It were making a right noise. I'm getting panicked, 'cos if Barry found us, he'd kill us. Somehow though, I cudn't tear meself away.

"Print one for me," I say. She really were dead pretty.

But he shook his head. "What," he said, "and have you waving it all over the shop for Call-Me Norman to see? No way."

"Aww, go on." But he's squinting at the screen. He's looking at a bit that says Present Location. *It says* Seven Sisters *and I wonder if she's got family. Maybe she's got sisters same age as me.*

"What's her name?" I say, as he's shoving her picture in his pocket.

He gives a big grin. "Grace," he says.

The murderous kick-off in the Social Room was showing no signs of diminimising. Barry Gorilla-Hands enjoyed that particular perk of the job.

So even though the Digit's no technical geek, the file dealing with the case histories of the Prisoners of Tenderness was simply unmissably opportunistic. Further fun was to be had.

"Come on, let's get out of here," wimped Alfi-Boy, "we'll get into trouble."

But I'd already opened up the Byron file. All of his horrible case history was there, mocking me in bold black and white. My younger, pathetic mug frowning up at me. Goodbye, loser. I pressed delete.

"What you doing?" Squealer-Boy was so shocked.

"Byron *Blank Space* is no more." I looked at Alfi Spar with deadly earnestness. "From now on, you must only address me by the name Citizen Digit."

Alfi looked less than impressed. Sure, it was only one file of hundreds. But it was *Call-Me Norman's* file. The one that counted. I went on, "And soon, Citizen Digit will be free!"

I opened up the Alfi Spar file. Least he could do was a bit of tampering of his own. "Let's see what we can do about your case history, while we're here."

But he started trying to tug my hand away, fully panic-attacked. He'd be terrified of his own bad breath, that boy. "No!" he was going. "No! We can't!"

"Oh, indeedly?" says me, clicking away like a fury. "But ain't you, Mr Innocence, always proclaiming your-self a victim of framing? This is your history, Alfi. One version at least. Don'tcha want the opp to rewrite it?"

I flipped the laptop so he could see the screen, and there was his file in all its gory.

"Dun't matter," said Alfi-Boy. "I *am* the victim of a Great Miscarriage of Justice." He pointed at the screen, where it boasted: *Reason For Relocation to Tenderness House*. In the little box was typed up one word: THEFT. "But even so," he went on, "you can't mess wi' this. It's against the rules."

At the bottom of the page, to prove the truth of all this, was one electronic autograph:

Approved by: Governor Norman A. Newton.

"You could just delete that one word," I tempted him. "Replace THEFT with something more suitable. Like *Needs constant supervision due to lack of life skills.*"

"That en't funny," he sulked.

"Aww, go on. Just delete it. Then you can type what you like."

I could tell he was tempted. "Should I?" he said.

"Shouldn't you?" said the Digit.

"No, it en't right," said Alfi.

"Thief," says I, all cruelsome. "Stinky thief." If this boy was going to default the document, he was going to have to do it himself. It was his life, not mine.

"Errr," fumbled Alfi, "ahh."

"Forget it then," I teased.

But he just stood over it like Chief Ditherer. I took a quick glance down the corridor. Down in the Social

Room, Barry was rolling on the floor, WWE-ing them rough girls.

"What could I replace it with?" said Alfi. "I can't leave it blank, can I?"

"Run away!" I yelled, all of a sud.

"Ahh!" Alfi yelled back, and scowled as I laughed at my little joke.

"Type: *runaway*," I rectified. Alfi always hates it when I pull those kind of crackers on him.

But suddenly he seemed to blank out. Just stood there, squitzing at the screen.

"What?" says I, but he don't say nothing back, just keeps on squitzing like he's seen Jesus or Michael Jackson or whatnot. I follow his eyes and I see a box that says: *Name of Mother*. And in it is typed: KATARIINA UNKNOWN.

"Katariina," he purrs, taking his time over the two *i*'s, enjoying the sound good and proper. "Katariina," he repeats. "Katariina."

From Alfi's rants, I always assumed they'd told him his mother's name wasn't known.

"Katariina," he purred again, like a hypnotic kitty.

"I guess *Alfi*'s a letter down, but your mum's got one extra, so that balances out."

He didn't answer, and then I saw he had a tear trickling down his cheek. I suppose it probably must have been a bit moving, suddenly finding out what your mum was called, after all that time. Then I saw he had tears trickling down both cheeks. The Digit's a bit emotionally embarrassed. I looked back down the corridor, hoping Barry might be on his way back, but he was still rolling round with the Psycho Girls.

"Come on." I start to hint we maybe should get out of there, and I see Squealer's chin all trembling, and the tears are getting worse. I'm reaching into my pockets, seeing if I ain't got a tissue for him, and he only starts moaning, doesn't he?

Then he starts wailing, good and proper. Next thing I know, he's got snot coming out of his nostrils, and his shoulders are shaking too.

The Good Citizen's never seen anyone sob as much as this before. It's a veritable tsunami of tears. I lay my hand on his back, dead gentle, try and help him through it.

Through the tears and sobbing, he says again, "Katariina," only it's all in a gurgle and he sounds like he's drowning. In his own tears.

"Come on," I say, even more gentle and kindly than the first time. But he can't stop crying, can he? He's all choked up.

What he needs is a surname, added on to Katariina. A proper one instead of a supermarket chain. I wish I could do the opposite of delete – add his real, lost name to his file. But I can't. So I stand there, don't I, like a ding-bat, and make *there there* noises of reassurance, and keep patting his back, gentle as I can.

*

I know who I am. I am the son of Katariina. I know me mother's name. I am Alfi Spar, son of Katariina.

If she has a first name, I can find her second name. She's no longer Unknown Unknown. She's Katariina. And when I get out of here, when I can live me life for meself, I can find who she was.

Katariina Somebody. My mother is Somebody.

When I find her name, I'll know mine. Nobody'll make jokes any more about us having a shop sign for a name.

I'm only Alfi Spar for now. Tomorrow – sometime – I'll be Somebody.

11. THE JIMMYS

Alfi Spar was doomed.

The Digit has seen many a WhyPee in a dreadful state. I've seen acts of violence and destruction, the head-buttering of Carers, the smashing of fists, the slashing of wrists, rainbows of bruises and overdoses of booze. Life is hard. I walked away from Alfi that afternoon knowing that the boy didn't have the strength in him to survive what was hanging round his next corner.

The Digit kept his nose to the ground. Sniffed what was afoot and heard the furtives. That night was going to be another party night.

The Jimmys. Alfi Spar was perfect fodder for them – without family, friends or respectabilities. Their big party was going to freak him out, sure enough, and then they'd put him down. Right down.

The Digit was outta there anyway, but Alfi had to get himself out of Tenderness House too, or he was going to end up such a damage case that he'd never be allowed back on the outside.

The Digit knew, because Byron himself hadn't been

in much of a better state. Only the Incredible Citizen Digit knew how to survive.

So, even though he didn't deserve it, on account of being a misery-guts goody-two-boots cry-baby snob, I decided – at great risk to my good self – to give Alfi a bit of a hand.

There was only one option. I had to invite him to join Citizen Digit in his Greatest of Escapes.

"You're nuts," I said. "How're you gonna escape anyway? Do you reckon it's really any better – out there?"

Byron had snuck up to us in the yard during afternoon break. He cudn't leave us alone, could he?

"Listen up," he said. "You remember in the newspapers, all that stuff about that freak Jimmy Savile?"

I had nowt to say to that. All of us had heard that horrible stuff. Byron knew that well enough. So he went on. "In all of them children's homes, yeah?"

"Yeah," I said. So what was he getting at?

"Well, it's like that here."

And he told us, all about it. How he reckoned that Call-Me Norman were grooming us, setting us up. He told us what Sniper and some o' them other WhyPees had been having to do to get all their so-called rewards. How Call-Me would have "parties" in his lounge at night, with all his posh friends coming round. How the WhyPees and WhyPettes would provide the entertainment.

I'd never heard such a load o' rubbish. I stood there,

shaking me head at him. "It's against the law, in't it. They
can't make you do owt if you don't want to. Anyway, even if
you did want to, for rewards or whatever, it's still against
the law. We're only kids."

"Doesn't make any difference," he said. "They make
you do it."

Like he knew all about it. Byron reckoned if he went
round calling himself Citizen Digit he could come out with
any nonsense and it made it true. But he din't know. How
could he? He were just trying to freak us out.

"No," I said. "I wun't let 'em. Not for an iPod. Not for
owt."

He laughed at us, din't he? Like I were a stupid littl'un.

"Anyway –" I weren't having it "– if they tried any o' that
stuff, they'd get in massive trouble wi' the police, wun't they?"

He laughed louder. Right in me face.

"I don't believe you," I said. "You're just saying it 'cos
you're jealous, 'cos I got given an iPod."

The trouble were, he had a funny look in his eye, dead
serious, like. And he grabbed me arm. "I'll prove it, if you
like," he said. "I'll show you. Tonight. You can see with your
own eyeballs."

Din't I have enough to worry about? Why wun't folk
just leave us alone?

"No. Forget it," I said. "This conversation is over. Right?"

He gave us a dirty look. Like he thought I were dead
pathetic. Not worth the effort. And he let it drop.

*

You know what? I was outta there anyway. Tenderness House was horrible enough even without taking the Jimmys into consideration. But the mood around the place the day after one of their parties was too miserable to bear. The place stank.

I had it all planned out. Citizen Digit could finally begin to make a proper life for himself. In London. I had Grace's details. All I had to do was track her down on Seven Sisters Road, see if she could help me out for a day or two until I settled into my brand-new life.

But.

Alfi Spar. He had no one watching out for him, did he? If he wouldn't see how much danger he was in, I'd have to open his eyes for him, so he could get to grips with the situation and sort himself out. I'd do just this one thing for him, and then I'd be off, out of Tenderness House for good and for ever.

So Citizen Digit, for better or worse, adapted his perfectly laid plan.

I waited for nightfall. Then, the first thing I did was pick the lock of Alfi's room, while he slept, and steal his iPod.

iPods have a video function, see? Not sure Call-Me Norman totally twigged that when he gifted it to Alfi. He pictured young Spar-Boy foot-tapping away to endless hours of dub-step. As if.

Boy was sleeping like an angel, not that that mattered because the Master Crim Didge was as light on his feet as a ghost. So the ghost took the angel's iPod and then floated away through the corridors of Tenderness. Sure enoughski, the corridors had more security cams than corners, but I'd studiously studied the blind spots. No nightshift Carers were going to spot the Citizen making his way out of the accommodation block and into the driveway. I was Mr Invisible himself, the Floating Shadow, Sir Citizen Digit esq. I was Night-time Plus. If the Digit wants to stay unspotified, it is a hundred and fifty per cent guaranteed that he will stay unspotified.

And so it was. I planted myself like a shrub in the driveway outside Call-Me Norman's office-come-dirty-den, between a rose bush and a hedge, and as the visitors came, I watched, and filmed.

First up, a Jaguar. Poshness itself. I filmed the number plate and the boat race of a man who oozed out the passenger door. He must have been full of influentia to have his own driver, and by the look of his threads he'd come straight from work. What kind of man wears a suit and works these kind of hours?

The chauffeur drove off and a few minutes later another car pulled up and, I kid you not, a *Sherlock* got out, in full uniform too. I almost jumped up in excitement, thinking for a moment the law's long arms had stretched all the way over to Tenderness to nick Call-Me Norman and his cronies. But the Digit knew better, and I kept filming.

A third car pulled up and a bald, fat man in a suit belly-huffed out.

Next thing, I see Barry Gorilla-Hands leading one of the WhyPettes by the wrist. She was a fairly new girl. I figured by the pale look on her face, and the way Ape-Face was dragging her, that this was her first time. They went in, and Barry came out a minute later, on his own.

Maybe I'd filmed enough already. All I needed was to convince Alfi of the need to get out of this place. But it made me angry, seeing the way Barry had rough-handled the girl.

"No way," says I. "I'm going to paparazz the lot of them."

Then Barry came back with one of the boys. Moses. I knew Moses had done this before, 'cos his room was practically overflowing with rewards. He was marching ahead of Barry, full of grimful determination.

Barry was away again, and returned a few minutes later with another girl. She was smoking a cigarette, trying to look cocky, and failing. I'd seen her in the games room the day before, practising a hand-clapping routine with one of her mates.

This time, Barry didn't come back out.

I should have left it at that, but I couldn't, could I? I'd caught the Squealer-Boy's righteousness.

And before I could instruct them otherwise, my very own legs were skedaddling towards Call-Me's doorway.

Dimwit legs.

I get to the door, ease my way through it and make my way down the corridor towards the back lounge.

Where's the Citizen's brains gone? Only gone and fallen out into the mud by the rose bush, ain't they? 'Cos at the end of the corridor, I slide the door open, just a tad, and keep on filming.

Never-been-seen, never-to-be-seen, that's me, yeah?

Classical music is flowing out of the speakers and you-don't-want-to-know-what is playing on the Widescreen. On a sofa, the flabby Groan and the girl with the cigarette, together. I really do not want to look at what's happening in the room. I turn my head away and just point the iPod.

I close my eyes. Try not to imagine what it is I'm not watching.

But I can hear it, can't I? Going right through my brain. Those two girls, and Moses, and the Groans.

I clap my hands to my ears. Block it all out.

Stupidity itself. The iPod clatters to the floor.

"Hush!" Barry hisses to the others.

I grab the iPod, run to Call-Me's office and leap into a hidey hole.

Barry comes through a moment later. Stands there, assessing the room. I left Call-Me's door open, and I can see him thinking about that, trying to remember whether he left it open himself or whether some fool WhyPee has just fled through it. Then he turns round, scans the room. He bends down by Call-Me's desk, to look under it. He pulls open the curtains, checks nobody's hiding behind them, pulls out some cabinets, checks no one squeezed between their gaps. Then he walks towards Call-Me's closet.

My heart is pounding like it wants to give me away. My breath whooshing like waves on a stormy beach. I can see him, listening. And I'm so loud!

He tugs open the closet door and straight away starts punching and kicking into the space.

Hush, boy.

Then he sticks his whole body in and starts rummaging, pushing aside coats and jackets and wholesale boxes of Bourbons and piles of confiscated WhyPee smokes. He pulls out a bag of golf clubs, which Call-Me probably uses to play rounds with the fat Sherlock. He pulls one out, measures the weight of it.

"Come out now," he says, turning to address the room. "It'll be better for you."

As if.

He whacks the club down on Call-Me's desk. All the stationery on it jumps. So do I.

Barry starts viciously jabbing the golf club at every space he can find. With each jab he goes *Hunh!* like he's stabbing as hard as he possibly can. *Hunh!* he goes, *Hunh!* Each time, I flinch like I've been stabbed in the gut. Then he stops. He waits.

He drops the club and he chuckles. He goes back to the closet and comes out carrying a baseball bat.

A baseball bat is exactly the thing that would make Barry chuckle.

He strides out of the office, a hungry look in his eyes.

From behind the ajoining door, opened wide against a corner of Call-Me's office, I step out.

From the inner sanctum, I can hear the men, enjoying themselves.

I wait, for as long as I can stand it, then follow Barry out into the courtyard.

Having filmed the evidence and shown it to Alfi, the Didge was getting the hell out of Dodge, preferably with Squealer-Boy riding side-saddle. I'd hotwire Norman Newton's car, which he always parked in the same spot in the driveway, pick the lock on the main gate and burn rubber all the way back to civilization. That was *the plan.*

But with Mad Baz on the warpath, the sensible option would be to Take My Leave by the nearest exit; aka leg it for all my life was worth.

Somehow, though, my feet weren't fitting into Citizen Digit's shoes. My toes defied all great expectations, like they were in shock. I was in shock from the toes upwards. As I zombie-walked back to the Tenderness House accommodation block, Barry was still in the driveway, literally beating about the bush. It gave me time. I sneaked straight past the night-keeper, who was half asleep on duty. He missed me in front of his very eyes, because – on the outside at least – I was smooth, sure and silent. Inside, my heart was bashing madly against my ribs, like a rat in a trap.

At Alfi's doorway, I momentarily lost the ability to pick the lock. I started pushing against the door while it was still locked. Byron sweat was dripping down my forehead.

I *forced* my senses to come back and, a half a mo later, the door creaked open. Over on the bed, I could see Alfi sleeping soundly, like a baby. I was jealous. I didn't think I could ever sleep again. My eyes kept repeating, over and over, what the iPod had recorded.

No way I was going to be able to take Alfi with me now. Once I showed him the evidence, he'd freak big time. And the two of us would never be able to sneak away without Barry spotting us, even when Alfi *wasn't* freaking out. Alfi carried a big flag around with him that said, "Hey, here I am! I'm Alfi Spar!"

I had to think triple quick. Soon as the Jimmys copped hold of me, they'd take the iPod and obliterize it. Then they'd obliterize me. Barry would grapple my ass to the ground and grind my brains into gravel.

But the evidence was going to do Alfi more good than me. When he saw it, he'd finally get the danger he was in. Blabber-Boy could use it better than me. I didn't want it. It was sick. I was getting out of there. The Squealer could pass the film on to the Sherlocks, sell it to the *Daily Mirror*, whatevs. Once I'd delivered it, it weren't my busyness no more. I'd done my bit. Thanks kindly and goodbye to bad rubbish.

I tossed the iPod across the room, onto the foot of his bed. He sighed in his sleep. I wished I was where he was. I wanted to lie down on the floor next to the bed, clutching my arms round myself. I couldn't stop shivering.

Citizen Digit doesn't shiver. He doesn't tremble. This wasn't in the plan. I could still hear the violin music wailing away, see the scene on the sofa, the WhyPette with the cigarette, and through the smoke, her shivering just like me.

I was going to get caught. I was going to get hurt. They would put a stop to me.

Mooooove!

I scribbled a note telling Alfi to brace himself and take a look at the iPod's video function, screwed it into a ball and tossed it onto the bed next to the iPod. I shut the door gently behind me. I invisibilized myself all the way back to Norman Newton's car. OK, slight Citizen Fib – I *panicked* and ran as fast as I could to Call-Me's car. There was no sign of Barry. He must have been searching around the other side of the grounds. I picked the lock with shamefully shaky fingers, slid behind the wheel, hot-wired it and slammed my foot down on the accelerator.

The car jerked forward and smashed straight into the security fence. It stalled.

The smash made the in-built ashtray pop open,

stale stubs scattering over the passenger seat, so the car smelled like Norman Newton had his tobacco-breath face right against you. The glove compartment fell open too, a grubby pair of boy's boxers dropping onto the seat.

I looked up, and in the wing mirror there was Barry's face, snarling at me.

I turned round and saw him charging towards me.

I hot-wired it again, reversed a bit, and slammed the car forwards again. The seatbelt cut against my chest.

The fence held.

Barry's baseball bat smashed against the driver's seat window and glass shattered all over me. Cold evening air rushed in at me like rage. I rammed the fence again. There was a crack and a crash, and the bonnet of the car rose up like I was going to be tipped out, as the wheels revved over the collapsing fence. Then a jolt as the tyres smashed back down on the ground on the other side. Another crash, as Barry's bat smashed uselessly against the car boot.

He yelled my name. *Byron.* He saw my face.

But I was gone, pedal to the metal in Call-Me's car, screeching and beeping across the fields behind Tenderness; smackeroo through the farmer's fence at the back of it, scattering sheep; across a few more fields and tracks and then *zoomerang* – straight down the fast lane of the M1.

It should have been an absconding act of the highest style – but I felt as smashed up as the car. As I drove down the motorway, all I could see was that girl, the cigarette smoke curling around her, like Norman Newton's greedy yellow fingers.

I hit London in the early hours. I drove to a gloomy industrial estate, burned the car out, grotty boxers and all, and Citizen Digit's been under the radar ever since.

The End. Happy Ever After. Goodbye.

12. THE RELAXATION ROOM

I'd never been as happy as when I went to bed that night. For the first time ever, I had some kind of idea who I was. I know it were only a name, Katariina, but up 'til then, I'd had nowt. It gave us some hope. Maybe I could find out about me mam after all. She must have had family, somewhere or other. I probably had grandparents, an't I? Uncles and aunties, maybe. If I could find out more, if I could track any of 'em down, I could find meself a home. A family.

It were a grand feeling, going to sleep wi' that rolling round in me head.

In the morning, o' course, it were all different. Summat had happened. Lessons were cancelled and Barry and t'other Carers were going round in a right strop. Turned out someone had nicked the Governor's car and actually smashed down the fence that keeps us in. Someone: Byron. He'd really gone and done it, then; done his Citizen Digit trick, and broken out of Tenderness.

After breakfast we were all sent back to our rooms and locked in. It were then that I saw his note, on the floor by the end o' me bed. And me iPod in the folds o' me bedding.

So I watched it, din't I?

I'd heard about videos like this, o' course, on t'internet, but I wan't prepared for seeing it.

I paced the room, desperate for fresh air. But o' course the windows didn't open. I were trapped. And I had to watch the film again, 'cos I cudn't believe it were as bad as it was. But the second time it were worse, and I started shaking wi' it.

Byron were right.

But now we were locked in. He'd exploded the whole thing, done a runner to London, and left me to face the consequences. I should o' gone with him when I had the chance.

Outside the room, it all sounded horribly quiet. It were like the whole of Tenderness had shut down. No one came. No one shouted. The whole morning ticked by, minute by minute, endless.

I needed someone to come and open the door, let us out. But I knew that when they came, they might just as easy drag me over to the Governor's den, and do all that stuff to us like they done to the other WhyPees on the video.

Dinnertime came and went. Normally, I hate missing me dinner, but this were the first time for as long as I could remember that I cudn't stomach any grub anyway.

Half the afternoon went by, and I began to wonder whether they were ever going to let us out again. I were thinking maybe the police had turned up and arrested Call-Me and Barry. Maybe Digit had gone straight to

Social Services and told 'em everything that were going on. Maybe the police 'ud turn up any minute and unlock me door and tell us we could all go home; that Tenderness were shut down.

Except none of us could go home, could we? We ha'nt got no homes to go to. And Digit wun't o' gone to Social Services anyways; he hates them. There's no way he'd have gone to the authorities at all. He'd o' gone straight off down to London, looking for that lass whose picture he printed.

So eventually, when Barry came and unlocked the door, and me and the other WhyPees were all called into the dining hall for an important announcement from Call-Me hisself, I knew it were up to me.

I had to say summat, din't I? If I din't, no one else would.

We were all crowded together in the dining room, full o' whisper and rumour about the Jimmys and Byron, but no one were saying it out loud, 'cos no one wanted to really admit how bad it were. Everyone were just sort o' muttering stuff to their mates, and you cudn't hear owt proper.

Barry kept throwing us thundering looks, and he even threatened one or two o' the lads, like he cudn't wait to give 'em a good smacking.

Then Call-Me Norman came into the room and went and stood at the front, so's we all had a good view of him. I could tell he were gathering hisself together to make a speech.

A hush fell across the room.

"You're all here," he said, "because you broke the rules. Many of you broke the law. Some of you are a danger to yourselves, or to society. That is why you are here."

That were a joke. Me head kept replaying the film. The only dangerous ones were Norman Newton and his pals.

"One of you—" he paused, for effect. "One of you has, over the last night, proved – yet again – what a dangerous, destructive and downright criminal bunch you can be."

Character assassination, in't it? I could see why Byron wanted to create a new persona when the ones we had at the moment were supposed to be so rotten.

I had to say sommat, din't I? But I wondered how it might be, if it were just my word against the Jimmys. For a moment I thought that might be OK – 'cos it'd be me who were telling the truth. But Call-Me's speech reminded us what happened wi' the Barrowcloughs, how nobody had believed us then, and I were telling the truth then, wan't I?

"Some of you have been in cahoots with this individual. This is not acceptable."

All of us knew, all of us in the room. None of us were in cahoots wi' anyone. It were them – the adults – who were up to no good. The whole room were full of our muttering. They cudn't ignore us all. So I stood up, meself.

I pointed at Call-Me. Straight at his head. And I yelled out, "Everybody knows."

Then Barry punches us in the belly. All the wind goes out o' us, and I'm hearing a big intake o' breath from all t'others, still sitting round, but saying nowt. I'm bent down, holding me belly, trying to get me breath back, and Barry gets us in a headlock and marches us out o' the room.

Once we're out, he punches us in the head. I fall over. Then he kicks us in me belly. I'm all winded and seeing stars, curling up wi' it all, and Barry kicks us again. It hurts too much for me to even yell out. Then he's kicking me arms, which are trying to protect me belly.

"Not his face!" I hear the Governor yelling. "Don't kick his face!"

Then I'm getting carried through, back into the main Unit, and I'm thrown down into a room, in the dark. I lie there sobbing and hurting, feeling sorry for meself. Through me pain, I'm feeling round, and I can't find owt to lie down on, so I curl meself up on the floor and have a right old cry. Ages go by and I can't hear no sounds 'cept me own sobbing, and no one comes at all, and in the end I cry meself to sleep, right there on the floor.

When I wake up I'm aching everywhere, and someone's switched a light on. I'm in a sort of cell wi' nowt in it but a fixed bench made o' wooden slats. Only one of the slats has been taken out, so you can't really sit on it. And there's no window. It's lit by a bare bulb, switched on from outside. That's it. This must be the Relaxation Room.

After a while, Barry comes in. He takes me arms and makes me bend 'em and straighten 'em, and he feels all round me belly and looks at me head. Then he says, "Nothing broken."

133

Some time later he brings in some soup. But he don't say owt.

I don't know how many days I'm in there, but I keep count o' the number of meals Barry brings us, and I'm still in there after he's brought in fifteen *meals.*

So I've been in there for a week. And I have to poo in a bucket, which Barry empties when he brings in the food. It's disgusting. Stinks out the cell.

I suppose Call-Me Norman and Barry thought it were funny, calling this place the Relaxation Room. But it in't funny at all.

It's the worst thing that's ever happened to us.

You can't do this to people. It's torture.

They won't get away with it.

I don't have owt to read, but that's all right, 'cos I'm planning me revenge. I've got to play this right, make sure it ends proper, with Call-Me and Barry getting properly punished. Me brain just keeps wondering about what they're going to do to us, and about what happened to Byron, whether or not he managed to get to London. Maybe he did go to the police. Any time now, I'll be freed and Norman Newton and Barry and t'others 'ull be sent to prison. I'll be allowed to go back to the Barrowcloughs, to make up for all this horribleness.

I wish.

More likely, Byron got caught and he were locked up as well. Or if he did manage to escape, would he have even looked back? Would he have even given a second thought about what might happen to me or t'other YPs? He just chucked the evidence on the end o' me bed and left us to it.

'Cos it is, in't it? Up to me. Byron gave me the iPod 'cos he knows I'll speak up, that I'll make sure the authorities find out about what the Jimmys are up to.

The door opens and the pong of stale cigarette smoke wafts in. This time it's Call-Me Norman. "Hello Alfi," he says. "How are you doing?"

How's he think I'm doing?

I had nowt to say to that, which seemed to tickle him 'cos he gave a smile and reached into his jacket pocket and brought out his packet of Bourbon Creams. "Biscuit?"

"You're quiet," he says, "for a change." He leans forward and shoves a biscuit under me nose, but I can't even smell it 'cos of his stinky yellow tar fingers. "I like you quiet." He munches the biscuit hisself. Then, while he's still chewing, he says, "I wonder if that's the way you'll stay?"

This one-person conversation goes on for a half hour or so, and Call-Me Norman never gets bored of his own voice, and he gets happier and happier wi' me having nowt to say, and he eats another six biscuits, one after t'other. Then he calls Barry in, and Barry's got a look on his face like he wants to kick me in the stomach again, but he dun't.

He takes us back to me own room. He drops us back onto me bed, and he says, "One word. Just one word, and you get everything you've had, all over again, only doubled. Understand?"

I open me mouth to say yes I understand, but he holds

his finger up at me, like a warning. "One word," he says. He glares at me until I have to look away and stare at the wall. Then he walks from the room and locks the door behind him.

I press me head against me pillow to stop meself from sobbing. Then I dig out me iPod from under the mattress.

Call-Me Norman dun't know I've got this, does he?

This is all the evidence I need. It's power, en't it?

I click on the video camera, and there it is.

I glance at the peephole in the door. No one. Norman Newton reckons he's scared us enough, hurt us enough, to make sure I never open me mouth about any o' this.

I switch off the iPod and hide it back under me pillow.

I lie down, and think.

What's the plan?

Think, Alfi. Think.

But I already know what I'm going to do.

I'm going to tell. Tell all.

But to start with, I never said a word.

Governor Newton and Barry and t'other Carers were watching me like hawks. There weren't no sign o' Byron, and they must've been dead worried that he'd gone to the authorities.

But nobody came. No police. No social services. No journalists. No one.

Meanwhile, Call-Me Norman kept paying visits to me room, leaving us little gifts, crisps and fruit and stuff. One *day he left a whole packet of his favourite biscuits. It made us sick. I shoved the lot of it into me backpack. There's no way were I touching it, even though I were starved.*

And he kept smiling at us.

"How you doing, Alfi?" he'd say.

I'd shrug.

"Got no more nonsense up your sleeve?"

Shrug again.

"'Cos you know no one would ever believe any of it. All it does is make people annoyed, you know. People like Barry."

I tell you, I weren't saying owt.

"I know you were mates with Byron, but that lad's gone now. He was trouble. Whatever tales he might have been telling you were a load of rubbish. You know that, don't you?"

"Yes," I said.

"Good," he said. "You're a good boy, Alfi."

I had no choice, did I? Another week went by and I knew any evening now, Barry 'ud come and drag us from me room and march us over to the Jimmy den and I cudn't bear to think about it.

So I did it. I escaped.

I'd been thinking it through. All that time in the Relaxation Room and ever since, planning every detail. Byron weren't the only one who could make plans.

I'd got some wire cutters from the caretaker's

137

storeroom, and I took me backpack full o' snacks and put on as many layers as I could, for the cold. It were "Owntime" after breakfast, before lessons started. I sneaked out into the grounds. There were part of the fence that had a whole load o' bushes in front of it, and I snipped a hole at the bottom and squeezed through.

I'd already figured that if I took the road to Bradford I wun't get far before being dragged back, so I went the opposite way, across fields, up to Ilkley Moor. You'd have to be mad to go up Ilkley Moor this time o' year. Or desperate.

I found an old stone hut and huddled down wi' me crisps and biscuits and me six layers o' clothes. I wrapped meself in a scabby old blanket I found, and waited.

Two days. Call-Me Norman 'ud have Barry and his mates scouring Bradford for us, but I bet they wun't tell Social Services that I'd gone missing. I bet they han't told 'em about Byron either. They wun't want the attention. Too many awkward questions.

Nice thinking, Alfi. Using your brains.

I had a bit o' money, and after two days waiting it out, I got a bus into Bradford. I bought some chips and went straight to where I knew I'd be safe for a while, to stop and think.

The library.

I like to hang around libraries. They're warm and have soft seats, and newspapers and computers, and no one gives you hassle, even if you're there for hours.

The library were the one place where grown-ups 'ud

138

look at us but not take any notice. They'd just think, "Aww, ain't it sweet, young lad coming here and reading books and learning stuff for hisself."

So I rested, made me plans.

At first, I were going to go to the village where Mr and Mrs Barrowclough live, tell them everything. They were solid, Jenny and Doug. Then me brain told me not to be a muppet. As far as they were concerned, I were just some low-life thief. They'd never believe us.

So after I left the library, I went to Social Services. I had a Senior Case Worker there who were a good bloke. He were a professional. He wouldn't have the wool pulled over his eyes like Jenny and Doug. He'd know if someone were telling the truth, or if someone were lying.

You can see the truth, can't you? In people's eyes.

I were going to show him.

I went right up to the desk and asked to see him, and then I went into his office and sat down and he looked at us dead calm, and he said to us in a slow, soft voice, "So, Alfi, shouldn't you be in Tenderness House right now?"

I told him everything – about the Jim'llfixits and Barry beating us up and the Relaxation Room and the pervert policeman and Byron – the whole lot. I even give him the iPod.

"It's all on here," I said. This were it. The Jimmys had had it now. Me Case Worker would send for the police, and before any time at all, it'd be Call-Me Norman and Barry locked up in Relaxation Rooms o' their own.

"Alfi," he said, "you know as well as I do that young people in secure units are not allowed to have iPods and mobile phones and the like. Remember how you ended up with Mr Barrowclough's mobile phone, before you went to Tenderness? What am I supposed to think?" He gave a sigh.

"It's true!" I yelled. Then I took a breath, made meself quieten down. "Honest. It's true. Go on. Have a look at the video."

He looked at us dead grave-like. "All right. Wait here." And he stood up and he left the office. I'd done it!

He'd go and play the film, and see the truth and tell his managers and Call-Me 'ud go to prison, and as a reward for my breaking up the Jimmy Ring they'd let us go back and live in the village wi' the Barrowcloughs.

So I sat there, and waited.

Then I heard a voice buzzing in me ear like a gnat: There's a paw in the flan, there's a paw in the flan, there's a paw in the flan!

Citizen Digit – in me head. Wittering on, his usual nonsense. A paw in the flan, a paw in the flan! *Irritating.*

And still I sat there, waiting.

After ages passed by, I stood up, shook me head to get rid of his buzzing. "Raaagh!" I said, but his Smart-Alec voice just kept going on at us.

I looked at the clock on the wall. Half an hour had gone by.

And that voice: The Digit knows, the Digit knows...

So I flung open the door and stamped down the corridor.

And round the corner, I heard me Case Worker, talking to Call-Me Norman.

At first, I thought he were just on his phone.

"Call the Youth Discipline Team," he said. "We've got a situation with young Spar."

A flaw in the plan.

Then I heard Call-Me answer him, and he were right there, in the room with me Case Worker.

"I'm sorry the boy's been up to his old tricks," says Call-Me. "I'll see this iPod goes back to its rightful owner. Sticky fingers."

"I'd wondered what had happened to that," said another voice. Barry. And in the pause I could picture him sticking the iPod in his jacket pocket.

My evidence.

Whatever happened to "Listen to the Victims"?

"Look," says Call-Me, "it was very good of you to get straight on to us. It's a serious breach of the rules, what's happened here. But Alfi is going through a challenging time at the moment. I'm not sure how helpful it'll be, bringing in the Youth Discipline Team. Unless, I mean – Barry, would you want to press charges?"

"Good Lord, no," said Barry. "That would be a terrible backwards step for him. I thought he'd been making good progress."

"Well, what do you propose?" said the Case Worker.

On your marks *said the Citizen.*

"Why not have Barry here go have a quiet word with Alfi, and we'll take him back to Tenderness and leave it at that."

Get set *said the Digit.*

"If you think that's best," said the Case Worker.

Run for your life!

And I ran back along the corridor quick as I could. But all the rooms were locked, wi' nowhere to go but the room I'd been in. I shut the door and looked round for an escape. There were a window, but I were three floors up. Barry was coming along the corridor, and if he got his hands on us I'd be in for the beating o' me life. I'd be locked in the Relaxation Room for ever. If I were Citizen Digit I'd be able to invisibilize meself, escape that way. But I weren't. I were Alfi Spar.

Son of Katariina.

You can't trust none of 'em, can you? Even me Case Worker trusted a creep like Norman Newton more than me.

I were going to have to take a page out of the Digit's book. Find me own skills; use 'em for me own sake.

I opened the window. I climbed out. The winter wind were blowing a gale. I looked down, into the alley alongside the building, like a great pit, waiting to swallow us. I shut the window behind us. I jumped.

I landed on the ledge of the building opposite – just. I had to roll forward, so's I din't fall back down the alley.

I clambered over the tiles, round to t'other side. I were up high, but there were a drainpipe and I shimmied down it.

I were doing well, until the drainpipe started to give way from the wall. Horrible backwards falling. Nowt I could do, but cling on as the whole pipe came off and took us with it.

I crashed through a tree, a load o' spikey branches, and I were lucky I were wearing all them layers, but I still got scratched and cut. I were a right mess, torn and bloody, wi' flaps o' skin hanging off me hands.

Citizen Digit were right. I'd never trust the authorities again.

It were us, and them.

I staggered to me feet.

I'd never stop. And I'd never shut up.

I thought about the message I'd left for Call-Me Norman back at Tenderness. I'd borrowed a marker pen from art class – indelible, right? – and scrawled a great big farewell message on me room wall:

NORMAN NEWTON IS A JIM'LLFIXIT
(AND BARRY IS TOO)
THE WORLD WILL KNOW

That were just for starters.

13. EYEBALLING

"Predictiv Tex takes total responsibility for this catastrophic turn of events," says Tex, snarkastically.

Our bus has long since left behind the view of
Alfi Spar getting bundled off into the back of the local
Sherlockmobile, siren blaring.

"If the hoodie fits..." says I.

"It'll be me gettin' zapped then."

"Tex." I'm reassurance itself. "Virus ain't going to
zap no one."

My boy has a faceful of doubt. He reckons Virus is
going to go through several ceilings when he finds out
we lost Alfi Spar to the Sherlocks. It's true, we were only
supposed to show Alfi the ropes, not tie him up with
them. It's tricksy, finding that fine line between accus-
tomizing a boy to the ways of the street, and handing
him a one-way ticket to Tottenham Nick.

Citizen Digit Esquire should have been more con-
scious of the consequentials, shouldn't he?

"Listen," I say. "He ain't got nothing on him that can
link him to Operations—"

"The only stress might be if he blabs to the Sherlocks that he's part of Virus's crew and leads them straight to base."

"Zackly." Durrr. "Oh! No, listen, that wouldn't happen. Alfi would never blab."

"'Cos Squealer-Face never blabs, right?"

Right now, Tex is being more irritating than an eyeful of Vindaloo. I lean in close. "It's like this, yeah? Alfi's going to claim total innocence, correct? Correct. And, having had Mr Dictiv Tex throw a freshly picked wallet at his angel face, he's twigged that *Cash Counters* is actually a den of dishonesty. Correct? Correct. So what good is it going to do him, how's it going to serve his plea of innocence, directing the local Sherlocks to a store full of liberated goods? Hmm? Predict *that*, Tex-Head."

In actual fact, I cannot even convince myself, Mr Citizen Digit, that Alfi ain't such a fart brain as to point the Finger of Accusation in our direction. As I said, the boy's a blabbermouth. And he lives under the insane illusion that if you only Tell the Honest Truth, all will be well in the end. What a div.

And me and Tex have put him straight into the hands of the Law. It's a right royal disastrophy. Virus is going to have our guts for pudding. I'm seriously thinking of doing a total vanishing act.

"Don't even think about it," says Tex. "You ain't disappearing and leaving me on my own to face the consequence."

145

"I've never been so insulted in all my life, upon my life," I fibricate.

"As if you would," says Tex.

"As if I would."

My mind is racing round and round like the rainbow wheel when your laptop freezes. Pretty, and pointless. The best I can think of is to put off telling Virus for as long as possible.

"Let's not get off the bus at our stop," says Tex.

"Let's stay on until it hits the West End," I say.

"Then we'll get off and have a buzz in the shops."

"Spend the day liberating goodies for Virus's window display."

"The whole day," says Tex. "Sweeten him."

"Sweeten him."

If anybody can describe to the Digit a better plan, I'll award them an MBE, an OBE and a DVD.

Tex and I have a deeply rewarding day: three purses and a wallet; two tablets, three BlackBerries, and a couple of iPods; more snacks and drinks than we can stuff in our gullets; the complete Harry Potter box set; one Gucci watch; one Bulgari necklace (snatch and run!); and a totally cool miniature torch. Wotta buzz.

It's dark by the time we're bussing it back up to Seven Sisters. We're smacking each other's backs over how Virus'll totally forgive us for slightly mislaying Alfi Spar. We're utterly convicted that Spar-Boy was probably let off with a police caution and is already back at *Cash Counters* digging into double burger and chips. Or, surely Shirley, Alfi made a great escape and returned to Operations with Poshboy's wallet, stuffed with cash. Or, yes indeedly, we're mos' definite in our view that Virus never liked Alfi anyway, and will be glad that we've helped get rid of him. Virus is probably planning great treats for us right now. Life is as sweet as it's ever been.

Tex is looking deadly pale.

"Nah, blud," he says, shortly before the stop for *Cash Counters*. "There's contacts I might check with, get me? Have some knowledge to share. Find where your friend is hanging."

My friend, all of a sud.

"You can let Virus know the Dictiv is on the case. He can rely on me, yeah?"

I'm saying nothing.

"I ain't bailing," he babbles. "You know it, yeah? I just – just got a lead or two I should pursue."

Bus starts slowing down for our stop. "Tex," I say, "it's better to risk a small zapping now, than have Virus save it all up for you. The Great Manager ain't no idiot."

But he's got his gaze fixed out the window. "I'm going to check out the Manor House crew. See if they've heard anything. Tell Virus – tell Virus: Tex is doin' his duty. Yeah. *Doin' his duty.* You got that?"

I stay with Tex for two more stops, in case of

Sherlocks tugging our tails. As I hop off the bus, loaded down with all our ill-gottens, I'm sad for him. I liked him. But I know we'll never see Tex back at Operations again. Virus is a man of discipline.

And yeah, if you want the God's honest, Citizen Digit is sweating it. We've compromised the whole *Cash Counters* set-up. Virus is going to go zap-happy. Needless to say, the Digit will be on the receiving end of Dictiv's share.

But you got to screwtinize the bigger picture. The Manor House crew ain't fools. Anybody running out of Virus's Operations is contaminated goods. Ain't nobody going to touch Tex now.

He is even more on his lonesome than Alfi Spar.

Nevertheless, Citizen Digit ain't simply going to stroll into a major zapping, any more than he's going to show his face to the Sherlocks or the SS. For certain, as I hover over the road opposite Operations, I'm spying for any sign of the Sherlocks. If Alfi has scattered them a trail of crumbs back to *Cash Counters*, no way am I walking back into custardy.

What a mess. I should never have brought the Blabber back to *Cash Counters*. I should never have gone out of my way to film the Jim'llfixits to warn him of the danger.

If they get me back to Tenderness, it's my life over.

As I scan the street, I wish I could tag Alfi Spar with the blame. Or Predictiv Tex. Wish I could blame Virus or even Jackson Banks.

And talk of the demon, I see JB's latest set of wheels mounted on the kerb outside *Cash Counters*. I can tell it's Jackson's 'cos it's illegibly parked and the windows are blacked out. He likes it that way, so he can see out, but you can't see in. JB's got no licence to drive and he buys his motors cash in hand. When they get clamped, he just leaves 'em, like busted toys left at the end of a garden.

Maybe I'll give it a miss. Last thing I want is a throttling from Jackson Banks as well. I'll spend the night on the buses. Face up to Virus in the morning.

Not safe in Yorkshire, not safe in London. Caught between the Devil and a deep blue seizure. Wretched as Byron, yet suddenly in the doo-doo as Digit. I need to disappear altogether. I need—

A shadowy figure is lurking dead suspish outside *Cash Counters* entrance. He's got a hat pulled down and a collar pulled up, but there's no disguising that fizzogful of hair perving out into the night air.

My kneebones turn to custard and I topple against a wheelie bin, sliding down into its dog-wee shadows. I'm here in Seven Sisters Road. But I'm looking at Governor Norman Newton.

I wedge myself deeper into the shadows. Suddenly desperate for the loo.

Call-Me Norman. But how? And why?

This is the worst development ever. Call-Me must have tracked us down. Someone must have blabbed.

Alfi. Boy probably wrote down a forwarding address, right underneath WE'RE GOING TO TELL. Yeah. AND YOU CAN FIND US AT...

No. No matter how football-stadium-sized Alfi's mouth is, he didn't even know *Cash Counters* existed, never mind where it is. If by any chance he blabbed everything to the Sherlocks, I suppose they *might* have contacted Tenderness, but even the Seven Sisters pavement-plodders wouldn't just immediately tell all to Norman Newton. Not with Alfi-Boy yelling *Jimmy This* and *Jimmy That* all over the cop shop.

What about the evidence? Alfi *swore* he had the evidence somewhere safe. But then he said he gave the iPod to his Case Worker.

Citizen Digit, you need to get your brain in gear.

Think. You need more inf. How do you get it? You do what you always do. Do what you do best.

Citizen Digit Esquire's Incredible Disappearing Act.

Oh, I'm impressive. I'd applaud myself if my middle name wasn't Humility.

So, I watch while Call-Me Norman stands by the *Cash Counters* side door, waiting to be buzzed up. I navigate four lines of traffic jam while Call-Me pushes the door open and steps inside. I glide over the pavement and wedge my Nikes into the doorframe just before the door clunks back into its latch. Softly softly.

Newton's stagnant smokiness creeps into my nostrils as I stand there, torn in two. I could disappear, for real this time. Go off after Predictiv Tex, never step foot in *Cash Counters* again. Or I can step up, refresh my vicinity with Call-Me Norman and let what must be, be.

I step up, and in.

It's late. Most of Virus's young henchies'll be beddy-byes, aside from his overnight hacking team, busily tap-tapping in the Techno Room.

Stair creak. The Digit is convinced Virus has no stair carpet in order to assistificate his earflaps with intruder-detecting. But Air-Max got extra bounce, ain't it? Don't the shoebox claim these trainers are like walking on air? Speshly when inched along each step-edge by Twinkletoes Digit himself. Hah, invisibility ain't a power any fool can develop. It takes dedicated Olympics-style training.

I'm hearing voices as I inch my way up, figuring how many, who, where.

Virus: tetchy.

Call-Me: blunt, businesslike.

And Jackson Banks: bonkers.

Busyness as usual then. They're gathered round Virus's precious dinner table. I gently lay down my ill-gottens and drift towards the open door.

I look through.

Oooh, this bit gives even the Digit the willies. It's like my eyeballs have floated out of their sockets and are roaming freely round the room, taking the closest peek-a-boo at the assembled. My gaze is right in Jackson Banks's chortling mush, but he can't see me. All he can see is whatever opportunity for gain is in front of his face. In this instance, Governor Norman Newton. Virus. If he clocked I was there he'd be instantly zippitty-zap-ping away. But *his* focus is on Call-Me's filthy fingers and the cigarette burning a long line of ash, threatening to fall on his luvverly varnish. He keeps shifting the ash-tray from spot to spot, try and have it in position for when the ash drops.

Obnob, leaning against the wall, would chew my face off if he got the slightest sniff of me. But Invisible Digit don't smell, does he? Odourless boy. And poor old Crow, slumped next to Obnob, hoping he's not going to get nipped by the dog or thrashed by Banks.

Lastly, Grace. How come Call-Me knows where to find Grace? I thought she was one of the runaways. *Cash Counters* is supposed to be a safe house. Has the Digit been played for a fool all along?

Then me and Alfi are doomed.

Ain't nothing to do but sink into a cooler space. Go all tranceydental.

And like this, in this state of coma-ness, sliding gently into listening position outside the door, Citizen Digit becomes all ears. And this is what he earwigs:

"How much?" Jackson.

"Three hundred." Call-Me Norman.

There's an awkward pause. Call-Me's taking a long toke on his cigarette.

"In total?"

"Per girl." You can hear Call-Me Norman's irritation. I picture him, reaching for a biscuit. Smoke and munch.

"I'm not particularly happy about these negotiations taking place on my premises," says Virus, wiggling uncomfy.

"Mute it," says Banks.

"Shall I remind you," says Call-Me, "of how you obtained the funds to set up this business of yours, Mr Virus?"

Virus says nothing to that. But it gets the Digit wondering. Virus and Call-Me have history?

"Once you have the girls," Call-Me continues, to Banks, "the profit is in perpetuity."

"In English," Banks demands.

"They'll keep earning for ever."

Call-Me's munching and crunching. Nervousness, ain't it? He likes to bite, snap and swallow, sharklike. None of this sogginess. How come he's so nervy?

Banks, ain't it. Obnob gives a whine.

"Hungry doggie," says JB.

There's a snaffling sound as Norman Newton tosses the beast a Bourbon. Gone in one gulp.

"Hungry, not peckish. Starving doggie."

I'm hearing the entire packet unrustling, followed by grizzling, snarfling sounds like when peeps get eaten down in a zombie movie. Bourbons demolished by Obnob.

"All over my floor!" whimpers Virus, but no one takes any notice.

"It's three girls," Call-Me goes on. "That'll be nine hundred pounds, plus transportation fee. Call it a straight grand. They're all sixteen, still children, but legal." He pauses for effect. "That means legally they are adults. Once they officially leave Tenderness House, they're off the system. Social Services don't need to bother with them any more. Effectively, they won't exist. Nobodies. Gorgeous nobodies with no home, no family, no job. They need *you*, Banksy, as much as you want *them*."

Banksy.

"Eight hundred then. All in."

"I won't take less than a grand. They won't need any training. They're already good at what they do."

I feel sick.

"Well, Banksy?" Call-Me wheedles on. "The poor girls are going to be homeless. They need a – a Responsible Adult."

"Hah," go Virus and Grace, in synch.

There's a thunderous silence. I picture Jackson's eyes burning into Grace's face; Obnob's glaring at Virus. An awkward moment.

"As I say: one grand. Non-negotiable."

"If we're done," says Virus, taking JB's further silence to mean an agreement's been reached, "perhaps you could take yourselves back to where you belong. I have tidying up to do." There's a shiveriness to his voice when he says the word *tidying*. It ain't just his varnish that's tarnished. He's got a mucky stomach.

I always knew the kind of nastiness JB had Grace up to. Now Banks is expanding the business. How can they do it, those girls?

But the Digit's seen the look in Grace's eyes when Jackson Banks's horseyplay gets a little too rough – she's been on the rough end of his tumbles. I dunno why she never just disappears.

"That's just it, Mr *Virus*," Call-Me goes on, emphasizing V's name like he's mocking it, like he knows what Virus is really called. What he *used* to be called. "I didn't arrange my business meet with Jackson to be here just for the convenience. I need to talk to you too. About boys."

"No." Virus is getting riled now. "That's not my type of business. Go elsewhere. I've told you."

"I need to talk to you about *missing* boys," Call-Me clarifies. "Absconders. Trouble-causers."

The Digit's burning ears start flaming. Virus gives an embarrassed little cough.

"We're all well aware of your, your kindness towards young runaways. There's one runaway in particular who wants to stir things up. Stir things up for me, and for Banksy here. And what's trouble for us, is trouble for you."

Another pause. My heart's thumping through my chest, loud as a heavy bass through paper-thin walls. What's he bringing Banks into it for? We've not crossed Banks. I'm not suicidal. Obnob gives another whine. His fight-tattered ears have picked up my heart-thump. And

155

I imagine Grace, through the wall, her own heart speed-ing up to match mine.

Virus leans in towards Call-Me Norman. "Names?" he asks.

"First boy: Spar," says Norman. "Alfi. Alfi Spar. He wants to bring us all down."

I picture Virus casting the tiniest glance in Grace's direction. They say nothing, but Jackson catches it. He clocks it. He giggles. "Then we'll bring *him* down. Hidey seeky. Catchy monkey."

"Don't know of him," says Virus, carefully. "Spar, you say? I'll put the word out."

"He's not to be hurt though," Call-Me insists. "He's to be brought back. Back to Tenderness." He looks at Jackson Banks. "In full working order. You understand?"

"What's the prize?" says Banks.

"Keeping out of jail." He waits for this to sink in. "He's a lovely-looking boy. Mop of blond hair. Blushes at the drop of a hat. Eyes like summertime. Make sure he stays that way."

JB snorts, but Call-Me professes not to hear it. He goes on. "Alfi Spar got hold of some incriminating mate-rial. Got as far as handing it to Social Services. We got it back, just in time, but it was a tricky job persuading them we'd caught the boy, after the runaround he gave us. Now we need to make it true, before they become suspicious. That boy *must* not fall into the hands of the police or the Social. We need him back where he belongs."

As if.

"And the second boy," Call-Me continues. Then he says it. My real name. "He's been gone for over a month now. Mouthy. You might know him."

"Byron *Blank Space*? No, don't think we've come across him."

"If we get him," says Jackson Banks, "return to sender?"

"No." Call-Me Norman goes all adamantium. "Dispose of him. He deleted his entire file – makes it easier for us. He's no one. And no good to anyone."

"Price on his head?" All Banks thinks about is profit.

Call-Me sighs. "He's trouble for you as much as Alfi Spar. But I tell you what. You make Byron *Blank Space* disappear permanently, we'll owe you a girl. Gratis."

"Deal," says Banks. "The game is on." He rubs his hands together, gleeful.

I can hear Call-Me rummaging around in a bag. "And you know what? Here's an added incentive to help you along a little bit. To do the job properly."

"Ooooh," says Jackson Banks, like an over-excited kid. "It's lovely this."

What is?

"It's a Glock," says Call-Me. "A gift, from a policeman friend. Use it wisely."

A gun. He's handed a gun to *Jackson Banks*? Citizen Digit is sick to his stomach. Luckily, Byron *Blank Space* was killed off a long, long time ago.

I'm already dead.

A gunshot blasts my eardrums and a sulphur smell trickles through the doorway. My hands immediately crawl all over my body, search for a bullet wound. Inside the room, Obnob is whimpering in terror.

"Banks!" yells Virus, forgetting himself. "Are you insane?"

"Use it when you need it, Jackson!" snaps Norman Newton. "It's not a toy."

Another deafening blast.

"Ooops," says Jackson Banks. "Twitchy finger. How many bullets, you say? I'll need plenty."

"That's enough," says Call-Me, in his sternest Governor Voice.

BANG!

Each time, I feel a bullet blasting through my heart.

"What are you doing to my wall?" I've never heard Virus so angry. "Please, just get out of here. Go on! Leave!"

There's a silence. I picture Jackson Banks raising the gun, aiming it, slow and steady, at Virus's sweating face.

"That's enough, Banksy," says Call-Me, again. This time soft, gentle-like.

"All right, all right, keep your hair on. I'm going for a slash."

Jackson Banks strides out of the room and walks right past where I'm huddled. If he looks up, I'm dead. But he's too busy admiring his new weapon.

In the room, Virus and Norman Newton are whispering together. My double-plus lugholes pick it all up:

Virus: "Are you insane? You'd be as well giving a grenade to a five year old."

Newton: "Nonsense. You're too mistrusting of Jackson. He needs his outlets."

Virus: "Outlets? I've seen the state of some of the boys who've come away from Tenderness House. You and your *outlets*."

A pause.

Newton: "Banksy always had a liking for weaponry. It's part of his nature. And we fulfil our remit. We satisfy the Reliance Plus shareholders – no thanks to *certain persons* syphoning off company funds. It might have been ten years ago, but I still know the name of that person, Mr *Virus*. Don't forget it."

"I retired my post."

"Nobody retires from Tenderness. It's a post for life."

"My role was only administrative. I didn't do what you did."

Another pause.

"I thought you were wiser than this. It's as well that I have Jackson Banks on hand."

"Banks doesn't obey *you*."

"What? Banks obeys *you*?"

Grace: "Stop it, both of you. 'E's comin' back."

The Mad Dog almost stands on my fingers, he

stomps so close. He's still waving the gun about like he's Billy the Kid.

"Well," Banks says to the assembled, "that's me a couple of pints lighter. Don't worry, Fairy Cakes, I washed me hands. Come on, Grace, we got a couple of boys to hunt down. Happy days."

"Have a nice evening, Mr Virus," says Newton, all gloatful.

For once, Citizen Digit is at a loss. I sink into the wallpaper as they make their way out. I smell 'em coming, Call-Me first with his stale tobacco clinging to him like rot; Obnob, like stewed meat; and Jackson, ripe gym sweat. Grace is the only one of them who smells good.

I'm cowering in the shadows. I'm a dead boy. The only reason I'm so invisible is because I'm the Ghost of Myself.

They trail past. If Norman Newton turns and sees me, Jackson will have me full of holes and gym-bagged within the minute.

But it's Grace who turns. Half a mo, she winks at me, then glides onwards behind these beasts. Her head held high, noble, her long locks prettying up the murk she's gliding through. Her chin trembles as she passes. I imagine her, going to lie on her back now, to make easy cash for Jackson Banks.

Crow, last of all, limping behind them, staring straight through me. His dead eyes meeting mine. Saying nothing, trailing past.

Nobody saw no one.

Down they go, creatures of the night. The door clunks behind them. I stay hunched, my face sunk behind my knees, thinking about the price on my head.

"Digit!" Virus's voice snaps me out of it. "I know you're out there. In here! Now!"

14. SERIOUS SHARPENING UP

First up, the Seven Sisters cops lock us in a cell. It en't much different to the Relaxation Room at Tenderness House.

"Been in one of these before, have you, 'Fred'?" says the copper, sarky. They've already taken me fingerprints, which were dead messy, and me hands are covered in smudge that won't wash off proper. And they put a swab in me mouth so they could test me spit. The copper put on rubber gloves when he did it, like he thought he were going to catch summat off us, like I were some sort of mangy dog they'd picked up from the gutter. I suppose I am really. And they took me picture too.

"Don't smile," said the copper. As if. I had a big bump on me head an' all, from when I landed on the pavement.

Because I were under fourteen, the police cudn't take me fingerprints when Jacob got us arrested for stealing from Doug's wallet. But 'cos I told this lot that I'm sixteen, they reckon they're allowed. But me prints aren't on the system, so they don't know that I'm really Alfi Spar, so the joke's on them.

I told 'em that I were just trying to give the bloke his

wallet back, and I had nowt to do wi' taking it, but they kept asking us a zillion questions. Who were I with? What were their names? Where do I live? But I can't tell 'em owt, can I? If I tell 'em the truth, I'm dead. They'll take me and Byron back to Tenderness House, and that's it, everything's up.

I hate it. I hate not telling the truth.

Me head hurts where I bumped it.

Think, Alfi, think. Got to get yourself out of here. They han't even given you no food, just some water. It's got to be illegal to lock you up this long wi' no food. If they knew you were only fourteen they wun't dare.

Always tell 'em sixteen, whatever happens.

I ought to stop doing what Byron tells us. He en't that bright, is he? He's always pretending everything. Trying not to be who he really is.

Not me. I know who I really am. Me mam is called Katariina.

KATARIINA.

Me head's on fire and I've had enough. I'm going to tell 'em.

I'll tell 'em about that Predictiv Tex lad stealing the wallet, and I'll tell 'em about Cash Counters *too – I bet they'd be dead interested in what's going on there. I'll tell them about Mr Virus – I bet that en't even his real name. But I don't need to tell them about Tenderness House 'cos they'll never believe us. And I don't need to tell 'em I'm Alfi Spar.*

When I'm free, when I'm safe, when it's right, I'll tell all about the Jimmys.

Me cell's got a buzzer. I think it buzzes for the desk sergeant. I'm going to lean on it, just keep on pressing it till somebody comes.

That's it, Alfi. Use your brains.

At last, someone comes.

"I'm only fourteen!" I yell. "I'm only fourteen! I shun't be here. I'm just a kid. I'm fourteen!"

The copper escorting us down the corridor looks really grumpy.

"Fourteen! Do you hear me? Fourteen!"

They lead us to an interview room, and there's a sergeant sitting at a desk, and I sit down opposite, and the copper who brung us in says, "Apparently, he's only fourteen."

"Is that so?" the sergeant says.

"Aye, and I'm only just turned fourteen too. I en't much more than thirteen."

"Well, I'd never have guessed." They love doing sarcasm, the police, don't they?

"And I din't pinch the stupid wallet either. I were trying to hand it back. I en't a thief."

"Well, we know that now," says the sergeant. "The man who owns the wallet has made a statement, saying that you were trying to hand it back. Someone else stole it, apparently."

"You can't keep us then! You have to let us go! And give us me phone back!" I jump up.

And down. Summat's the matter.

Sergeant looks at us all clever-dick. "Definitely not. You can have your phone back – but that's all. You've just confirmed that you're only fourteen. As we thought. We have a duty of care. We can't put you out onto the streets. You're only a kid."

"What?"

They're going to stick us back in that cell. That can't be right.

"Listen, 'Fred'. You need to understand, we're on your side here. We've only held you for this amount of time a) because you had a knock on the head, and it's our duty to watch you for a while and make sure you don't go fainting or anything. And b) we've been trying to establish who you actually are. Up to the present moment, we've failed to achieve b. Perhaps you'd like to tell us now?"

"I'm – I'm..."

And I want to. I do; I really do. But I'm remembering me Case Worker in Bradford; how he got straight on to Call-Me Norman.

Me head hurts. Throbbing. "I'm nobody."

The sergeant sighs. I can tell he's getting tired. Dead tired. "We know you're not called Fred," he says. "What kind of kid is called Fred?"

He looks at the copper who came in wi' me. "Did the Council get back to you?"

The Council?

"Yes," says the copper. "They're sending the Welfare Team over now."

Welfare Team?

"What's going on?" I ask.

"Well, 'Fred'. Obviously we can't keep a young kid like you in the cells overnight, and neither can we turn you out onto the street. As – at the moment – we aren't able to establish who you are, and who you belong to, we're going to have to set you up in short-term emergency foster care. Do you understand what that means?"

I blink. "A foster family?"

"Short-term," says the sergeant.

"When?" I say.

A family.

"Soon as they get here," he answers, closing his file.

Yes!!!

I'll have a family again.

That's the way, Katariina's son. Played a blinder. And I managed all this without having to drop the Digit in it, after all.

Result.

The Good Citizen is in for the zapping of a lifetime.

I think about running, here and now. Get to street level and do a Mo Farah. But in my chest I know Virus would have his henchies track me down in no time flat. And if any of them find out I used to be Byron *Blank Space*,

I'm dog meat. Literally, if JB has anything to do with it.

"Digit!" Virus yells. "You're trying my patience now!"

Okily-doke. This is it then. In I go. Take a deep breath.

I won't bite my tongue off when I'm zapped, lose my brightest attribute. I won't.

"Come," he says. He's lounged on his sofa as I inch in. "Make yourself comfy. This is your home, Didge." His eyes widen in joke surprise. "No Tex? Surely our faithful friend wouldn't be so unpredictable as to ... lose his way?" He mock tuts. "Not when we need his talents so much –" he snatches my wrist and pulls me next to him "– to get back Alfi Spar!"

The Digit figures it's prudish to stay shtum at this point.

Virus has enough vocab for the two of us. "That's Alfi Spar, who as you have just eavesdropped, is even as we speak conspiring to bring everything tumbling down around our heads!"

"I think he's—"

"I *know* where he is, Digit. I have him tracked, don't I? Have a guess. Go on, I'm sure you'd make a highly informed go of it. Well, boy, where do you think Mr Alfred Spar is residing at this point in time? Where?"

"Err..."

"I'll tell you. Tottenham police station. The police station, Digit. Which is most peculiar, because I distinctly remember the last time I set eyes on him he was in the safe and reliable hands of one Citizen Digit."

"See, what happened is—"

"Save it. I can guess only too well. Trouble at our door, boy, trouble at our door. Look around. What do you see? Nothing! No one! Where are our friends, our little playmates? All gone. Shipped out to safe houses around the borough. And half our electronic items bagged up and shipped out to trusted associates. Because of you, boy, because of you!"

I can't hack the wait. "Go on, then. Go on." I close my eyes. Clench my teeth. In the scrunched starriness of my lids, I wait for the jolt.

"Open your eyes, little soldier."

I can't.

"Open your eyes."

"Please," I say, "just do it."

I can take the pain. Not the waiting. In the dark.

"Open."

I do. He's not got his zapper aimed at my face. His hands are praying, on his lap. "Do you see the police around you? No. Do you see your Manager sitting in handcuffed indignity? No. If they were going to come, they'd have come by now. I'm prepared. We have nothing to hide here. Not now. What I'd like to know, Citizen, is what's going on? What's the story? Why is Alfi Spar so important?"

Ah. I get it. You can't bleed no info out of a zapped-out zombie. Virus is the kind of gentleman who likes to know all the right angles. Ask questions first, shoot later.

"Well?" he prompts me.

"What do you know about Norman Newton?" I blurt.

"Aha, ha," Virus muses, fidgeting with his phone. "What do *you* know about Norman Newton?"

Careful now. "According to Alfi," (hah, see what I did there?) "he runs a Young Persons Secure Unit. Place where Alfi comes from. I think Alfi did a runner."

"Oh, you do, do you? How bright. What a bright young man you are, Mr Digit. And why, why do you think it is that young Alfi felt the need to flee from this place?"

"Well, you know, we all hate those kind of places, don't we?"

"Do you now? Why's that then?" He's trying to squish me into a corner, ain't he?

"Do you think –" I play the game like a triple-crowned champ "– Alfi might have something *on* Norman Newton?"

"Something on him? Oh, that's an interesting idea. Any thoughts as to what that might be? Any vague ideas?"

I shrug, like the sort of fool boy I'm not. Don't over-play it, Didge. "Up to no goodness?"

"Mmmm. Maybe."

What's his game? I need to know his game, otherwise how am I able to play him?

Virus says, "So Alfi never told you then?"

I could spill. But if I overflow, the link to Jackson Banks is too severe. If Call-Me is passing on girls for

Banks to pimp out, then Alfi (and me) can bring the Sherlocks directly to his door. And from JB's door to Virus's is an untidy litter trail of house-burgled goodies. Half of *Cash Counters*' Tru Valu merchandise comes straight out of JB's gym bag.

So I say, "I was trying to find out from Alfi. I think he dug up some sort of evidence. Some sort of wrong-doing."

"What's it to do with Jackson Banks, do you think?"

"Dunno."

"And what about that other boy?"

My heart brakes. "Other boy?" I say.

"Other boy." He leans in close. His eyes flick down to his phone, but he ain't checking no text, is he? "This ... Byron *Blank Space*."

He's setting the voltage.

I am cool. I am cool. But I'm sweating, ain't I? I can feel beads of it building up on my forehead, squealer-sweat. "Don't think I know him," I say. "Byron... Byron what's his name?"

"*Blank Space*."

"*Blank Space*. Byron *Blank Space*. Nope. But I'll let you know if I hear of him on the grapeline."

"Thanks, Digit. I knew I could rely on you. Oh, here's a funny thing."

"Yes?"

"It's Alfi Spar. The other night, when we were all having so much fun. I could have sworn – I might be wrong – but I thought for a minute I heard him call *you*

Byron. Is that possible, do you think?"

That's it. I'm getting zapped to smithers.

"No," I say. "No, no. That's crazy. Oh, I get it. It must have been when he called me by my other name. My birth name. Brian. I hate it when he does that."

"Brian?"

"Yeah. Nasty, isn't it? Now you know why I call myself Citizen Didge."

"Not Byron?"

I hold out my hands, all nonshalonse. "Do I look like a Byron?"

He ain't convinced. "Do you look like a Brian?" he counters.

"Exactly."

This conversation's on a fast train to Nowheresville. Better reset the Sat Nav. "Listen, Mr Virus, I know I messed up today – big time. I should never have let Alfi Spar fall into the Long Arms. If I can talk to him, I can get you all the answers you need. I'll do the mission, make up for my misdeeds. It's dangerous, I know, but if I go to the police station I can say I witnessed it all – I'll even give them a description of Tex's mug if it'll help convince them. I'll say I know Alfi from the street, and get the goodies from them about what's going on. I'm hot. I got skill. The Digit's the best. You know that."

"What good will any of that do?" he snaps.

"See, I get to Alfi, one way or another he needs our help, yeah? He can let us know what's the score with this geez who runs the Secure Unit. Norman...?"

"Newton."

"Norman Newton. And once you know what's a what-ness, well, you hold all the cardies, don't you? You can figure out what works out best for us here, can't you?"

Virus is silent for a long time. He's thinking it all through. "You think I don't already know?" he says. My heart goes boom. "Norman Newton is a nasty piece of work. He's bad news for everybody." My heart goes phe-ew. "He needs to learn a lesson or two. Let's put it this way, Didge. Alfi might not just be a liability to Norman Newton. He might be of *value* to him. And if he's of value to Newton, then he can be of value to us. Always follow the money, young prince. Always follow the money."

Virus is nutkins. He surely realizes the extent of the nastiness that takes place at Tenderness. He reckons everything boils down to *blackmail this* or *bribe that*. Alfi *of value* to Call-Me Norman? Hah! Like a one-pound note.

So I ask Virus the million-yen question. "What I don't get," I say, "is what's the connection between you and Norman Newton. How come he seems to know you?"

He clenches his fist. I've overmarked the step. I brace myself.

Then his shoulders go all saggy, like he's as tired as me. "It's true. Norman Newton and I go way back. You didn't think I was christened *Mr Virus* did you?" He pauses, and makes his confession. "Norman Newton knows my real name."

Then it's worse than I feared. We're all in it, up to our throats.

I try to hide my surprise. "So what's the plan then?"

He doesn't answer for ages, like he's lost in the annuals of time. "We'll see," he says, right when I think he's not going to answer at all. "Tomorrow. If Alfi's still in custody, seeing him might be an appropriate plan. But for tonight, Digit, I'm afraid you can't stay here. It's possible the law might still come a-knocking."

"Comprende." I stand up. Surely I'm not going to get away with it? "I'll make myself rare for the night. I'll pop back in the morno. I can take your directives then."

"Very good."

I turn to go.

"Oh, Byron?"

"Yes?"

"You need to do some serious sharpening up, Digit, some serious sharpening up."

Byron.

A bolt of pain sears through my arm. The bolt knocks me off my feet. I'm on the floor, jerking.

"Won't we ever learn?" I hear him through a squeal in my brain.

He zaps me again.

15. HOMELINESS

The desk sergeant gives us back me mobile phone. The only thing active on it is the clock. It's well gone midnight. No wonder I'm famished.

The Welfare Team ask us a zillion more questions – twice as many as the police did. But I'm saying nowt, for now. Tell 'em I'm Fred, and no more. Katariina's son is keeping his options open. No one need know about Alfi Spar or Call-Me Norman or any of it. Not yet. Not if I'm to stay with a proper family again.

It takes for ever before they finally let us see 'em. They lead us through into the Victim Support Lounge. I en't a suspect any more, am I?

I go in and there's a couple o' sneaky-looking crooks sitting there, and I'm wondering where me emergency foster family are, when this dodgy pair stand up and smile at us.

Oh, what? You're pulling me leg.

"Hello, Fred," says the bloke. "I'm Danny."

He's got a big, bald head like Phil Mitchell in Eastenders, and he's wearing razor-blade earrings. He's got a T-shirt with THE DAMNED on it, and a bunch of blokes dressed up as vampires and in maid outfits and stuff, and below them the words SMASH IT UP.

"Hiya," says the woman. "I'm Scarlett." And they both stand up to shake me hand.

This en't right. Scarlett's got a big mop of unwashed hair that looks like a giant Brillo pad. Black and silver, wi' flecks o' colour like it's been used to paint a few walls. She's wearing charity clothes. She pongs like skanky socks.

They en't exactly Mr and Mrs Barrowclough. But I say hello and shake their hands 'cos it's right to be polite.

Everyone puts their signatures over twenty sheets of paper. The Welfare Team and coppers watch very closely to see whether I sign me own name, but I en't that thick, and I put down Fred X. I like that. Fred X. Citizen Digit 'ud like that. I'll have to tell him. Or, I would, if me and him weren't done wi' each other.

Maybe I'll be able to get rid of Alfi Spar for good. That boy were nowt but a loser. But me mam named us Alfi, so I better stick wi' that. I could be Alfi X. Dun't sound as good as Fred X. Wait on – Citizen Digit's still got me birth certificate, han't he? I'll have to find him, get it back. Nobody gets away wi' taking me birth certificate.

"...must be pretty hungry, hey, Fred?"

Grub!

Scarlett is smiling down at us. She's got silver-plated teeth. In't it illegal to let people with silver-plated teeth foster kids? I reckon the Welfare Team have placed me wi' *these two 'cos they think I'm a villain, 'cos I won't give 'em me proper name. Still, got to be better than Tenderness.*

Grub. I realize I'm nodding like one o' them nodding dogs folk put in the back o' cars, and they're all laughing at us. But it's friendly laughter, and I smile back, and we're walking out the cop shop into the night air. Danny's got his hand on me back. It's physical contact, that is, which is against regulations. But I don't mind. Funny, in't it, how you can tell the difference? Between bad hands and good, I mean.

Scarlett drives us to their house in Finsbury Park. She drives fast, like she's in a bumper car at a fair, and keeps saying "Oops" and "Go! Go! Go!" The Digit 'ud like her. They should foster him. They're just his type.

Danny keeps asking questions, like, "Have you been in North London long?" and "What do you make of Finsbury Park, then? It can be a bit scabby, but we like it", and "Have you ever been to Hampstead Heath? It's like the countryside, only in the middle of London."

I en't really answering, just hmming and ahhing and nodding me head, and Scarlett says, "Don't mind Danny Boy. He's a right nosy sod."

Swearing's against the rules too. Then she says, "Hold tight: sharp left!" and almost crashes us into a wall. Then she's tooting her horn like a psycho and saying, "They all drive like lunatics round here, Fred. You'll get used to it."

Get used to it. Maybe, once I've settled in, I'll let 'em know I'm really called Alfi.

We get to their house. "It's no palace," says Danny,

"but it's got to be better than Tottenham Nick."

They push open the door and there's a yipyipyip and Scarlett switches on the light, and there's what looks like a wig zooming across the floor. It skids to a halt against Scarlett's boots, and starts to jump up and down, scrambling at her knees, a big pink tongue licking at her kneecaps.

"Iggy!" she says. "Hello, darling, did you miss us then? Did you miss us?"

"I hope you don't mind dogs," says Danny.

Iggy starts jumping up around us, and I bend down to pet him and he's licking me fingers like I'm his oldest pal from years back.

"Shall we show him round then, Scar?"

They lead us into the kitchen. It's got an old wooden dining table and in the middle of it is perched a black cat, on a place mat, totally still, like a catty vase.

"Evening, Patti." Danny ruffles the cat's head. Patti narrows her eyes and smiles at us, purring like a phone set on vibrate.

"Go on, Fred," says Scarlett. "Have a poke around. It's a free country."

So I do. First up, I look in the fridge, which is a bit of a letdown, if I'm honest. It's got a couple o' cans of beer, a tub o' margarine, some crusty-looking cheese and an onion. Where's the scran they were going on about?

I look in the cupboards. Only one of 'em has any food in, and that's a tin o' kidney beans, a packet o' lentils and a bag o' flour.

"Oh, yeah," says Danny, "we're not much cop at cooking."

What?

He tosses us a takeaway menu.

"It's a late-night one. Indian grub. Is that all right? We can do a chips and kebab shop if you like?"

"No. No, that's great. I love curry."

"Go on then," says Scarlett. "Pick what you like, and we'll make the order."

Just hold it right there, Alfi. Don't let 'em think you're greedy. You mustn't mess this one up, on top of all t'others. "Err," I say, "I'll just have whatever you two are having. I don't mind."

But I've got me fingers crossed that they'll order plenty of good stuff.

And they do. Scarlett orders three pilau rices, a stuffed naan, chicken tikka, lamb curry, aloo ghobi, channa masala, two dhals and four samosas.

"We have to get enough for Iggy. He's a complete curry hound."

So am I.

Citizen Digit manages to stagger himself onto the street, out from *Cash Counters*, his legs warm and damp, head screeching. Traffic roars. Headlights like light-sabres. Tumbles off the kerb. Angry horns and squealing breaks. Keep it together, Didge.

Had a little accident, trouser department. Bladder storm.

Keep walking. Keep on walking. In big, mad London no one will offer botheration. Walk away, down the road to nowhere.

Somewhere. The Digit has to get somewhere. Away from Virus and his zap-happy teaching method. Away from this ache.

Oh, yeah, I know where. Safe house. Tender ... ness. Not Reliance Plus. Not Call-Me and his Fixits. No. The tender touch, the soft hand: Grace.

To change me, wash and dry me, blanket me.

Blank it.

The Digit walks and he walks and he walks and he walks, cool damp strides, cold clammy socks. Squidgy Didge. Citizen Digit looks messtastic, his head abuzz. I'm a face ache. But on I walk, because if you stop moving, they catch you. You stand still and the game's Kerplunk.

Grace lives and works in a one-bedroom flat – kindly installed there by one Jackson Banks – above a newsagents up the Arsenal. JB's place is only a street or two away, so he can keep a close eye on her proceedings. She'll be there now.

So that's where the Digit goes, same as the other Joes, to see the sister who'll tend the blisters, past the point of innocence, no more nonsense—

SHUT UP! SHUT IT, DIGIT! ENOUGH NOW!

On I walk, in silence.

To Grace.

*

I hardly remember floating up to bed. The pile o' curry sent us dozy and full.

"This is your room," said Scarlett, "for as long as you need it. Your space. Tomorrow, you can rearrange it however you like. And me and Danny will only come in if you ask us."

I sink into the mattress. It dun't stink all bleachy like at Tenderness; it smells all soft-like. Got Spider-Man duvet; keep the baddies at bay.

Luminous stars stuck to the ceiling.

Just think, Alfi, scrunched up in an open skip, staring up at frozen sky.

But this en't any skip.

Patticat curls up at the end o' the duvet. Purring us to sleep.

Hammering on the door. The code, the secret, safe rhythm. I hammer the pattern over and over. After for ever, Grace finally unlatches the door, lets me stumble in.

"Digit? You're a late one." She sees the state of me, tries not to look shocked. "Who ruffled your feathers, Didge?"

"I was a naughty boy, wasn't I? Needed a bit of a reprimand."

"Virus."

"Gotta learn, don't you? Don't learn your lesson, keep makin' the same mistakes, over and over."

She hugs me to her. Holds me, in the hallway.

After a while, I say, "Jackson?"

"Workin'. Doin' a house. With Obnob and the boy. Don't stress, when he's done he'll go straight to his gaff with his pillage."

As I hoped. "Can I borrow your washing machine?" I say, looking down at my mess.

"Long as you promise to give it back."

She finds me a dressing gown, and puts the wash on for me, telling me to go take a shower. I have it hot as I can stand, steaming. I stand under it for ages, sweating the bad stuff out of me. I feel like I'm washing away all the poison that Citizen Digit has been so busy absorbing. I remember other showers, ages back, washing off the stench of Byron *Blank Space*. Emerging clean, well-scrubbed, as Citizen Digit. Brand spanking new. Now, I see myself in the bathroom mirror, just a boy.

When I feel clean I come back out and Grace tells me she's finished working for the night. She's in a long, technicolor skirt, covers her flesh, flows with her soul. She already had her shower, she says, and she feels cleaner too. We sit on the sofa and she puts her arm round me, and we're warm.

She says, "You're riskin' it, comin' here."

"I had nowhere else. Anyway, Jackson knows me."

"Lucky for you, he doesn't." She pauses. "Byron."

"Aww ... how do you...?"

"Same way as Virus. Usin' my ears. Alfi named you, the other night."

181

"Blabber-Boy."

Damn. It's as if the more time I spend near Alfi Spar, the more Citizen Digit's power of invisibility disappears. Like Alfi's hi-vis glow sheds its own spotlight on me too.

"Doesn't matter now," I say. "Me and Squealer-Face are finished. We're bad for each other."

"You don't mean that."

She's right, as ever.

We're 'cosy, me and Grace, feeling the night draw by.

"You need a bed – you're done in," says Grace. "I can kip on the sofa. You use the bedroom."

But the bedroom is where she works.

"You sure you're finished for the night?" I ask.

She nods.

"Grace," I say, "how come you do it? For Jackson? All these men."

She shrugs. "'Ow come you're always on the nick?" she asks.

"I ain't got no choice, have I? What am I going to do – go ask for a job? They'd drag me back to Tenderness in no time."

"Well," she says, "same with me, wasn't it?"

"Yeah, but that was years back. You're an adult now, you can do what you want."

She laughs at that. "Tell it to Jackson. I belong to 'im, don't I?"

"No, you don't. Just walk away."

"'E's a bit precious about his personal playthings.

182

Gets ragin', don't he? I ran once before. 'E found me. Let's just say, I won't run again."

Is that it then? Are we like this, for always?

"When I done a runner from Tenderness," she goes on, "I thought the world was me oyster, yeah? But you've been on the streets, you know what it's like. When Jackson found me, 'e was a proper charmer. I thought I'd scratched the winning card. Even when it turned out 'e used to be one of Newton's boys 'imself – an' 'e was still runnin' favours for 'im – 'e never gave me up."

"Favours?"

"Not for the Jimmys. He used to keep the other boys in check, yeah? Before Barry came along to do official discipline."

"Humph. He must have been much more fun back then," says me, snarkylike.

"We 'ad a laugh."

"A laugh? With Jackson Banks? He ain't exactly Mr Tickle, is he?"

She smiles. Her eyes take on a glaze, like she's thinking about the distant past.

"Yer'd be surprised. So I put meself in 'is 'ands – like a barbie doll with a terrible two year old. You don't wanna know 'im, in 'is tantrums."

No, I don't.

"Then, when I came of age, 'e started getting ideas, didn't 'e? Ideas and Jackson Banks are a bad combination. I been workin' for 'im since."

"And the Authoritariacs? Tenderness House? They didn't come digging for you?" I'm jaw-dropped.

"Less 'assle that way, weren't it? Easier – and quieter – for them to let JB keep 'is little pet."

"When you were at Tenderness," I say, "was Governor Newton up to his tricks back then?"

"Call-Me Norman."

My brain blinks a bit. "Then he was."

"Course he was," she says. "He always was. It ain't just these days things are 'ow they are. Why d'yer think I ran?"

I'm sitting up straight in bed. "You know?"

"I know all about the Jim'llfixits. And their little parties."

"Oh, Grace."

The Digit's all a-shudder. Got the terrible trembles, haven't I? Sunk in her arms. She's holding me tight.

"So what's the plan, Didge?"

"Plan?"

"You're comin' undone."

She's spot on. It's hard to keep up. Sometimes you don't even want to think any more. She squeezes my hand. I'm squeezing back. Try and focus.

We're holding each other and this time it's my eyes that are leaking. All over my face. She's right; I'm all undone. We both are.

"Oh, Grace," I say again. The Digit's lost his vocab.

"You know it ain't even me real name, don'tcha? I

let meself lose that a long time back, same as you lost Byron. Same as Virus lost whoever he used to be. You know the funniest thing, Didge?"

I shake my head.

"I ain't even a bleedin' Cockney, am I?"

The Digit smiles at that. Course she isn't.

"We do what we need to, to fit in. No one wants to stand out, do they Didge?"

I feel so sad and happy at the same time. Sitting here, arms round each other. It reminds me of home. Citizen Digit's doing his best to stop his peepers from leaking. In this single instance, his best isn't quite up to it.

"Don't you have no one else?" I ask. "No family?"

She snorts at that. Stupid question, Didge.

"Any youngers come find me from Tenderness, any WhyPettes – I direct 'em well away, don't I?" she says. "I know a gang of squatters south of the river. It ain't ideal, but it 'as to be better than Newton and 'is pervert mates. I'd 'ave done the same with you, D, if you hadn't of found *Cash Counters* first. Sorry you got a zappin' tonight."

"Me too," says I.

She pulls me tighter into her arms.

Later. She's got me all tucked up in bed, put clean sheets on and everything. She's stroking my head.

She asks again. "What's the plan, Didge?"

How can Citizen Digit hope to answer that? It's a mess. All of a sud, I'm busting with bitterness at Alfi Spar.

"Plan? Plan was to get as far away from Norman Newton as possible, make a fresh start and live happily ever after. But Alfi Spar brought Call-Me straight to our door, didn't he? Ruined it all."

"Did he?" she asks.

"Yes." I'm sulkiness itself.

"So it ain't you, then," she says, "what brought Norman Newton to my door?"

"No." Double-sulk.

"It ain't you, then, who started blabbin' and squealin' and upsettin' Call-Me's apple cart?"

She's outraging me. "I *warned* Alfi, that was all. I gave him the evidentials. The Citizen was doing him a favour."

She's silent. I can hear her thinking. "Then maybe it's time you finished what you started," she says.

"Me?"

"Digit."

I pull myself together. "I gave it all to Alfi, didn't I? It's Alfi who's got the evidence."

What's it up to me for? Why's it always up to me? Citizen Sort-It comes with full responsibilities, don't he?

"Where?" she asks.

"He gave it up, to his Senior Case Worker." I laugh and Grace joins in. Alfi Spar. What a doughnut. If he had a brain, it'd be made of jam.

"He actually reckons it's safe though. He started to tell me, just before he got long-armed. I don't know how.

Even if he made a copy, he ain't even got no friends to have left it with."

"Everybody's got friends."

"Not Blabber-Boy. He's the only sucker in the universe who don't even have a single Facebook friend. Can you believe—"

I stop myself right there. Start again. Focus, Digit, focus. "He ... wanted ... me ... to friend him on Facebook."

Grace gives me a *so-what* look, as I'm bouncing my knees from under the duvet. "Facebook, Facebook," I chant. "Quick, Grace – laptop, Smartphone. We need Facebook!"

She goes into the living room, reappears with a laptop and we log in. "Go to your Facebook page," I tell her.

"I ain't got one. Go to yours."

"Ain't got one neither." We're invisible, ain't we? Offline.

So we do the unheard-of, and set up our own Facebook page, pseudononymously of course. And we search *Alfi Spar* and there it is. But *Alfi only shares some of his information with his friends...*

"So –" Citizen Digit brainzaps this through "– if Alfi posted the video onto Facebook, it's effectively as secure as it gets, because—"

"'Cos 'e ain't got no friends."

"So all we got to do is put in a friend request and we've got the evid-errr..." The Digit limps to a halt.

Alfi-Boy ain't in no position to be responding to friend requests, is he?

I squash my head. "Aaaaaagh... We're going to have to hack into his account. To do that, we'll need his password."

Which could be any of a billion weirdies. Virus has the technical gadgetry to do this kind of hacking in a matter of minutes. But for the Good Citizen and Grace, we're just going to have to guess. We're going to have to use our brains.

So we sit and think. Me cosy and soft under the duvet, Grace resting on the edge of the bed like it's bed-time storytime.

We think for a while.

And we keep on thinking. My eyes can hardly keep themselves open. I'm feeling myself nodding off. Then, from behind my lids, it comes to me, all a-flash.

Ah-hah! Digital thinking conquers the world.

So I grab the laptop, and type in the magic letters:

K – A – T – A – R – I – I – N – A

A round of applause and a gold medal, please, for the one and only world champion Mr Citizen Digit, code-breaker extraordinary.

We're in. And it's right here:

Call-Me Norman Newton and his Jim'llfixits in all their horror. It's ugly, but it's real.

Grace doesn't watch. "Don't need to," she says.

I'm forgetting. She's seen it, first-hand. I switch it off.

"So," I say, over-cheerily, "we have hope."

Grace's mouth twists into an ugly line, and she wipes away a tear. "We have hope."

What else is there to say? I shut the laptop, so there's no light but the moonlight coming through the window, and I've got Grace's warmth around me. I'm all plumped up like the pillows, and she's wrapped around me, as soft as you could want, and that's how we stay, with our thread of hope. And after a while, I guess I fall asleep, feeling safer, softer. It's almost like in the olden days, when Byron still had some family.

Who knows how long I sleep like that. I'm awake soon enough, alone in the moonlit room.

Something woke me.

There's a CRASH. Then there's a load of THUDDING. I hear the living-room door slam open. I hear Jackson Banks through in Grace's room. He's yelling at her. He sounds like murder.

16. SHUT-EYE

"J!" Grace sounds as surprised as me. I imagine her sitting bolt up from the sofa, wrapping herself in her safety-net of sheets.

"Don't sound so pleased," he snorts, all sarky-snark. There's a thud as he drops his gym bag where he stands, like it's too heavy to hold for a second longer.

Obnob gives a whimper. "Shut it!" says Jackson. Then there's a silence, like he's looking around the room, sniffing the place. He'll be wondering why Grace is a-kip on the sofa, and who's occupying her bedroom. Grace'll be trying to read his face. I can read it from here, through the wall – it's a poison pen letter.

"Where's Crow?" I hear her ask.

I hear the gym bag unzipping, then the clatter of the crowbar, clanging onto the table top. That ain't right. That crowbar lives down the side of Crow's trackies.

"Where is 'e?" Grace repeats.

"Gone."

"Gone where?"

"Gone!"

He's opening the cupboard where Grace keeps her whiskey. Unscrews the cap and there's more silence while he swigs.

"No," she says. I guess he offered her the bottle. "What's happened? What happened to your face?"

He wails. Sounds like a grieving hippo.

"There, there." Stroking him. "There, there." I think I can hear him sobbing. Because he's hurt his face, or because of Crow?

This is the worst thing ever. If Jackson Banks clocks that the Digit's heard him crying like a littl'un, he'll bash the Good Citizen's face in.

But then he speaks again, and starts chuckling. "They'll never find him, young Crow. He's down the river. Sunk without a trace. Weighed down by his worries, ain't he?" He laughs out loud. "But you know what, Grace? You know what? Apart from weighting the body, I never touched him. I never. He fell, didn't he, bashed his brains? Like a stupid amateur. Slipped off a window ledge, woke the household, panicked, tripped over Obnob. Smashed his own head in."

Obnob gives another whine from wherever it is he's skulking. Is he collaborating JB's account – or protesting his own part in it?

"Crow. He's really," says Grace, "really dead?"

"Dead?" roars Banks. "Dead as a donkey! Dead as a zombie! Dead useless to me now, and stiffening with it!" He laughs like a Looney Tunes.

"It's all right," she soothes him. She'll be putting a gentle arm round him, reassurance itself. That's her job. I bet he's resting his head against her chest. The Digit feels a pang of jealousy.

For a zillisecond.

"All right?" Banks booms over her soothing. "Course it's all right! What am I, a Fairy Cake like Virus? Stupid boy should have watched his step."

Oh, he's a sensitive soul.

"What we goin' to do?" says Grace.

"Do? Do? Lay low is what we'll do. And get a replacement for the useless lump. Norman Newton can sort it. It's about time he delivered something worthwhile. Poor old Crow was always too feeble. Newton should have toughened him up, shouldn't he, before sending him my way."

"It's not Newton's fault," says Grace.

"It's *all* Newton's fault. Newton, and that Fairy Cakes Virus. They make their promises..."

"We could move," says Grace, all in a hurry. "We could stop all this nonsense. Go abroad. Somewhere sunny. Open a bar, take it easy."

Even the Digit knows how sad and pathetic that sounds. It makes Banks laugh again, guffawing like he's fit to burst. Then he stops.

There's a long silence. Uh-oh.

"Who's in the bedroom?" he says.

I duck my head under the duvet. Shut my eyes, tight as I can. Hold my breath.

"It's the Digit," says Grace. "'E's coppin' a couple hours' shut-eye. Virus give him a zappin'."

Jackson Banks makes an electrifying *bzzzz bzzzz* noise, dead sympathetic. "Best say hello then, hadn't we?"

All of a sud, I'm aware of the weight of the laptop, still sitting on top of the duvet, frozen on the page with the Jimmy footage. I scramble to get it tucked under the bed, just before JB comes a-barging in.

He flicks on the light. "Didgi-Boy!" His arms open in greeting. I've never seen him so deranged.

Before I can blink, he's got my head between his hands, ruffling my hair and rubbing my ears in rough'n'tumble greeting. I can feel his nails digging into my scalp. He's shaking me like a rag.

"Stop it, J, stop it!" I'm hearing Grace's voice through the roar of air inside my head. He stops, pushing his palm into my face, flipping me back against the pillow.

I open my eyes. He's got his fists raised in front of me, like a boxer and we're going to spar. I reckon he's given himself a triple-strength steroid jab. "Having a laugh, ain't we, Didgy? That's all. Just having a laugh."

I fake a smile.

"Drag in my bag," he orders Grace. He leans in towards my face. "Lucky for us, Crow had the good timing to wait till we bagged the loot before going and bashing his brains in. How you doing, Didgy?"

He's sizing me up, ain't he?

"I thought I'd come here, get a bit of shut-eye," I say.

Is the Good Citizen still small enough to fit through the kind of spaces Crow does? *Did*, I mean.

I puff myself up, trying to be bigger.

Grace comes in, lugging the gym bag. Obnob limps behind her, stopping at the rug, where he rolls onto his side and lies there looking sorryful.

"Unzip it," he tells her, without taking his eyes off me.

He leans his face into mine. He's all eyeball. I'm discomfy.

"Go on then," he says, beaming.

He looks like he's going to nut me. If I wet myself twice in one night, I'm going to have to move towns. He doesn't move. He doesn't blink. It's one of those awkward moments you laugh about later. I can't get up, 'cos he's leaning in too close.

"Go on then," he says, again.

"Go on *what*?" I ask.

"Shut-eye."

I close my eyes. I hear him chuckling satisfaction, feel him turning towards Grace. I hear him upending the gym bag, then the clatter of liberated goodies on the floorboards. If I open my eyes, he'll kill me. I try and shuffle further under the duvet.

"We need to be calm." Grace tries to sound calm.

"Dead calm?" Banks jokes back at her.

He starts moving about, depositing his ill-gottens around the bedroom. Grace is following him, like she's his other dog. I'm not even invisible any more; I just don't count. It's a relief.

"Where's Alfi Spar?" I hear him suddenly demand, from behind my shaded eyeballs.

She's taken aback. There's a pause. "Ah, you're askin' me?"

His hand jolts out and seizes her throat. I know because I hear her gasp, then her voice sounds all strangled. I could open my eyes, just a slit, take a peek. But I'm not going to.

"No," he says, "I'm asking Obnob."

"I don't know, J."

"Virus knows. So you know."

"Please, J…"

He's crushing her throat.

I say, "He got arrested." But I keep my eyes closed.

He slams his fist down on the bedroom table. Everything clatters. He stromps towards me. His hand comes round my throat. But gently, oh so gently.

"Open your eyes." His fingers tickle me beneath my chin. Eyeballing again. "Speak."

I try my best. "He was out with me and the Dictiv. He got fingered. Then long-armed. He's at Tottenham Nick. Virus has him GPS'd. That's all I know."

"Shut your eyes." I do. "Tomorrow, we get him." There's a pause. "That'll be a laugh, won't it?" I dunno if he's talking to Grace or me. Both of us mumble in the infirmative.

I keep my eyes closed. I hear him moving back

towards Grace. I can sense her, trying to stop herself from backing away from him. He stinks of brute.

"Where's Byron *Blank Space*?" His hand is back round her throat.

I ought to leap up, leap through the window. But if I make a move, he'll know.

I won't see another day. I ought to run.

He's waiting for his answer.

"I dunno no Byron *Blank Space*," she gasps. "Jackson, please, you're scarin' me."

Silence.

Don't open your eyes. Don't run. Just breathe.

Silence. He's scrutinizing her. Obnob whines. Jackson knows when Grace is lying.

Through the silence, we're all breathing, me and her and him and the dog. Living breath, in an empty space.

Finally, he lets her go. "You find him," he tells her. "Then I'll do the fun stuff."

She's nodding. She's trying not to let her eyes flick in my direction. I'm trembling. Byron *Blank Space* isn't any good for Citizen Digit. Like I said, that Walking Dead Boy is a shuffling liability.

"Breakfast!" he barks at her. "Yum yum. Hop to it!"

It ain't even three in the morning. I hear them heading for the kitchen. Jackson saying, "Shame the Digit ain't small enough to squeeze through windows. Smart lad like him 'ud make a good replacement for poor old Crow."

There's a silence, then he carries on muttering. "Poor Crow. He was my one and only. Poor old Crow. Who'll look after me now, hey, Grace? When we get old. We'll always need a Crow..."

I could open my eyes now. I could get to my feet and grab my threads from the radiator, run for the door, get out of London, flee the country. I could.

But I don't. I keep them closed. I slow my breathing. I calm my shaking. In my darkness, I reach around in my head, calling for the Citizen, seeking him out. Citizen Digit must use his good-given talent to get through this coming day. He's there, in the dark, and he says *Don't you worry. If anyone can pull us through this, the Digit can do it, the Digit can do it...* Over and over again. *The Digit can do it, the Digit can do it, the Digit can...*

Over and over and over. *The Digit...* Eventually, he lures me into sleep.

17. GOLD DUST

The Digit awakes!

I cry out in terror. My eyes are convinced they're going to be greeting the face of Jackson Banks, twisted in hilarity.

I sigh in relief, breathe in the silence. The house feels peaceful. Don't know how long I slept, don't even know *how* I slept. Exhaustion, I guess. But it's a new day now, and my fuggy mind is reminding me that there's chores to be done.

First up, I remember how me and Grace dug up the evidence. What a clever legs Alfi Spar turned out to be, thinking of putting it on a Facebook page that doesn't have any friends. Intellectualism itself.

All we need now is a plan. Sunlight streaming through the window inspires hope and hippiness to all and sundry. It's basic. Citizen Digit is going to get killed to death if nobody calls off Mad Dog Jackson. Call-Me Norman is the man for that job, as he set the psychonut on Digit in the firstness. There is, of course, a crumb of hope that Call-Me might do that, if we threaten to expose him. Give him no alternative. Then we can all shake hands and go have a picnic.

On the other hand, he might just have JB take me by the throat and shake me to death before I even reach the end of my threat. I ain't got no authority, have I?

A softer option might involve going to the Sherlocks and having Call-Me locked away for what's left of his calendars. We like that one. The only paw in the flan is that in the meantime JB might kill me anyway. He hates time-wasting, and the due process of the law is slow-poke central. Jackson would have me throttled faster than it takes to say *You're nicked.*

And JB would fall into a murderous rage the nano-second he hears we've blabbed to the Sherlocks, your honour. He's got his little fingers wrapped up in this, up to his knuckle joints.

And yes-but-no-but-yes-but, we need a mediator.

I wander into the kitchen, see if I can't find Grace, borrow her opinion. She ain't there. Neither, I'm massively relieved to see, is Jackson Banks. Guess they've made starters of the day.

Rewind: threaten Call-Me to call off the Mad Dog; dial 999, Emergency Sherlocks, please; or find a mediator. Somebody who has some degree of influence over JB.

I can't believe what I'm actually thinking.

My ears are still buzzing from the shock of it. We need a sane mediator, not Electro Supervillain with the Power to Shock.

Is this it? Is the Man To Go To In A Crisis – really, truly, deeply – the lunatic with the Zap App? Can't Citizen Digit think of one single other *Responsible Adult* to foil the evil conspiracy?

Oh, you should just go back to bed if this is the best you can do, Didge. Surely, somebody, somewhere, somehow, can help us out?

The thing is, there is not a single trustabubble Groan out there. Either me and Grace and Alfi Spar defeat the gang of Psychopaths and Jimmymen ourselves or—

Or we work with one of them. The only one we can half trust. The only one not so utterly depraved or violent that it's a danger to share the same room with him. And, even then, he's an itsy bitsy depraved, and a tiny-weeny bit violently tended.

How can I even think about going back to him?

Because I'm desperate.

Grace's fridge is empty and there's no bread. Jackson's wolfed it all. So I make my way back up towards Seven Sisters Road, to *Cash Counters*, to pop some toast with the Devil's not-quite-so-evil half-bro.

Virus himself.

He seems to be expecting me. "Ahh, Citizen," he says, rubbing his palms together, warmlike, as if last night's incidentals hadn't happened at all. "To what do I owe this pleasure?"

His eyes flick feather-light over my features, see if

he left any burns or marks with his zaps.

"Perhaps the Digit would like some tea. Toast?"

He's guilt-rid, ain't he? The iron knee of it is that Virus is always most approachable after a zapping episode. Like he wants to set things right again, after making everything skew-whiff. After some bad boy made things skew-whiff first, of course.

"The Good Citizen's found something of keen human interest, ain't he?" says me, all swaggerlike.

I'm not going to waste precious tick-tock by molly-coddling round the matter. We both of us want to put the zapcident behind us, and the Citizen's got urgent matters at hand. So I go straight to one of his screens, sign into Facebook, and show him the vid.

He watches it and says nothing. Then he presses *play* and watches it again. Still he says nothing. Then he plays it a third time, turns to me and says, "It's worse than I feared."

Worse. How's that then?

"What? You eyeballed this before then?"

He closes his eyes. It's what he does when he's run out of patience. Has the Digit been impertinent again? In for another zapping? I close my eyes. Brace myself.

But nothing happens. Instead he says, "I let you all down."

"You can't have," I say. "You're Mr Virus, the Great Manager. You're here, at *Cash Counters*."

But he's shaking his head. "If I'd known it was going

to end like this, I'd have ... intervened."

"What are you talking about, V?" I say.

He lets out a long sigh. "Oh, we go back, Norman Newton and I. Many, many years. Long before *Cash Counters*. I used to be on the board of an organization – you might have heard of them – they're called Reliance Plus. Of course, they've expanded a lot since then. The first children's home they ran was up Enfield way. Mr Newton was the manager."

"You knew!"

He closes his eyes again. Like he doesn't want to see what's right in front of them.

"No, no. I didn't. But ... I suspected. I always suspected. I mean, none of it was on the straight and narrow exactly. There's a lot of money to be made from the care system, you know."

"Oh, is there?" says me, all snarkastic.

"But it does a lot of good too!" he puts in. "That was what drew me to it. I never simply wanted to make money – I wanted to help the young people."

"Instead, you made your money and you left the *young people* to the hands of Norman Newton. You fiddled the books, and he – just fiddled." I can barely conceal my disgust.

"No. I promise you, no. Well, I admit, I was syphoning funds, but not to the detriment of the home; it was all government money. But there was an incident. A serious incident. And a nasty rumour, regarding Newton's involvement. It was enough for me."

"Enough? So what? You had him long-armed? Got the Sherlocks on the case?"

I'm pushing my luck, I know.

"I challenged him, Digit. I promise you, I challenged him."

"Excellent," says me. "And that stopped him there and then."

"Well, of course, he denied it all," Virus stutters on, "and then he showed me copies of documentation he had that would have brought me down."

What's he expect me to say? He's squirming, like he's sat on his zapper. "I'd have gone to prison," he pleads. "I'd never have bought the building, this building, that eventually became *Cash Counters*, and I wouldn't be able to give you and all the other boys the support you have. Don't you see?"

The Digit doesn't know about *seeing* Virus's support. I've certainly *felt* it. My skin is still sensitive from last night's punishment.

"I see." I'm going to say more. I'm going to switch on the Citizen Digit sarcastical button, and give him the rattatat verbals he deserves. But I can't. I need V's help, not another zapping.

The Great Manager stands up and leaves the room, muttering. He leaves me there, with the ugly image frozen on-screen, and an anger, from the balls of my feet to the brows of my eyes.

He's gone into the room next door and he doesn't shut the door properly. After a moment, I hear the electric buzz. I hear him wince. I hear him thud against the floor. And in that moment, it seems like Citizen Digit is the only sane person left in an insane world.

Fifteen minutes later, he comes back in. He's carrying a tray, with tea and biscuits. He's smiling like a tea-party chimp.

We drink the tea and dunk the biscuits. He picks at the stray crumbs, and without another word, he gets straight back to business. He's perkiness itself.

"So. You guessed that Alfi's password was Katariina?"

"Yes," I say, all warylike.

"Katariina is the name of Alfi's mother, you say?"

The Digit nods, affirmativelike.

"And you remember this all from looking at the file at Tenderness House?"

The Digit nods, affirmativelike.

"And you worked all this out yourself?"

The Digit's bored with the nodding.

"Digit, you're a genius. You do me proud. I always knew you would. Tell me though, would you have any idea at all as to who Alfi Spar's *father* might be?"

"Does it matter?"

"Everything matters," he snaps, more at himself than me, but his voice echoes shrilly in my ear, the side he zapped. "Look at this number plate." He's frozen the film on the shot of the Jaguar driving into the Tenderness grounds. "Any idea who this belongs to?"

"The man in the suit, who gets out and walks into Call-Me's office."

"Don't get *too* facetious, Citizen, it's not a pretty habit to fall into. Do you know the *name* of the man?"

The Citizen shrugs it.

"Well, see, it just so happens that I have an app here that allows me access to every document belonging to the DVLA. Know what the DVLA is, Didge?"

Shrug it again.

"It's the Driver and Vehicle Licensing Agency. Means that in less time than it takes to make you some toast, I will know who this fine old gentleman is. In fact, Mr Didge, this little film is gold dust, I say, gold dust! Do you know why, Didge?"

Gold dust. The only type of dust Virus approves of.

"Why's that, Mr Virus?" I say, all duty-bound.

"We have the technology," he purrs. "See these men here? The Sherlock? The man in the Jag? The other one? They have made themselves high visibility, haven't they? I will have their identities and personal details in a mere moment. Digit, you are a star!" He lays his hand on my leg. "I'm sorry about last night," he says, all remorse. He sighs and adds, "But, you know, you did rather bring it all on yourself."

"I know," I fib. I move on. "So we can expose them all?"

I'm all a-flush. A bunch of kiddliwinks bring down the evil predator ring. Rewarded with all their dreams come true.

"Expose?" Virus frowns. "No, no. *Threaten* to expose."

Oh, what? I'll be jibjabbed. Virus can zip me with the zapper all he likes – but these Jimmys are getting long-armed.

"They're," I say, "they're." I can't think of a word. Then I know. "They're *shit*."

Normally, Citizen Digit is more imaginatious.

"Language, Digit," says Virus. "I completely agree."

"Then all you have to do is persuade Jackson Banks to lay off his boy-hunt. The Sherlocks can dive in mob-heavy – and *bam!* The Jimmys get banged up for ever."

He thinks before he answers. "Digit, these men certainly merit the severest punishment. But, believe me, I've had acquaintances who've faced stronger evidence than this and still avoided court."

"Not possible," I say.

"Possible," he insists.

"Only if you own the court."

"That," he agrees, "plus bribery, intimidation of witnesses, technical loopholes, corrupt judges, Sherlock stupidity, cross-contamination of material evidence, flight to a sunny island. Need I go on?"

"The Citizen comprehends. But, even so..."

"Oh, look," says Virus, peering at the screen. "Very interesting."

I await his expansion.

"Turns out," he says, "your man in the Jag is rather important indeed. His name is Chris Primrose. Guess his job. Go on, Digit, take a wild stab."

"World-famous hip-hop star?"

"Oh, ho." He thinks I'm so witty. Not. Virus feeds me the most serious look. "He's actually a politician. A Member of Parliament, no less. And a front-bencher. Know what a front-bencher is, Digit?"

"He always sits on the front bench?" The Digit was always didgy-doo at tests.

"Bright boy!" He's all a-mock. "And he does indeed sit on the front bench. Very close to the Prime Minister himself. Call-Me Norman's nasty little gang is only headed by the Minister for Urban Development. Ohh, I've waited years for this kind of opportunity."

Citizen Digit shakes his head, like a dog spongy with water.

No I almost say *it's just Call-Me and his weirdo pals...* But I ain't such a peanut brain. What I say ain't much higher wattage. "Are you sure?"

He throws me a look of mild reproach. Of course he's sure; the computer knows everything. But this can't be factual. It's a politician. A minister. What's he doing joining in with Jimmys like Call-Me?

Virus reads my mind. "Men," he snarls. "You never know."

For all his other faults, Virus clearly ain't no fan

of the Jim'llfixits. You can see his headcogs whirring, trying to figure out the best course of acting.

"What's this mean, then, V?"

"It means we have him. It means blackmail. It means extortion. It means making them sweat. We're going to have a lot of fun. I'll fetch you that toast."

Off he goes, letting the fact of the matter settle into each of our heads. Virus is obviously now as happy as Larry, but the Good Citizen has to think it through a tad.

Shouldn't we just yell for the Sherlocks?

'Cept a Sherlock was one of them, wasn't he? Brilliant – the Long Arm gets long-armed!

"That Sherlock," says me, when V comes back in. "Just wait till his Chief Constable finds out what he's been up to."

Virus rolls his eyes. "He *is* the Chief Constable."

Ah.

Virus hands me a plate of toast. And a napkin. He goes on. "Anyway, the Minister for Urban Development will be, shall we say, closely related to the constabulary in London."

He throws me a look. I get it. The Digit should know much better than be thinking we can rely on the Sherlocks.

And we're on the wrong side of the straight and narrow road as it is.

If we *threaten* them, will we be able to make Call-Me Norman stop his evenings of evil?

Will we make money out of it? (Virus will.)

Virus can do all the negotiating, via his gadgets. Me and the Alfi-Boy will sit on the sidelines, watching YouTube and eating toast.

V seems to be waiting for the Citizen to think all this through. Like there's something he's missed. A paw in the flan?

A fuzzy, fuggy point of order starts harrumphing around inside my headcase, raising a point of utmost vitality.

Ah. Last night. I blabber-boxed, didn't I?

"Err, Virus," I say. "There's something you might need to know."

He feeds me his quizzicals. I've set him up, haven't I? Set the Mad Dog on V's own tail.

"Last night," I confess, "I let it slip, didn't I?" I'm in for another zapping, high wattage this time. "I told Jackson Alfi's whereabouts. I'm sorry!"

I close my eyes. Twice in two days. But I feel his hand, gently, on my shoulder.

"It's all right," he says. "Just because Jackson is Norman Newton's dog, doesn't mean I can't get him to perform a trick or two for me."

"What d'you mean?"

"He came round a while ago. You need to rise earlier, young Citizen. Early birds: worms? Don't worry. Despite his obvious disgruntlement, we reached an understanding."

Oh the Digit is slowness itself this sunny morn. I need to catch up. *Previously, at* Cash Counters...

"You see," Virus continues, "when push comes to shove, Norman Newton isn't Jackson's master at all. You need to observe more, young Digit. Money is Jackson's master. Money! JB is now of the belief that Alfi Spar offers more financial reward if he's in our hands than if he's back at Tenderness."

"You lied to him?"

Virus doesn't answer that. Instead, he looks at his watch. "I have already dispatched Jackson Banks. I checked the present whereabouts of Alfi Spar. He's now at a less conspicuous address than Tottenham Nick. Jackson should be with him, right about now."

"But Jackson Banks is out of control! You have to stop him!"

"Too late."

"This is ugliful!"

He attempts reassurance. "Call-Me Norman ordered Jackson not to hurt Alfi. I myself reiterated that instruction. And now I can prove to Banks where the profit really lies."

I'm bunching my fists. "Do you think he'll bother to obey?"

"You can rely on it."

But there's something he's not telling me. The Digit is being kept out of the loop. Virus gazes at the cushion, checking against stray crumbs. There are no crumbs. He closes his eyes. Again.

The Digit's wondering. What exactly *is* Virus's perfect master plan?

18. THE PERFECT MASTER PLAN

I sleep in. Danny's already gone to work and Scarlett's realized there's nowt in for me brekkie. She knocks on me door, says we need to go to the shop. It's 11.30!

I leap out o' bed.

"If we're quick, we'll be in time for breakfast," she says.

"Hunh?"

"Trap it, kill it, cook it, eat it. Thirty minutes. Beans on toast. The deadly beast."

She's la-la.

Still: beans on toast. What's not to like?

London corner shops are pretty much the same as Bradford's. Scarlett spends ten minutes gossiping wi' the owner. I can't remember last time I stood in a shop this long, not without getting hissed out. Scarlett likes talking.

The thing wi' beans on toast is you have to heat up the beans nice and slow. If you just bring 'em to the boil the heat won't seep through. They'll go cold. And you need room-temperature margarine, so it melts upon touch o' the toast, rather than making the hot toast go cold. And lastly; hot toast fresh from the toaster. Be ready wi' the marge, slop on the gently bubbling beans, grind some black pepper and serve on a pre-warmed plate, wi' fresh, steaming tea.

Oh, aye, I'd have some o' that.

Scarlett says I'm worse than Iggy, dancing round her feet while she's trying to cook. She won't even listen to any advice, but, to be fair, she makes a cracking beans on toast.

"Danny's on half-day today," she says, "so we thought we could spend the afternoon down the park."

She's got a big grin on her face. "Unless," she goes on, "you'd rather play computer games all day?"

Is she teasing? "No," I say, "I like the park."

"Just as well, 'cos we ain't got no computer."

That sentence literally dun't compute. "Everybody has a computer," I say. "What about a laptop?"

"Nope."

"So you've all the info you need on your Smartphone?"

"It can take messages," she says.

See? Weird.

Then a thought hits us. I need a computer so's I can check on me evidence. "I need Facebook," I say. "What do you guys do when you need Facebook? Or email?"

"Don't panic. We do it the old-fashioned way."

"Smoke signals?"

"Library. That's what it's for."

So while we're waiting for Danny to get back home from work, Scarlett takes us to the library. We get a screen each, next to each other. Private but friendly. And I'm glad

213

about the privacy, because I have to play the film, test it, don't I?

But first up: I'm a bit put out to discover I've got a friend. And one "like" for the video. It en't right, 'cos I an't got any friends. Nobody can "like" me video, 'cos there en't nobody seen it. And nobody can be me friend unless I like them and they like me.

So how come I've got a friend?

I glance across at Scarlett. She's engrossed in social work documents.

Who could have broken into me account? I had the perfect password and everything. Nobody even knows that Katariina is me mam's name, apart from the Digit and Call-Me Norman. And Barry.

What if the Jimmys have tracked us down and hacked us? They could be making their way here right now. I look all up and down the library. It's creepily quiet.

I click on the "friends" list. Me "friend" is called City Zen *and his profile photo is me actual birth certificate.*

Relief. It's the Digit fair enough. It's a message, letting us know he's still on me side. But, actually, I think I can manage quite well without him at this stage. Clever or not, that lad's nowt but trouble.

In fact, I wun't put it past him if he's even gone and done summat dumb like disabled the video. Trying to move it somewhere "safer". Got to have it all, dun't he?

So I press play.

First up all you get is a rosebush and all you hear is

Byron breathing, dead nervous. He en't so cool. Then you hear the first car, and he starts to work the camera. It's deadly dull. It just feels like a bad lad spying on some grown-ups, and any second now he's going to get caught and probably get a fine or summat.

Then there's movement, and you can hear Byron breathing heavily again, as he makes his way to Call-Me's office.

And me heart's beating here in the library and Byron's hand is shaking holding the camera, but on he goes. It's just an open corridor, they don't even have the door shut at the end. You can see a bit of a porn film playing on a screen on a wall. It's all well lit. Then he shoves the camera through the gap in the door.

Then you see 'em. Then you see the faces, wi' their crawling eyes. And their hands, creeping. Then it gets all shaky and falls on the floor.

I click off the screen.

"All good?" says Scarlett, leaning over. "You look pale."

"I think I'm a bit peckish," I say. It's only half a lie.

So we meet Danny for dinner, and then we go for a walk around Finsbury Park. It en't a bad park, even if it is surrounded by traffic and big buildings. It's got all kinds o' facilities, like running tracks and children's play bits and a duck pond and a big football pitch.

For half a mo, I think I see Citizen Digit, sitting on a bench on t'other side o' the football pitch, watching us. I'm

215

about to wave, when I realize it's not him at all, just some other lad.

No way is Citizen Digit bothered thinking about anyone other than hisself. It's t'others I need to be watching out for – Call Me's crew.

Danny sees me eyes scanning across the playing pitch and reckons I want to join in the game.

"Go on," he says. "Go play. We don't mind."

No way. Running round the middle of a field? I might as well wave a sign over me head saying COME AND GET ME! *I feel all right wi' Scarlett and Danny. I en't leaving their side.*

We pass by a bloke on a bench, wearing shades, reading a paper. Seemingly reading a paper. I think he's watching us. I huddle in close. "Can we feed the ducks?"

Danny raises his eyebrows. "You sure?" He and Scarlett exchange a look. I s'pose they expect lads like me to be into drugs and gangs.

Scarlett buys some duck feed from the café and the three of us stand and watch while ducks, moorhens and seagulls go ape over the crumbs in the water. They're funny, dive-bombing and splashing. Danny does a spot-on impersonation of a mad seagull. We all laugh like crazy. Then we go back to the café and buy cola and crisps. Scarlett rips open the bag so the crisps are spread across the table and we all dive in, pretending that we're the different birds, fighting over the crumbs. It's a right mess.

After the café, there's some big swings and we go on

them, and a big climbing frame an' all. Danny and Scarlett stick close by. They allus have their eyes on us, but it dun't feel like it's 'cos they don't trust us. It's like they're watching out for us.

Other folk are watching too. People always stare; you get used to it. The tricky bit is figuring out why they're watching. Some folk just stare 'cos I've got blond hair, catches their eye. Other folk are thinking other things when they stare at us, like the Jimmys. I know that now. But you can never tell which is which.

See this bloke on the bench ahead of us. Looks like a right psycho. His dog's going nuts after the squirrels, racing round like a loon to try and get 'em. He reckons that's hilarious, this bloke. I bet he's, what's that word? Care in the Community. Chuckling away to hisself, like he knows summat dead funny that the rest of us don't. His hands are big as spades, and his fingers are clutching in and out like he's exercising 'em. He gives us the weirdest look as we walk by, all red eye and glaze. Gives me the creeps. We speed up a bit.

Next thing, his dog scurries past and manages to get a hold of a squirrel. I allus thought dogs weren't fast enough. It gets this squirrel and shakes it. It makes a horrible squealing noise and dies. Then the dog starts chomping at it, trying to swallow it down.

Behind us, the bloke is laughin', like it's the funniest thing he's seen ever. Scarlett takes me hand, like I'm eight, and I don't mind.

217

Fifteen minutes later, when we're leaving the park, I see this bloke again. He's stood up this time, and I can see he's a proper giant. He's leering at us, and his dog starts sniffing round me ankles as we go by. It's missing half an ear, and its tail's got no wag.

I can't wait to get back home to Scarlett and Danny's.

The Digit and the Great Manager go to work on email blackmail. Virus's scam is straightforward. He has thousands of fake web identities, all set to serve Operations at the click of a mouse. Connected to forums, chat rooms, Facebook pages, Twitter.

He's going to drop a Rumour Bomb. A mass attack of libellous suggestions and outright lies by people with fake names at untraceable addresses, who don't exist anyway. You can't exactly sue them, can you?

Chris Primrose is this. Chris Primrose did that. Apparently, Chris Primrose. Primrose is part of a secret network. The track always leads back to Chris Primrose.

And Virus, techno-whizz that he is, got the identity of the Chief Constable too. Name of Wedderburn. Search the name online now – Chief Constable Wedderburn – and it's fair to say the Force Is in Disrepute.

None of these terrible rumifications, of course, flow from *Cash Counters,* Fair Deal For All, Seven Sisters Road, N7.

But Virus will – anonymousely – email Call-Me Norman a copy of our magic film. Call-Me will be Virus's cash machine, collecting the money from his sick associates, with V collecting all the crinkle direct from a ghost bank account.

"It's all so beautiful, Didgy-Boy," Virus brags.

True, but.

"Call-Me and the Jimmys will want to obliterize Byron twice as much now, won't they? And Alfi. It's obvious that I made the film, and that Alfi's in on it."

The Great Manager dismisses this with a wave of his hand. "Well of course. But Byron *Blank Space* is already a marked man. They can't kill him twice, can they? As for Alfi – well, you're just going to have to trust me on that one."

Making mockers at me. But the Digit don't care. I'm worrying more over Alfi's bones. If Mad Dog Banks and Obnob have already sniffed him out, will there even be any bones left?

"You sure Jackson isn't actually going to *do* anything to Alfi then?"

"Well, he's not going to bring him back here, is he? *Cash Counters* is a marked site now – thanks to *certain persons near by*. I suppose he'll – I suppose he'll keep him safe somewhere."

But before I can ask where, the intercom's all a-buzz, and when Virus goes to answer it, it ain't Jackson Banks.

No. It's the Sherlocks. Sherlocks at the door.

Virus throws me the evils. It's the Citizen's fault for letting Alfi get long-armed. If he's blabbed, it's a disaster.

If he's blabbed? This is Squealer-Boy we're talking about.

Virus claps his hands at me, impatient. "Vanish, boy!"

I hide in the cupboard. It ain't clever, but it is tidy.

The Sherlocks make their way up.

So I eavesdrop a crack, listen for the catastrophic news. The Sherlocks are certainly not happy. They are seeking one Jackson Banks. Yes! Resultification.

Then they say it's in connection with having found a body – a WhyPee's body – and I almost fall out of the cupboard.

Please, please, don't let it be Alfi Spar.

Virus is as cool as a clue-comber and polite as a teapot.

"You'll already have tried Mr Banks's home address, I suppose?" he says to the Top-Notch Sherlock.

"No one at home. We're of the understanding that Mr Banks is an *associate* of yours." Here Virus gives a disgusted snort. "And we're keen to speak with him. We have an unidentified body—"

Alfi. No. *No.*

"We aren't able to make any connection with dental records, fingerprints or DNA. The boy is off-system."

Alfi's off-system.

"But he did have one distinctive physical feature."

"Ohh?" says Virus, all nonshalonse, couldn't give a monkey's buttons.

"A scar, running down the left side of his face."

Thank you!

I guess Jackson didn't sink Crow as deep as he reckoned. Poor kid, denied a life *and* a decent burial.

"I see," says Virus. "Mr Banks, of course, being foster parent to a young man with a scar, you need to establish with him whether or not the poor body might be that of young, what's his name? Raven?"

Oh, he's a sly one, that Virus.

"Of course," says Top-Notch Sherlock. "You can understand the urgency. If the body is that of Banks's child, we need to speak with him. This is a murder enquiry. Should you hear from Jackson Banks you need to contact Tottenham police immediately."

Soon as the Sherlocks leave, I clatter out of the cupboard to find Virus checking his Smartphone for Alfi Spar's whereabouts.

"Your talkative friend remains at the same Finsbury Park address," he tells me, "and I can confirm that it is *not* a mortuary." He's silent for a moment. "Poor Crow."

"Poor Crow," I echo. I'd always had the shivers about that boy not making life past his teens. What a short, horrorful existence.

"And Jackson?" says Virus. "He was ... quite agitated over the loss of his young assistant?"

Crow wasn't so much an assistant as a slave, but now's not a wise time to be correcting Virus over such matters. So I agree. "He was bonkers as ever."

Bonkier than bonkers. Banks was *thinking*. He was looking at me – like I might be the next Crow.

"Hmmm," says Virus.

Hmmm? What's that supposed to mean?

I don't like it.

If the Sherlocks are going to long-arm Jackson, and he's got Alfi with him, it could get bloody.

"So what do we do?"

"We wait. We sit tight and wait for Jackson Banks to return."

"Call him off. Isn't that simpler?"

Virus gives me a stern look. "When Banks is on a job, he's switched off. Incommunicado."

So that's that, then.

Cash Counters is on skeleton staff. Virus still has most of the WhyPees packed off to safeholes, and the bulk of his gadgets hidden away. There's not much for us to do, other than watch his Rumour Bomb splattering all over the internet.

Afternoon turns to teatime, and still no JB.

Virus tries to perk me up with a steady supply of tea and toast, and I try not to make a mess. ("Crumbs, boy! Crumbs!") He puts on some tunes – old soul stuff – which seem to flow out of every electronic screen scattered round us. He normally surrounds himself with the chit-ter-chat of his henchboys. It's funny, it just being me and him.

To kill time, he teaches me a few magic tricks. Coin-out-of-the-earhole type stuff: the Magic Knife (it's there/it's not/it's there/it's not) and the Not Knot (very handy for kidnappy-type situations). He teaches patiently. "You have to get it wrong before you can get it right, Digit. Do it wrong two hundred times, then the two hundred and first, you're a winner. You've got 'em bamboozled, boy, bamboozled."

Oh, yeah, that's the Digit – the Mighty Bamboozler.

Early evening. No Alfi. No Jackson. Citizen Digit is beginning to stress. Virus starts to sweat it too. But we don't hear zilch from the Sherlocks, so we just gotta sit safe and soundless. Grace must be with JB or we'd have heard from her, surely to goodness. If Grace is there with him, then whatever's descending, Alfi'll be all right. In fact, he's probably a thousand times all righter than the Digit, who's still in fear of a grievous bodily harming that's officially owed to Byron *Blank Space*.

That's right, Didge, *convince* yourself.

Before cooking up supper, Virus teaches me a few online scams. The interweb ain't usually the territory for a finger-slick invisible fiend like Citizen Digit, but it never hurts to have a bit of wisdom up your sleeve.

Alfi'll be just fine and dandy.

The Rumour Bomb, meanwhile, has been gun-powdering across the network. Where there's smoke, there's money.

JB'll just be laying low somewhere, is all.

We email Call-Me Norman. It's a cracker. 'Cos of course it's not us sending him an email, which would be simplicity itself. No, we play with his nerves. Virus hacks into the account of Chief Constable Wedderburn, and wha-lahh, it's Bent Sherlock who sends this message:

NORMAN, HAVE YOU SEEN THE VIDEO OF OUR LAST NIGHT AT TEN-DERNESS HOUSE? IT'S NOT IN SAFE HANDS. AND SOMEONE'S BEEN SPREADING DANGEROUS RUMOURS. GOOGLE OUR DEAR FRIEND CHRIS PRIMROSE. GOOGLE CHIEF CONSTABLE WEDDERBURN. IT'S NOT NICE.

GOOGLE YOURSELF, NORMAN. GOOGLE YOURSELF. TAKE A GOOD LOOK. AND LISTEN CLOSE: I'M NOT EVEN ME. I'M HACKED. WE ARE BEING THREATENED WITH EXPOSURE FROM CRIMINAL MASTER-MINDS. THEY WILL BE IN TOUCH. DEMANDING MONEY. IT'S THAT OR THE FILM GOES VIRAL.

I AM NOT ME.

I DIDN'T SEND THIS. THEY DID.

THEY CAN HACK YOU TOO.

PAY THEM THE MONEY!!!!!

Rinky dink.

I wanted to get Virus to add: LAY OFF ALFI SPAR but he thought it was buttering it a bit thick.

And then, Virus cooks us steak. With onion gravy, roast potatoes and steamed broccoli. He must be trying to convince himself, as well as me, that Alfi is in no danger. Alfi: if the human Monster Munch known as Alfi

Spar was with us now, he would die of culinary overload. The steak is perfecto, but it all feels a bit Last Supper. There's none of the racket of the other WhyPees; Jackson Banks still hasn't made an appearance; we've no idea where Grace is. Virus lights a candle over the dining table and puts out napkins. One point, the Digit swears he's even about to say *grace*. Talk about sacrifistic.

Maybe Jackson Banks has done a runner. And maybe Alfi is just away someplace, living a life. Yeah, that'd work. Banks gone. Grace could come back, move in here with me and Virus and any other stray WhyPees, and we'd eat steak and play picky-pock and whatnot.

I pester Virus to check Alfi's whereabout one more time.

"If Banks is off the case," I say, "what are we going to do about Alfi? I could get him, bring him back home. He must be worried shirtless."

"Please!" Virus snip-snaps. "Don't fret about young Alfi. We'll reel him in. You Facebook-friended him earlier."

"I did?"

"Well, City Zen did."

What the Hull? Virus created a false Facebook ID for me? What an intrusion on my personal liberties. "So," I snap, "what did you do, post an ID pic of Byron *Blank Space* with it? Call-Me and the Jim'llfixits will be round any minute!"

He reaches into his jacket pocket. "I told you. You

must stop fretting about your online presence. Earlier today, you mislaid this. You ought to be more careful, Didge. I used it as the ID pic."

Alfi Spar's Birthday Tificate. I snatch it back. Throw Virus the evils. "You know what he's like about who his mum was. He's obsessed."

"Exactly. Who can blame him?" Virus replies. "If I was him, I'd be searching everywhere."

"He deserves some answers, and soon." I wish I was hopeful of it. I disappear the Birthday Tiff into the folds of my threads.

"He needs to look in the right place, doesn't he," says Virus, enigmastically, "young Alfi?"

"Meaning what?"

He pauses. Looks at me, deep. "Sometimes," he says, slow like a numb-tongue, "we have to go back to where we're running from. To find where we're going."

"Oh, yeah," says me, all sarko. "Like Tenderness House?"

But V gives the slightest of nods.

"You're nutkins!" Virus really *is* nuts. "Alfi would have to be insane to go back to Tenderness now."

"Perhaps. Either way, Alfi knows you're watching out for him," says Virus. "He may feel he's better off where he is now, but he'll come back to us soon enough."

"How d'you reckon that?"

"For starters, he hasn't blabbed to the Sherlocks, has he? And he'll want his Birthday Certificate back. If

Jackson Banks really is off the scene, I expect we'll be hearing from Alfi pretty soon."

I'll certainly be happier once his squealer-slot's safely back in front of us. And I hope he's getting as good grub as the Digit is. But what Virus says about Alfi needing to return to Tenderness House is so bonkers, the Digit almost puts it right out of his mind. Almost.

Virus gives me a room with a big double bed. "You need a proper rest," he says. He goes back down to his living space, to check the networks and plan the next day.

Then there's a knock at the front door, and it ain't the safe, secret rhythm. It's the Sherlocks again. I'm all Agent Lightfoot in my socks, tippytoeing through the upper rooms, until I'm close enough to eardrop.

They're *still* seeking Mr Popularity himself. They had a bluebottle parked twenty-four hours outside JB's house, and he never returned. I suppose you wouldn't, if you had guts on your hands and the Sherlocks parked at your front door.

Virus is as politely unhelpful as ever, and the Sherlock leaves, happy that Mr Virus is As Good a Citizen As It Gets, and full of surety that he'll let them know in the immediate, if he hears of Mr Banks's roundabouts.

I'm back in the room. Virus is practically rubbing his fingerprints off in glee. "He's gone," he sings out. "Done a runner! Jackson knows he can't avoid being long-armed for Crow's death if he stays around – even if, as he claims, it was a genuine mishap – so he's gone!"

The Digit pretends to be not *too* delighted, but can't resist a skip and a jump and an eensie *whoop whoop!* or three.

Let's wishful-think that he's gone and left Grace behind too. Imagine.

Virus goes all misty-eyed. "What a lovely way to finish the day," he says. "Digit, you must get your rest. Tomorrow, we'll plan our next step against Norman Newton."

"Yes," I say, "yes. But what about Alfi? We've got to bring him back. Tomorrow. We have to!"

Virus sighs. "All right. Tomorrow. First thing. But now, you need a proper sleep, young man."

Indeed the Digit does, and he tries to sleep, he really does. Animals like Banks are never gone – they're just lurking round different corners. But who cares? He's off Alfi's back, on the run from the Sherlocks, and V and me have got Call-Me Norman cornered in a cyber-trap.

Tomorrow, perhaps, will bring us all our heart's delight. Just like it always happens in the Grim Feary Tales.

19. THE FUR-PECKED PLASTER MAN

Me second morning waking up at Scarlett and Danny's. It's a sunny day and Scarlett says she's going to take us ice-skating up at the Alexandra Palace. It sounds posh. She says you get a view o' the whole o' London. I like that, being able to look down at a city, when the city can't look back up at you. I don't care if nobody ever sees us again, apart from these two – and Patti and Iggy, o' course. Patti slept on me bed again, and she's lying on me chest with her paws resting against me chin. I think she's trying to hypnotize me: feed me breakfast, human boy, feed me breakfast and tickle my chin.

While Scarlett makes us scrambled eggs for me breakfast (hah, I don't need to hypnotize her) I soak up more o' their space. They've got a zillion books for starters, a whole load o' boring ones about politics and philosophy, but also a huge pile o' graphic novels, and a whole wall full o' children's books. A big pile of old-fashioned board games too, like Buckaroo *and* Monopoly *and* Cluedo.

"How come you have so much stuff for kids, but you don't have any computer games?" I ask Scarlett.

She laughs. "Are we grumpy, out-of-date losers who don't think computers are fun?"

"No." I suppose not.

"The thing is," she laughs, "our young guests usually only stay with us for a few days, tops. And because we're Emergency they've had quite a few things going on that they've got to think over. We like to offer space, and time to think. What about you, Fred? Would you rather be playing Grand Theft Auto *or chasing Iggy and exploring the area?"*

Durrr. Grand Theft Auto, *obviously.*

"If you had kids stay for longer – more permanently – would you let them play computers?"

She laughs again. "Sure." Then she frowns. "But our kids always move on, to someplace else."

"Don't you ever—"

"Here it comes! Get it while it's hot!"

Oh my God, what a fantastic breakfast! Can this woman cook, or what?

Toast. You can't beat it. I'm about to enjoy my first chomp when morning is broken by the intercom buzzing its coded rhythm. V and me look at each other – both for a mere nanosec hoping it's Alfi, back to collect his Birthday Tiff. I leap up, happy as a fizz-crack firework.

But it's Grace.

She is on her own, and by the look on her face she's not a funny bunny.

"You seen 'im?" she says by way of greeting.

"'Im?" queries Virus.

"Alfi?" asks me.

"Jackson."

"'*Im*," says Virus. "Laying low. Many miles from here."

"*Was* laying low," she corrects. "Like a hunted beast. And much nearer than you'd hope. 'Cos now 'e's flipped, ain't 'e? Proper bad, this time."

This time? Does JB make a habit of flipping? Personally, myself, I'm of the belief he's permaflipped.

"It's your doin' too," she says to Virus. "You and your fancy forgeries."

The Digit's right out of the loop. "What forgeries?" I say to Virus, and to Grace, "What's Jackson done?"

"'Opefully nothin' yet. But what with the Sherlocks crawlin' all over the postcode, and 'im bein' so terrified of gettin' nabbed for Crow's death, I'm worried, Vi, I reckon 'e's got an insane plan. 'E reckons if 'e can show that 'e ain't missin' 'is young assistant, the Sherlocks won't be able to make any connection between Crow and 'im. So 'e's after a new Crow."

"Well, how's he going to manage that?" The Digit is well and truly slow on the take-off.

"Alfi."

I ain't getting it. The Digit turns into Citizen Blank Face.

"If Crow ain't missin'," Grace explains, "then Crow

ain't the dead boy. Know what I mean?"

"But, Grace," says Virus, his face all deadly pale, "Alfi isn't Crow..."

He trails off, as Grace chuckles, horribly, like she's caught JB's insanities.

"Crow had a great, ugly scar running down his face," I put in. "Alfi's face is smooth, no marks."

She gives us a withery look. "And Jackson's got a cut-throat razor. Solves both problems." She pauses, for it to sink in.

"No!" grumps Virus. "This is all wrong. Alfi Spar is not Crow Bar. They will never swallow it."

"They will," says Grace. "Didn't you drum up the documentation for Jackson yourself? 'E only 'as to swap the official photo on record for one of Alfi. Maybe you'll be doin' that for 'im later, V."

Virus goes bright red. I've never seen him look so guilty before. "That was quite some time ago. Crow was in need. And back then, Jackson wasn't as ... edgy as he is now. It doesn't entitle him—"

"'E says it does," Grace cries.

"It doesn't!"

This all sounds like a horrible mess.

Grace crosses her arms. Virus is fidgeting with his Zap App. He feeds me the most pathetic look, like he's a messed-up toddler, and I'm the responsible adult. But I won't return it with any softness. Instead I look to Grace. "Can you lead me to where Alfi is?"

She nods. "Jackson had me stake out the place."

I take her hand and out we bolt, heading straight for Finsbury Park, leaving the Great Manager behind in his HQ, to survey the ruins of his fur-pecked plaster man.

Suddenly, I feel all panicky. Short of breath and sweaty. Scarlett has her coat on and car keys in her hands.

"Let me come wi' you," I say.

"I'm sorry, Fred, on the way back from the super-market, I have to pop in for a private meeting at Social Services. You wouldn't be allowed. But you'll be all right here. There's loads to do. I'll be back before you know it, then this afternoon we'll do the skating rink. Deal?"

I don't like it.

"You han't told me the rules," I say. "The House Rules."

She pauses lacing up her boots. "There are no rules," she says.

"What about what I can touch and do, and what I can't touch or do?"

"Well, keep out of our room, and we'll keep out of yours. The rest of the house is shared territory. Don't tread on Iggy."

She grabs her keys and turns to the door. Pauses. "Don't answer the door." Pauses again. "Oh, if you want to spin some tracks, feel free."

Spin?

She gestures to a wall stacked wi' records. I've seen

this kind o' thing before. One twelve-inch disc gives you twenty minutes o' music a side. Neat idea, but they've used up all their wall space.

She's out the door while I'm looking at the records.

I pull a few out, grubby old cardboard covers wi' bands called Toots *and* Jam *and* Upsetters *and* Dead Kennedys *and* Skinhead Moonstomp *and* Stiff Little Fingers. *Is this music? Scarlett and Danny have one o' them record-player machines, so I pick a disc and put the needle on it and it sounds horrible, like blokes having a scrap next to a road-drill. But Patti likes it, and purrs even louder.*

Iggy gets jealous of Patti looking so chuffed and leaps up at us, clambering over me face. He has a zip-zap sticky tongue which he zip-zaps all over me face, tickly and cold. "Gerroff!" But he won't gerroff. He sticks it down me ear. Uurgh. I like him. Patti is sitting there, staring at us with a look on her face like everything's totally cool, front paws pressed tidily together like she's the happiest cat on the planet. She's defo trying to hypnotize us.

Iggy finally curls up. This noise must be relaxing for animals. Iggy looks so chilled I don't want to disturb him by getting up to stop the noise, so I sit through twenty minutes of it. When it's done, he gives a little yap and points his button nose in my direction. Does he have eyes? I can't tell. He yaps again, like he's asking for more noise, so I choose another – Deep Bass Space Dub Ape Mash. *It's mental. Iggy and Patti love it. Makes me sleepy...*

*

The Digit's hot-wired a motor, but I'm of the opinion we'd make faster progress hot-footing it. How can so many thousand vehicles crawl along so slow? There ain't no fast lanes on Seven Sisters Road, that's for sure.

"Does Jackson have his motor?" I'm asking.

"'E's been livin' in it. With its blacked-out windows it's the safest 'ide-out. The cops were even stakin' out my gaff. I ain't surprised 'e's so panicked." She feeds me a look of utmost severity. "You saw 'ow 'e was the other night. 'E's ten times worse now. Gone right over, 'e 'as. Take a left 'ere, Didge, there'll be less traffic." She stops talking for a moment, like she's chewing something over. She looks over at me and whispers, "I'm leavin' 'im."

"What? You told me you'd tried it before – and it ain't safe."

"It's a lot less safe stayin' with 'im. 'E's finished off 'is testosterone stash. 'E's like fifty kids at a birthday bash, all rolled into one giant bun fight. Smashin' everythin' in 'is path, jus' for the fun of it."

"How far now?"

"Jus' round this next corner."

If we're in time, I'm going to get Alfi out of there. I promise, I'll never let him down again.

Summat wakes us.

Someone banging at the door, sounding dead urgent.

I open me eyes and see Patti has her back arched and hackles up. She's hissing. There's a bang against the door.

Iggy jumps off me lap and hides behind the sofa. Another bang, and the catflap explodes into the living room. Through splintered wood I see fangs and bloody eyes, a monster dog snapping its way through the debris.

Patti's going ape. Claws out.

Another crash and the rest of the door smashes in. A giant man. "Obnob," the giant snarls at the beast. "Kill."

It's the bloke from the park. And the dog with the torn ear.

I'm still sat in the chair.

The dog bounds in, snapping its jaws around Patti's head, shaking her madly, like a rag doll. The cat is screeching.

She stops screeching, and the dog drops her. She's dead.

The giant bloke's got a big crowbar and he smashes it against Scarlett and Danny's record player, so bits of it go flying everywhere and the music dies. He laughs like it's the start of the party. Fixes his eyes on me. He nods, like he's giving hisself approval.

Iggy pounces, nipping at Obnob's back legs. The beast spins round, snapping its fangs. The two dogs race round and round the room, smashing everything over as they snap and yelp.

The giant pulls down all o' the record racks.

I'm still in the chair. He lurches towards us. He grabs me phone. Chucks it on the floor and stamps all over it, till it's a million pieces.

"Proper off-radar now, ain'tcha?" he spits, and then laughs. "Crooooow-Boy!"

He's a lunatic.

I try and leap out o' the chair, but he jabs me chest with his finger and it's like I've been stabbed with a great stick. I fall back.

He unzips his gym bag and puts it on the floor in front o' me chair. He brings out a tea towel and a bottle, which he starts unscrewing and there's a nasty stench like cat pee and he's pouring it all over the towel.

I'm shrinking deeper into the chair. Giant man has a look on his face like he wants to eat us up. He pushes the towel at me face and there's nowhere for us to go. It reeks. I feel sick. He lifts us up by me collar with one hand. Can't breathe. I'm floating up like I'm part of the spacey bassy ape music. Fumes in me face making me fadey...

I drop face-first into the bag. Thunk. Black hole. No pain. He's folding me legs and arms, bending me into shape like I'm luggage squeezing in. Sleepy-face baggage.

Zip, zip, zipped away.

Blackness.

Nice quiet side-street. Tree-lined, lazy cats on garden walls. I bet Alfi's been loving it here. No wonder he had no hurries to return to *Cash Counters*.

I'm waiting for Grace to direct me to the right house, but there's no need. What I see makes my heart go cold. Somebody's had a riot or a party. Citizen Digit ain't happy. When you see a big holiness where a door used to be, you can assume there's more than the doorbell bust.

I park the motor up the road, gesture to Grace for softly-softliness, and cast a bit of my invisibility over her natural brightness.

Inside, first thing we see is a load of spilled records scattered all over. Then, lying in the middle of them, is a dead cat. There's a horrible pong, and Grace mimes holding her nose, show she can sniff it too.

No Alfi.

I spot somebody's hair beside the coffee table. Were they *scalped*?

The hair starts crawling towards us. Despite being Hero of the Nth Degree, I jump in fright. The hair goes *Yip, yip!*

I see. Grace makes soothing noises and the dog stops yipping and creeps towards her. She lets it have a good sniff of her fingers, and then she strokes its head. The dog rolls over onto its back and shows us its tum.

Little doggie needs to go to doggie hospital.

Soon as we see the bite mark, it's confirmation who's been and paid a social visit to this tidy part of Finsbury Park. Wig-Dog is lucky to have any wiggle left at all. It must have squeezed itself underneath a sofa or something, where Obnob couldn't get to it, finish it off.

Me and Grace don't say nothing, on account of the scene says it all already.

I hear a car pull up out front, footsteps getting out,

238

making their way up the garden path. Instantaneous, I'm seeking a hidey-hole. Grace too, but the Citizen's got keener peepers from years of practice. These good Groans have long velvet curtains for their windows, hanging down to the floor. Drawn open, they're all a ruffle. I guide Grace to one and slip behind the other. Stock still, like we're playing Statues.

Grace keeps herself fully within the folds, but I can risk letting an eye out.

This woman comes in, and she drops her bag at the sight before her. The wig-dog whimpers at her and she bends down to pet it, going all *coo, coo*. Then she sees the dead cat and a horrible sob comes out of her, and she leaves the dog and she's taking in the debris and sits down on the sofa and bends her head, like she's in church. Maybe she's crying. Then I realize she's texting. I guess she's texting her man. *Get home. Now.* Then she looks like she's sending another text, but she's not, she's making a call. She puts the phone to her ear, and I can hear the tinny voice at the other end, *Emergency services* something, and *What's your name and* something. And this woman, sitting there with what's left of her living room, amongst the absence of Alfi, and her dead cat and mauled dog, she's all at a loss of words, just goes *err* for a moment, and then she is, she is crying, and it's time for the Digit and Grace to make our disappearance. Leave the lady to her loss.

So much for Alfi's perfect new home.

The Digit's waiting for the opportune mo to slip away, but the sobbing lady won't stop her sobbing. I'm thinking she's just going to sit there right in front of us, sobbing away until the Sherlocks arrive, and it's really curtains for me and Grace.

Then she stops, and she's looking in our direction. I wonder if she's just gazing aimlessly out of the window, but she says, "I can see you."

Impossible!

But of course, it's Grace she sees, and Grace knows it. She steps out from behind her curtain.

"It ain't 'ow it looks," she says. "I'm a friend of Alfi's."

"Alfi?" says the lady.

Grace gestures at the mess around her. "Alfi." Like that clarifies that.

"The boy?"

"'E's in proper danger."

The lady scoffs at that, understandably enough. She's cradling the wig-dog like it's all she's got left.

Grace takes a step forward.

Lady starts back. "I called the police."

"What's your name?" says Grace, unfazed.

Lady studies Grace's face, like she's trying to decide whether she's a goodie or a baddie. Finally, she says, "I'm Fred's – Alfi's foster mum. What have you done with him?"

"I'm…" says Grace, "I'm Alfi's sister. I didn't do this. It's 'orrible." She tails off. "'E's in danger."

"Well, the police'll be here in a minute."

Grace gives a sad laugh, shakes her head. "You tried to make a home for him, didn't you?"

"Till someone came along and smashed it all up – yeah."

I've seen places more busted up than this. I've lived in them. Some people like ruins.

"It's a nice 'ome," Grace says. She goes all wobble-kneed and plonks herself down on what's left of the coffee table. "Do yer mind?" She asks permission, polite as ever.

What's she playing at? We don't have time for this!

Table cracks beneath her and a leg gives way. Table and Grace crumple carpetwards.

"Make yourself at home," says the lady.

"I'm sorry. I'm so sorry. We can get it all fixed. Replace what's busted. 'Onest. It'll be even better than it was."

She ain't saying how she's going to fix the busted pussycat. She puts her head in her hands, and I'm thinking this ain't helping Alfi one bit. Now ain't the time to be cracking up, along with the furniture.

Lady stares at her. Precious seconds tick-tock by. But I see her face slowly softening. "Do I know you?" she says. "You remind me of a girl who stayed with us once?"

Grace straightens her face, offers her a little smile. "No," and the smile sort of slides off her face. "Well, we're all the same pretty much, ain't we?"

Then the two of them are just sitting there, saying

241

nothing. The Digit don't get it. Grace is looking round, at the photos on the wall. And the lady is looking at Grace, in a sad sort of way. "I'm sorry," Grace says again. "I'm sorry. We break everything."

No, we don't. Everything's already busted, before we even arrive. We just get plonked on top of it all, the last scrap tossed on the scrapheap.

"It's just things," the lady says, all kindly. "Home isn't made of things, it's the people in it." She reaches out a hand and touches Grace's shoulder.

"I'm Scarlett," she's says.

Grace bites her lip. All of a sud, she looks a lot younger, and she's gone all red-eyed.

"I'm Grace," she says. She's an insaniac. You *never* give your name.

And Scarlett says, "Shall I make us some tea?"

That cracks Grace up. She starts crying. Not sobbing and wailing, just sitting still with a thin trickle running down each cheek. Doesn't even try and wipe them away.

The Digit's getting fidgety as a flea-bit dog. Scarlett leans forward and wraps her arms round Grace, and Grace sinks into her. Last human touch she had was JB play-throttling her throat. "There, there," says Scarlett. "It's all right. It's OK."

But it ain't OK! I hear a car pulling up, and through the front window I can see blue light reflecting on a wall. Sherlocks.

We're out of time. Grace is getting mothered. If she

ain't careful, she's going to get long-armed.

She pulls out of the hug. Pulling herself together. We're on the wrong side of the thin blue line. Not even Alfi was safe here.

"I have to go." She leaps up.

"Wait!"

But she's already making for the back door. I hear her yell, "I'll save him. I'll save Alfi – I promise!" Then there's a slam, and I see her hurtling through the garden.

Another slam, and Scarlett appears in the garden. But Grace is gone. There's nothing for Scarlett to do but come back through to the front and face the Sherlocks.

I myself glide through to the kitchen, open the back door, soft as a feather, and ease my way into the back garden.

I vault a fence. I'll leave the car, it hardly being much faster than legging it. I hop over several garden fences, quick and agile, and race back towards Jackson Banks's Arsenal bolthole as fast as a flash. I pray one of us will get there in time to save Alfi's face.

20. THEY ALL LOOK THE SAME, MORE OR LESS

There's summat round me wrist. Me face stings. I smell like cat wee. I open me eyes. Where am I? Somewhere stinky and dusty and dark.

Handcuffs? Handcuffs attached to a big metal chain like folk use to lock up posh bikes.

A chain. I'm abducted. Call-Me Norman has caught us. Barry's gonna bash us up.

The Jimmys! I'm chained up in a Jimmy dungeon.

Dogs. They've got dogs. They killed Patti. Iggy too?

I'll get blamed. Scarlett and Danny'll think I killed their cat and trashed their house and ran away. Another foster home ruined.

I'm back in the hands o' the Jimmys.

They're going to do stuff to us. Like in Digit's film. One after t'other.

I hear breathing. Heavy breathing. Like someone's watching us.

Focus. Concentrate. I'm still wearing me clothes. Good. I'm Katariina's son. Who's watching us? Are they filming us? Where's the breathing?

Me eyes adjust. There's a bit o' light. Daytime. Little window. It's an attic. A house. Tenderness House?

"Hello?"

The breathing stops. Now it's a snorting, a snuffling.

There. Sat in an armchair. The dog, Obnob, curled up, asleep. He wakes, I'm dead. He in't even on a leash.

They've left him as a guard dog, han't they? Only this dog in't no guard dog – it's an attack dog. Big difference, that is. A guard dog'll only stop you escaping. An attack'll have your throat out soon as look at yer. Like this one, here.

I take a step back. The metal chain rattles against the wall, where it's attached on a big hook. Dog opens its eyes, glares at us.

I'm dead.

It curls back its lips and its fangs are ragged and raw. It bounds off the chair, snarling right in front of us, lip trembling like it can't control its rage.

Allus said I wanted a dog o' me own.

I take another step back, but I'm up against the wall, and the dog lunges at us. Its teeth snippy-snap, threatening to take a chunk from me leg. Sizing us up. Licking its lips. I'm cornered, chained.

It's time to employ me dog-whispering skills.

But this dog's mental, in't it?

What's its name? Obnob. Obnob killed Patti, probably Iggy an' all.

"Hey, little fella."

Dog stops snarling. See? Dog-whisperer.

"Hey there."

"RRAFFF!" Lunges again. Fixes them bloodshot eyes on me throat.

I en't got no choice, have I? I bend down. I get me head lower down than its head, me face looking up at it. All I can see is teeth, hungry eyes.

I look down, take me eyes off it. I make a pathetic, whimpering noise, into the floor.

And I wait.

"Grrrrrrrrrrrr..."

Is that a friendlier growl? I en't sure. Whimper again. It din't bite me face off the first time.

"Grrrrrrrrrr?" goes the dog. Ah-hah. Now we're in conversation.

From down on the floor, I raise me eyes. Look at him direct. "Cht-cht-cht," I go, "Ob ... nob... Who's a cute little fella then?"

He barks. Not a bad sign. He stamps a paw. A good sign. Reckon he wants to play.

"Who's a good boy!" Barks again. "Is it you? Is it? It is! Obnob what a good doggie, what a hero doggie. En't yer! En't yer! Yes, you are! Ohh, Obnob, en't yer the best? Good boy! Good boy!"

He starts dancing his paws up and down in excite-ment. In anticipation – of boy food, or a belly rub?

Let's find out. I waggle me fingers in front of his snout. "Yes, yes! Obbynobby good doggy! Time to play! Oh, yes! It's me! Yer old mate Alfi?"

He sniffs me fingers and gives 'em a lick. "Obnob! My friend. Awwwww, en't you the cutest?"

The beast lunges at me face and begins to lick me cheek. Cool. I say more nice things and he rolls on his back for a belly tickle. He loves it. His leg gets that happy twitch dogs get when you do their bellies. No dog in the world can resist a good old belly rub.

See? Citizen Digit in't the only lad wi' special powers. Just see if he in't.

But that in't going to get us out of here, is it? Where am I? This dun't look like Tenderness House, and I can hear too many traffic sounds.

"Help!" I call out. "Help!"

If I can hear traffic, maybe the traffic can hear me.

"Help!" I yell at the top o' me voice. "Help!"

I've actually got quite a loud voice. "Help me! I'm chained up! Help! Help!"

I listen for a moment. Nowt. "Help!" I yell. "Help! Help me! Help me! Pleeeaaase! HELP!"

Obnob starts joining in wi' us, barking and yapping in excitement.

But still no sign of anyone responding. I'm going to try screaming. Good idea.

"AAAAAAAAAAAAAAAAAARRRRRRRRRRRGH!"

That were dead loud.

"Help!" I call. "HELP! HELP! HELP!

WOOF! WOOF! WOOF! WOOF! goes Obnob.

Listen again. I hear summat. Movement at the bottom

of the stairs. Don't be the psycho giant. Please don't let it be the psycho giant.

"Help!" *I call. If it's someone coming to help, that's great. But if it's that giant bloke he needs to know that I've already let all the world know he's got us here.* "I'm being held prisoner! I'm chained up! HELP! HELP!"

Sound o' footsteps running up the stairs.

WOOF! WOOF! WOOF! WOOF!

"HELP ME! MURDER! TORTURE! HELP! HELP! HELP! I'M A PRISONER! AAAAAAAAAAA-AAAAAAAARRRRRRRRRRRGH!"

The door of the room smashes open. A giant shape. Blink, try and focus. A giant duvet? *The duvet dives on top of Obnob, so the dog's covered with it, wrestling with it.*

"Shoot me dead, Squealer-Boy, what a fu-roary. You cut? Need the parametics? Show us the wounds."

Citizen Digit. I'm saved.

JB's palace, up the Arsenal, at the end of a dead-end street. Any other crim wouldn't settle there for more than five mins. No back exit, no way out. But JB thrives here. Face your enemies, see. Come out punching.

Mounted halfway up the pavement is a beat-up old pimpmobile. Windows blackened. Personalized number plate: SH4NK1. This is a different set of wheels to the one Jackson Banks had two days previous. His old car is vanished, just like poor boy Crow.

But Alfi's here right enough. The Digit can hear him

yelling from all the way down the street. It's fair to say that Banks isn't with him at present, or Alfi's screams wouldn't be lasting more than a second and a half. It seems the Good Citizen is in luck, and in time.

Then I hear the dog, and Alfi's screaming gets worse. It's horribleness. I bankcard the lock double quick. I dash into a bedroom, grab a duvet and fly up the stairs, to the room at the top. I'm not thinking of my personal health and safety. I'm not even thinking. In factuality, I've gone a bit thick. 'Cos somewhere at the back of my head there's a memory that if you throw a duvet over a dog and wrap it tight enough, you can subchew them. That might be fair enough with any normal dog, but with a Hound of the Basketcase like Obnob, it's more a matter of poor choice for suicidals.

So I'm rolling round with the hound and calling for help and everything, and Alfi stretches out the hand that ain't cuffed and gives me the flat-palmed *stop* signal. Then he grabs hold of the edge of the duvet, throws it back and says, "Good boy!"

The Digit is struck double-dumb. Beast is licking Alfi all over. At the same time, I'm taking in the chain cuffing Alfi's wrist to the wall, the *size* of it, and I realize we've had it. These ain't the sort of locks even a picky-pock like the Digit can undo.

"Well, howdy doo-doo," I greet my old pal.

"Howdy doo-doo yourself," he grumps, ruffling the psycho-dog's head.

"Whoah. Ain't I the cavalry, come to rescue you from the bad boys?"

"You're the bad 'un, Byron. A thief and a traitor."

"Digit," I correct him.

"Byron," he insists. "Me and you, we're finished with each other." He looks all earnest at Obnob's face. "Don't trust him, Obnob. You don't know what he's like. He's a backstabber."

You've got to laugh. Alfi's still whinging on about the little scene with that Groan's wallet. I reach into my pocket and bring out his Birthday Tiff. "You gotta stop losing this," I say. "One day, you'll have no one to find it for you."

He snatches if off me, with a complete lack of gratis.

"That's all right," says me. "No problemo. I s'pose I shouldn't have looked after it for you, then the cops would've thrown you back to Tenderness."

He doesn't hear me. He's reading it, word for word, like he ain't even memoried it a million times already. Once he's satisfied it's still the same wordies in the same order, he looks up and glares at me.

I glare back.

"Thanks," he mutters.

I shrug. Suppose that's us best pals again.

Defo. 'Cos he grabs my arm and gives me the most pathetic look I've ever seen in my entire lifelihood. "What are we going to do? Where are we going to go?"

"Haven't the foggiest doggie. Anywhere away from

here. Away from Jackson Banks. You wouldn't want to hear Virus's plaster man. Reckons it's foolproof."

"What's that then?"

"Only for us to go back to Tenderness House."

"What?"

I throw him my *What-can-I-say?-Groans-are-insane* face. "Chillax. We won't do that. How about Ibiza? Tenerife?"

He ignores my sarkiness and rattles his chain at me. Like I'm supposed to solve everything for him.

"Don't worry," I say, "the Digit'll sort it. But listen up, Alfi, this is serious, big time. Jackson has you tagged as his new boy. You're going to be Crow. You get me?"

But he's confucious, ain't he? I forgot, Alfi never met Crow. But he's met Jackson all right.

"Is he that great big headcase?"

"That's the one. Listen, he'll have the key for this lock on his bones. We need cutting gear. A hacksaw. Bolt-cutters. I'll go look."

"No!" Alfi cries. The Digit lifts a hypoquizzical eyebrow. Alfi throws me a pleading look. "Don't leave me!"

"Well, I know how much you love the Digit's company," I smile, "but we don't have the time to be hanging out together. Work to be done!"

And before he can objectify further, I'm out of the room and working my way to the cupboard where JB must keep his tools.

I start rummaging round for some cutting gear. JB

must have something that'll do these chains – he's a burglar, ain't he? They're the tools of his trade. We've got to be quick – if his pimpmobile's outside and his dog's up here, then he can't be too far away. If he catches us, we'll both be dog meat – even if Alfi is Obnob's new BFF. Come on, Didge, shake a leg.

At last, bolt-cutters. Big heavy ones like Sherlocks use when tree-huggers chain themselves to local greenery. Perfecto.

Dash back. Flash the cutters at Squealer-Boy soon as I'm in the doorway. Then I hear the front door creak open. And slam shut.

Quick – vanish!

But it's Grace's voice. Relief. But who's she talking to? Virus? All rightiho, then let's go. *Go go go!* It's all good.

Then I hear what she's actually saying:

"No, Jackson, you can't. Please, Jackson, don't do it to him. Don't hurt him. Jackson, please."

Ah.

It en't often you see the colour drain from Citizen Digit's face. But right now, he looks white as a cloud. And he's looking round, in a panic. He never panics. Citizen Digit dun't do panic.

"Are you going to use the bolt-cutters?" I say. "You've got to cut me free!"

He's ignoring us. He's looking round, for somewhere to hide.

He ducks under a table, sinks hisself into its shadows.
I'm staring right at him, but you'd never know he were there.

What about me?

Jackson Banks is stomping up the stairs. There en't no
time. Back to Plan A. I open me mouth and yell.

"HELP! HELP! THERE'S A MANIAC! I'M CHAINED UP!
HE'S GOING TO TORTURE ME! HELP! HELP! HELP!"

Nice one, Blabber-Boy. Jackson bursts into the room and
gives Alfi a slap. Knocks him right over, so he's hanging
by the chain. Alfi gives a sob, then zips it.

There's only Grace with him. She must have had
the misfortune to bump into Jackson on the way here.
Drawn to him like a magnet.

He's red-eyed and phlegmy. I reckon he's been out
and scored himself more testosterone. Prepare himself
for what he's about to do.

Jackson produces his razor. The Digit's never seen
one like this in real life. It looks like it's from the Museum
of Murder Weapons.

"How'd you like a haircut?" Jackson says to Alfi.
"And a shave?"

Alfi looks all confucious. I guess he doesn't know
about Crow's shaved head. Or his scar. But Grace does,
and her face betrays it. Alfi clocks her clocking it, and
then I can see it on *his* face too. The realization. Alfi
sort of groans and looks like he's going to lose his lunch,
outta both exits.

The Digit curls himself in as small as possible. An insignificance.

Grace says, "No, Jackson. No."

"No?" he booms. Enough velocity to knock a Full Groan off their feet.

"No," says Grace. The Citizen can't hardly believe his eavesdroppers.

"No?" Banks whispers, softlike, amused. "No?"

"Please..." pleads Alfi, cowering in the corner.

JB likes that. "Please?" he mocks, in his best high-pitch, his hands held together in prayerlike. He throws his dagger eyes back at Grace. "Oh, but poor me. My darling Crow is gone. Gone for ever. And I need another. Please?" He's loving it. Testosteroned up, and set for nastiness.

Grace throws herself forward. "J," she says, "Newton won't pay up if you harm the boy."

Banks's free hand grabs Alfi's face like a vice. Alfi's eyes try and flee round the back of his head, sliding round the sockets, all helpless. Banks gives a gasp of delight.

"Please, J." She's got her hand on Banks's wrist. "J, there's no need. Virus is blackmailing Norman Newton and his gang. Alfi Spar is part of the plan. Think of the money. The money, J."

She'd make more impact with a swift knee to the groinals. Or maybe not. When JB's in his rages, even his nuts are made of steel.

"It won't work," she's pleading. "There's evidence, a video – V's going to make it public, blow it wide open. The Sherlocks'll be looking for Alfi. It'll be all the worse!"

All useless. Banks is lost in his own nutty role-play.

"Sherlocks need to know whether the boy corpse they've got belongs to me. *'Who is this dead boy corpse, Mr Banks? Is it your young Crow lad?'* 'Indeed it's not, Your Honour,'" JB smirks, chuckling at his own lines. "'For I still have my assistant, safe and sound.'"

"No, you don't," says Grace.

"Yes, I do," says Banks. "What a lovely young Crow he'll make."

He flourishes the cut-throat blade in front of Alfi's face. "You all look the same, more or less," he laughs.

"No, they don't!" She's pleading, desperate. "No, they don't!"

Obnob whimpers and does a widdle on the floor. Jackson Banks frowns, like a thought is trying to happen. Then he bares his teeth and steps towards Alfi.

"Don't worry, be happy." He reaches into his jacket and pulls out a rag that reeks of nastiness. "I'll put him under first."

"Jackson. No!" Grace throws herself between them.

Alfi, for once, is lost for words.

"No, Jackson!" She flings herself at him, surprises him, snatching the rag from his hand.

"Give it back."

But he's going to have to chase her for it. He lunges,

she dodges. He trips over his dog, falls flat. He yells. Grace sees her moment. She thrusts the rag into JB's face, over his mouth and nose. She clambers over his face, wrapping both arms round the back of his head, forcing his face and the chloroform into her chest. She hooks her legs under his armpits and latches her ankles round his back. Obnob has a grip on her top and is tugging at it, trying to pull her off Jackson Banks.

I wonder if JB is really going to black out. He's spinning round and round, trying to Buckaroo her. The Digit keeps getting flashes of her face. Grimful determination. We both know it's our only chance; we can cut Alfi free and flee. But we're forgetting about JB's big metal bolt-cutters, ain't we? He's feeling for them, where I left them leaning against the wall, and he gets his fingers round them, swings his arm, smashes her head. There's a *thunk*, and she falls sideways off him, like she's given up in a sudden huff. But it's the force of the blow, streaking down through her limbs, killing her every muscle.

JB is snarling and his dog whimpers, fretful. JB's red eyes flame down at Grace.

"J…" she murmurs. A red trickle flows from behind her head. She's banged it when she fell. Hard.

Her eyes roll up into her head. Like it's all another predictable irritation, and a sigh escapes her, like she's had enough. Or a final breath.

Ain't Banks her sweetheart?

Banks has a brick heart. He roars and raises the bolt-cutters. His rage is heartrage. He's going to finish her.

21. WITNESS

Blank Space. Blank Space. Byron *Blank Space.* He's only little. He loves his sisters, now that Mum has gone, they look out for him. His sisters, his assisters.

His dad is mad. Drunk and mad.

"Hide, Byron. It's just a game of Hide'n'Seek. You're so good at playing."

Byron's sisters in a fluster. In the cupboard they want him to go. Behind the sofa. Under the bed. Running round in a panic. *Hide, Byron, hide.*

Where did Byron go? What did Byron do? How much did Byron see? Why did he survive?

He didn't! He didn't survive. Citizen Digit survived and thrived. Grew big and clever. Decided he could live without having to watch further badness.

Didn't wanna see no more Bad Dads.

Idiot Byron just hid, and watched, and died of the watching.

Tricia and Dee pushed and shoved and squeezed little Byron into the washing machine, shut the door on him. Closed him off from the world.

How could he fit? It was such a little space. The only space for a tiny speck of a boy.

I watched, a heavy load, through the round glass screen. He tore the house apart. He swore and slapped and threatened and shook those fists, but my sisters wouldn't give me up, they never would. Then he knocked Tricia to the ground, fell on her, and began punching. I could see his fists as they raised back up, taking aim again, bloodying. And Dee, hitting him on the head with the iron, and him grabbing her and smashing her against the wall. His knees clamping down over Tricia, and his big hands smashing Dee, over and over like she was a dolly. Byron hiding, dumb, hearing the moan and the smash and the grunt, and Tricia whimpering all the while.

Obnob shuffles in next to the Digit, watching his master about to make murder, his sniffer tortured by the stench of it. But the Digit can still see past the dog's earflaps, can see what Jackson Banks is about to do to Grace. Byron is watching it all, again.

When my dad was done with Dee, he focused back on Tricia. "Where is he?" he slurred.

She never gave me up. Even as he dragged her final playtime out of her, she never gave me up. Her face was turned towards my round glass window. My sister looked at me and she never gave me up and then the life went; her eyes turned to marbles, dolly's eyes.

259

Grace.

The Digit is shaking memories from his head. We don't need Byron's old and ancients right now. But we don't want to be reliving them either.

So Byron leaps out from his hiding place. I show myself.

I stand between Grace and Jackson's killer blow.

I don't know what I can do. Grace isn't dead, I'm sure of it, but he will finish her off. So there's only one thing I can do. I tell a lie, and I tell a truth.

"She's dead!" I yell at him.

He blinks for a second, stopped in his tracks, drops the bolt-cutters. Daddy played too hard. Tears before bedtime. But this won't last for long. He's got further murderousness coiled inside him.

It's time to blind him with the truth.

I let him see who I really am.

"You may as well know," I say. "It's me you've been looking for. I'm the one. I'm Byron."

At last.

I suppose I thought I was going to have him chase me out of the house, away from Grace and Alfi, but my legs won't let me move. I'm standing there, not Citizen Digit, but a real boy.

Byron.

He blinks at me. Looks down at Grace, slumped. Wails, despairing, desperate. Looks back at me. Blinks again. His fist smashes forward, and my lights go out.

*

Jackson Banks is still gripping the razor. He don't say nowt, just glowers.

I'm saying nowt either. I'm fixed by his looney mad-dog eyes.

Burning at us. Like he's going to do me too. I don't care. I see who he is. I can't turn away. There's nowt here, just his eyes and mine, the dog whimpering from under the table, Grace and Byron lying silenced on the floor.

He shudders, looks away towards his dog. Anywhere but at me. Anywhere but at Byron. Anywhere but at Grace.

Jackson Banks has seen what he has done. I see what he has done. He turns back to me. If he's going to do us in, let him do it. I'm only a boy. There's millions others.

I don't really count.

Grace dun't count.

Scarlett and Danny will take in other kids. Jackson Banks will find another Grace, another Crow. Call-Me Norman will hold other parties, with other men and other kids. Virus will gather a thousand more Citizen Digits. Byron ain't owt special.

We might not be owt special, but so what? We are who we are.

So I look at the man.

"I en't Crow," I say. "My name is Alfi Spar. Me mam's name were Katariina. She were young, just like Grace. You can do what you like, but you can't take who we are. I'm Alfi, son of Katariina, friend of Byron, friend of Grace."

I meet his eyes, and I say, "Who are you?"

He drops the razor, and the bolt-cutters. He grabs Grace's coat off o' the table and chucks it over her, like she's some dead pet run down in the road. So you can't see her face.

Then he grabs the bolt-cutters. But instead o' clobbering us, he starts tapping them against the side of his head, like he's trying to drum sense back into hisself. Clank, *it goes, and he smiles like he's realizing how funny it is.* Clank, *again, and he tilts his head sideways to greet its beat.* Clank, *again, and a red trickle flows down into his ear.* Clank, *smiling like an idiot. Then his fist gripping the tool wobbles, like it's suddenly heavy, and he holds it out towards us, and cuts me chains. He frees me.*

I'm rubbing at me wrists where the chains were chafing, wondering if it's all over, finished at last. And his hand comes round to me face, wi' that stinking rag, and I can't breathe. I'm going to go under. Again.

22. WHOOSH

Byron's eyelids may well be drawn, but Citizen Digit's found a tiny gap between them and is peeping out.

My head is laid against Grace's chest, where I fell from Jackson's punch, and I can feel her, still breathing. And here's me, pretending not to breathe, let JB think he's done for the two of us.

Watch, and wait.

Alfi Spar is staring at Jackson Banks. Jackson Banks is staring right back at Alfi. The Digit ought to be doing something right now.

Alfi Spar's eyes are bright, round, innocent. Baby blues. They fix themselves on Banks's bulldog eyes, blazing murder.

Alfi's angel gaze will not waver. Jackson relaxes his grip on the weapon. Obnob pauses in his scratting at the door, turns to stare at them both.

It's me, the dog and Jackson, all caught in Alfi Spar's clear blue wonder.

Alfi Spar is a witness.

Alfi won't free Jackson from his gaze. He shifts his

head, slowly, taking Jackson with him, round and down to the floor where Grace lies. Alfi lets Jackson's gaze settle on her.

Alfi knows. And he shows him. Blabber-Boy lets Jackson Banks know what he's done.

The dog howls to be free, free of the stench, and the spell breaks, and JB grabs Grace's coat from the table, hurls it over her head, so you can't see her face.

Breathless, I see my sisters' faces.

We remember the bad dads. Mean old daddies with their bunches of fives.

What does Jackson do? He does what he's learned to do, don't he? He picks up the bolt-cutters and strikes. He smashes. Each time he bashes the bolt-cutters against his own thick skull his eyes widen a little more, like he's getting pleasure from it. Like he thinks it's Alfi he's bashing. Over and over with the greatest of pleasure.

Is this how it'll be for all of us, if we ever reach Groandom? Once we're too big to be clobbered by others, we do it to ourselves? Self-administer, like Virus and his zapper? Is this how it'll be?

Jackson bashes himself and glowers at Alfi. Battering the child.

Then he turns to Alfi, raising the bolt-cutters up over his head, and gives an animal roar.

He cuts Alfi free.

Then he knocks him out with the chloroform, and

he packs him back into the gym bag, and casts one final look of horror at the coat on the floor, the coat that makes the shape of Grace.

He shudders, and throws open the door. Obnob barks relief and flurries out, fleeing the scene.

When my father was finished with my sisters he fled the scene. Little Byron was left, scrunched up tight inside the washing machine, not wanting to climb back into the world.

Just waiting. Wishing everything different.

It's like that now.

My eyes are awake, but my face is a few moments behind, and my arms and legs several minutes after that. That was some wallop Jackson hit me with. Grace still ain't coming round. I crawl my way towards the kitchen, find a tap, water. I let out a sob, I can't help it, and I go over into the corner and curl into a chair and tears are leaking all over, leaking for Grace, and for my sisters.

Then I gulp the water and I gain the strength, and I pour more for Grace, and this time I'm going back on two feet rather than two knees.

Truly deeply – it may be minutes, or more, or less – I have the water to bring Grace round, I dab a finger to her forehead, cool against her burning pain, when there's a screech of brakes. It can only mean JB went away. It can only mean he went away and he is back. I hear him bashing his way through the door and stromping up the stairs. I hear him sloshing liquid from a can all over everywhere. I smell it.

I know what. I know he's pouring it all over the house, but he won't come back into this room, won't look at what he's done. What he thinks he's done. I know he's trailing a stream of it through each of the rooms and back down the stairs. I listen and sniff as he fumes back through the house towards the front door. I'm immobility itself as the door thunks shut behind him. The click of a lighter, the snap of the letterbox and the whole building, with us inside, takes like a lit-up gas ring.

Whoosh.

23. TO HELL

I'm watering Grace. She's coming back to the world. I got a pan, with water, I poured it, I soaked her. There's a fire licking at our toes, and I have to get her out of here. I soaked myself. I'm hearing the sirens as the fire trucks arrive. We are meant to live. She splutters and coughs, and I'm tending her, bruised and battered and burned and smoky.

We are at the top of the house and there is only a skylight, out of reach. Smoke is flurrying upwards, mobbing us. I heave her up. I drag her down. She's heavier than me, but I have sister-memory muscling my arms. I won't be stopped. I am Byron; I am Digit; and Grace is loved and I will not let her go. I clunk her down the stairs, *biff* goes her head on each stair, *biff*, and I try to cushion her as I drag her, tell her I won't let her cinder. She knows it's true; she flutters those eyelashes and the flames will not flicker too close to us. Though we are inflammable, *whooooosh* goes my breath, blowing the flames away. Yellow and red and orange like one of her billowing skirts. Grace is the kaleidoscope of life.

Little brother flesh melts away from me, fresh muscles bulge and bubble with air and heat. I doused us with bath water, see us through the baptism of fire. Is it a game, or life? *Fire, Fire, Pans On Fire.* Byron and Sister playing on the stairs, coughing and staggering, hamming and heroic, skin and blister, secret cigarette smoke killing young lungs, the darkest, greyest dream...

Daylight drags us through the doorway, cold pavement kissing our singes, traffic fumes cooling our airwaves, coughing up ashes into North-London drizzle. Grey and wretched and all Groan-out.

"Digit." She splutters to life, from the dusty gutter.

"Yes," I say. "What? What?"

"It's *Cash Counters*," she rasps. "That's his deal. He's going to get Virus's stash, so he can start again. Whatever he's got planned for Alfi, the stash comes first. *Cash Counters*. You got to get to *Cash Counters*."

Even now, she's thinking how to rescue Alfi. I'm of the same infurious state. Whatever our own personal ills, JB's animal verocity is shifting to *Cash Counters*' vicinity.

I rest her on the pavement, ambulances and fire engines sirening up to us, and I know she'll be OK, but I have to go. I have to save Alfi.

It's simplicity itself.

Banks's Bentley is jack-knifed across the kerb outside *Cash Counters* and the front door is smashed wide open.

Hulk-Head has torn it off its hinges.

As I take my cautious pause across the street to check out the scene, I realize I'm a little too late. Again. There's a gunshot from within.

I take two giant leaps into the next-door shop doorway. And I watch. Jackson Banks marches purposefully out of *Cash Counters*, gun in hand, metal safebox under his arm.

He wastes no time, tossing it into the passenger seat, flooring the accelerator and screeching away.

Alfi, gym-bagged Alfi, no doubt stuffed in the boot.

Citizen Digit feels a sudden sadness pass through him. I'm all Predictiv Tex as to what might be found up them *Cash Counters* stairs.

The Good Citizen spirits his bones across the road and up the stairs, following the stench of murder. As he reaches the top, the stench turns, again, to that of blood.

The word of advice is: leave no prints, leave no marks; this is the scene of crime – of the first degree – and the Digit must engage with no part of it.

And, oh, but it's sadness itself. For what do I find upon the floor of *Cash Counters*' fine dining room, but Mr Virus, the Great Manager, breathing and berating his last? I'm bending down to him, cradling his head, and his redness is juicing up all over his floor.

"Oh, Didge," he says, "I knew I could rely on you to see me through." He coughs and splutters. "I'm all messy, aren't I? Bloodstains on the boards."

"It'll mop," I say. "Don't be fretting it."

He points his eyes towards a hole in the wall, where one of his fancy artworks hung. The artwork is snapped and ripped, and the hole behind is empty like a slurped-out breakfast bowl.

"He took my safebox," says Virus. "Much good as it'll do him. He could never get the lock code out of me. I tried to stop him, you know."

"Surely you did." His Smartphone is still vibrating in his fingers, the Zap App sizzling to find a target. But the bullet hole in Virus's stomach shows he was evidentially outgunned.

He says more, but his voice is faint. I lean in close. "He's got Alfi, you know."

"I know."

"He's taking him back. He thinks you're dead." His eyes go all watery. "And Grace?"

"Grace will be fine." I wipe the sweat from his forehead, with one of his hankies. "Back where, V? To Tenderness?"

He blinks agreement. "He has to do something to silence him. Alfi's now a witness to murder, so he thinks. Now you're dead. Grace. And me. And Newton will keep Alfi quiet... Then Banks can go off somewhere – start again. With my savings. That was my pension."

I'd figured as much.

"Newton'll never let Alfi go. He knows too much, and he means too much."

The Digit understands that there's still more to this than meets the eyeball, but the one thing I'm sure of is, if Virus could have, he'd have protected us – Alfi, Grace, and me as well. He was just a bit rubbish, is all.

"Tell me, Didge," he says, "I wasn't too bad, was I?"

I smile at him, shake my head.

"And Newton." He stiffens in my arms. "Newton. If there were no Newtons ... well, there'd be no Jacksons. Isn't that so, Didge?"

"Sure, V, and if there was no Mr Virus, there'd be no – well," I say, "there'd be no fun and games, would there?"

"Did we?" he goes on. "Did we have fun?"

I make myself nod. His voice is fading now. He whispers, and I lean in closer. "I did you that favour," he says.

"You shouldn't be worrying about that now."

He smiles, feeble. "You get what you deserve. We all do."

I nod again. "What happens now?"

"Let's end it." He coughs and splutters.

"End it?"

"All the badness comes from Tenderness House. It's where it all started. Norman Newton. You've got to bring him down."

I snort. Can't help myself.

His eyes gleam back at me. "You know what *is* funny?"

Everything? We're having a right old laugh.

"He started paying up. Our plan was working. He

just transferred the second sum of money. Meaningless now. Let's do it."

"Do what?" I say.

"Tell."

"Tell?"

"End the silence. How many more years should we let them get away with it?" His fingers twitch themselves towards his phoney. He forces a lopsided smile as I pass him his box of tricks.

"I have a magic app. In the *untimely event of my death*. I believe it's time to activate it." His eyes fill with a fierce warmth as his fingers clutch the Smartphone. "This is for all you boys," he says, "and all the girls."

His thumb dances, its final dance. I watch as a series of images and info flash merrily one after the other across the display. First up, mine and Alfi's horrible *You've Been Framed* Jimmy clip – faces of the kids pixilated out – directed to YouTube and shared with several hundred Facebook "Friends". Then, some choice Twitterings to all and sunny.

Next up, names, addresses, photo ID of Chris Primrose, Minister for Urban Development, and top cop Chief Constable Wedderburn, as well as all details of Tenderness House, hacking themselves into what looks like dozens of media, government and police websites. Telling. Telling all. Instantaneous tittle-tat, blabber-mouthing to the whole wide world. Alfi would be so proud. It's what he wanted all along.

Finally, instant imagery of Mad Dog Jackson's sh4nk1 mean machine, sent to every media outlet Virus could find.

All good. All flashing by in the space of seconds.

Virus looks content. He lets the phoney fall from his fingers.

"And Digit?"

"Yes?"

"I'm sorry."

So I smile again, soft for him. And I let him go.

24. GYM-BAGGED

I'm floating. I'm floating up in the blackness, and I can smell the oil and petrol fumes. Floating around in the stinking dark.

I'm dreaming me mother's name. Katariiiiiiina. But not her last name. Not my last name. It's what I were going to do, find me name. Find it, wi' Digit, and wi' Grace. But I lost Grace. Digit's probably dead an' all.

I'm rattling now, bruising me ribs. An engine starts. I'm in Jackson Banks's car. He's driving us away. Away to?

Where? Back where I came from? Back to Tenderness?

Me eyes bust open. Darkness! Me arms wave and me legs kick, but they won't wave and they won't kick, and I yell, I yell me loudest, me voice muffles back at me, and I wiggle and I yell more. But I'm stuffed in a bag. I'm stuffed in a boot. Am I, am I really going back?

Call-Me Norman Newton just won't let us go. It en't fair. He let Grace go, and all t'others. How come I have to go back? I wanted to stay wi' Scarlett and Danny, make them my home. Not Call-Me and the Jimmys.

I'm crying now, en't I, like a little kid, and what 'ud me mam think? She'd think I were a right crybaby. There's no point in it, is there? I need to think instead, and work out what's the best I can do.

I need to use me ears.

First up, Jackson Banks is talking to someone in the front o' the car. No. Not someone. Obnob. Obnob's all he's got left. He's droning on, all about Grace.

"You miss her already, don't you?" he's saying to the dog. "She looked after both of us, didn't she? Proper good, she was. And we had a right laugh, the three of us, didn't we?" And then he adds, "And Crow." Then there's a pause, 'cos he dun't want to talk about Crow, really, does he?

Obnob whimpers. I bet Banks is tickling him behind his ripped-up ear, giving him reassurance.

"She never did as she was told, that was her trouble. You do as you're told – don't you, dog? – and there's no problem. I always did what I got told by Mr Newton and there was no problem. No problem. Do what you're told."

Obnob whimpers again. What Banks dun't get is that Obnob in't his dog any more. He's my dog, in't he? He's only in the car, 'cos I'm in the car. I'm his master now. What the dog hears, I hear.

He's only letting Banks tickle behind his ear 'cos he's too soft-hearted to let him know that he's on his own now. He's got no one.

Banks is sniffling.

"Ohh, we had some laughs," he calls out. "Made some good old messes, me and Grace and you ... and Crow."

There's the sound o' summat smashing. Obnob barks. Banks must have just punched in the dashboard.

"I never meant to!" he wails. "It were just more funnies, weren't it? Squiggle a line on the kid's face – would have only stung for a minute – and then boom boom, on we party. Me and you and Alfi-Crow and Grace. Grace my real true-to-life dolly-girl. She were the best gift I ever got given. Thanks, Mr Governor Call-Me Norman. So much. I never meant to!"

Smash again. Another punch to the dashboard. And again. "Never, no, never! I can't replace her; one of a kind. She – she's all I ever. I would've twisted necks for her, busted up anyone for her."

The car jerks to one side and I bash against the side o' the boot. Someone toots their horn. I can feel the steering going all wobbly, and hear him sobbing in the front, not really steering at all.

"Grace!" *he's wailing.* "My straight and narrow... My bleeding, bloody heart..."

Obnob gives a bark, and there's a soft thud against the seat behind me bag. There's a whimper next to me ear – he's jumped into the backseat, away from the loon, close to me as he can get. Good doggie...

Up front, Banks is punching Hell out of the car. He's mad. But he's right. I'm crying too. How could he do it? Grace were the best thing ever. The best sister, the best mother...

He killed her.

They kill everything good, the Groans.

My mam should never have died.

Or Digit's sisters.

Or Didge.

It's Newton, in't it? Newton and the Jimmys. Destroying everything.

It were Call-Me's lot that turned me into Alfi Spar. And now they're going to bury me back at Tenderness House.

Bookmark this. Here's the Citizen plonked and plumped up in the driver's seat of a spanking Jag. I zig and I zag like a cabbie on laughing gas, hogging *all* the lanes, and the pavement when I need to. Citizen Digit is a natural born roadhog. The North Circular Road ain't never seen anything like it.

Jackson Banks's pimpmobile Bentley is going to have to zoom full throttle to outrace this mean machine.

Virus fired all our shots. But he didn't think it through. Newton is finished and Barry, and Banks is finished as well, and when that penny drops, it's going to be curtains for Alfi too – because the apes are going to go *ape*.

But then again, Virus didn't fire *all* our shots. Citizen Digit is a bullet in a gun, aimed right at the bad guys' heads.

You want to mess with the WhyPees, do you? 'Cos you think we're too weak to fight back? 'Cos we're so small you think you can do what you like to us? Shave our heads and beat us and burn us and feed us to the Jimmymen?

Your mistake, Guvnors.

Jackson's going to take the most direct route back to Tenderness, so all the Citizen gotta do is the same; keep my peepers peeled for a red Bentley with blacked-out windows and SH4NK1 plates. He'll be speedy, but I'll be speediest. JB won't be wanting to be pulled up by the Traffic Sherlocks when he's got Angel-Face stuffed in his boot. Citizen Digit, on the other finger, doesn't give a monkey's hooter. The more Sherlocks chasing my exhaust pipe the merrier.

The Digit don't even bother checking his watch because a) he doesn't have one and b) he's going so fast he's leaving time behind. It's a matter of mere moments before Londinium is left behind too, and we find ourselves jet-fightering up the M1.

Once you're on three lanes, you can chill a little and check the car radio news reports while Top Gearing along. Three or four junctions pass by and then *bingo!* Breaking News: *Scandal that goes to the heart of the Establishment. Maniac on the motorway* (hey, is that him or me?). *Police forces across three counties on high alert.*

I check the rear-view mirror, see if I'm being trailed by any Sherlocks, but there's none behind. The Digit has never needed the Sherlocks, indeedly has spent his entirety avoiding their long arms, and what happens the one day you need them? Nowhere to be seen. *On high alert* indeed. Let's see if I can make this silver machine go a tad faster, find out if I can raise their alertness levels a bit.

Breaking News: *A video has appeared on YouTube, which appears to show Minister Chris Primrose...*

Whoo-hoo! The media's beginning to get up to speed alongside my liberated car and my agitated heart, both roaring along at 100 mph.

...apparently in breach of YouTube's decency code has been taken down...

Decency code. That's been well and truly prised apart by Call-Me and the Jimmys. Is it only now that the Authoritariacs have actually noticed?

...available now, in a censored version, on the Guardian *website. Meanwhile, Chief Constable Wedderburn—*

Ah-hah!

I crane my neck upwards and spot a Heli-Cop hovering over. I'm just thinking this is the final showdown when my peepers clock the media logo on the copter's belly. I see: *literally* Sky News. Makes sense, they're going to get on the case quicker than the old plod.

Citizen Digit needs the police, needs the police, needs the police...

...numberplate SH4NK1. Motorists have been tweeting its location, just north of Junction 27 on the M62. The Transport Minister is advising drivers not *to access social media while dri—*

Hold your horsepower – I've just passed that

junction – and, yes indeedly, there he is ahead. Citizen Digit spots the fleeing villain first. It's the Digit who knows whowhatwherewhenand*how*! JB may well be oblivioned to the attention he's getting from the media, but I seen his eyes. The Mad Dog knows he's gone on one rampage too many.

I slow the Jag, cruising behind him. He's doing a steady hundred in the fast lane, which is just breaking the speed limit enough to *not* get pulled up.

And ta very muchly, I guess Banks has too many voices guffawing round in his head to bother listening to the radio, because all of a sud he's indicating in and slowing up, the fool! He's going to pull into a service station.

Beautilicious: Banks has got all this way – the turning for Tenderness House only a mile or two off – and he's run out of petrol.

I follow suit. This is it. This is my chance. Alfi, I'll save you yet.

I pull up and wait. Banks fills up, twitching and jerking so much he spills more than he fills. He probably thinks the sound of the media-copter is his own head-cogs whirring. He lurches towards the shop.

Paying for anything is against Jackson Banks's religion, but I suppose he's trying – *thinks* he's trying – to keep a low profile. I can see him all red-eyed and sweaty, like he knows he's wiping his bloody boots on Satan's doormat. I clench my fists. Alfi Spar is right there, mere feet away, locked in the boot of the Bentley.

Still no handy Sherlocks hereabouts. Typical.

Okily-doke. I can break into a car boot quicker than any Sherlock anyway.

Keeping my eyeballs on the slow-moving queue, I casualize myself over to the Bentley, dig out my precious magic paperclip and begin to fidget with the lock of the boot.

That's when the Sky News starts to hover lower. I swear I can feel the wind made by the coptor blades stirring the hairs on the back of my neck. The Digit hates to have an audience. Don't film *me*; film the mad psychopath! That's what your viewers want.

I drop the paperclip.

Can you believe it? I'm on my hands and knees trying to spot where it fell with a live audience getting an aerial view of my clumsy butt. And *now* the copter blades are sending a strew of litter across the forecourt. My paperclip'll be blown to Stationery Limbo.

Jackson's reached the front of the queue. I surrender. Leap to my feet, bounce up and down, throw my arms in the air like a waving Mexican. All right already, the whole world is watching me, I might as well make use of it. So I'm sweeping my arms in the direction of the shop, gesticulating and pointing, trying to force the media chopper to focus on Banks – like I'm a bonkers farmer trying to herd clouds.

Dunno if they see him, but he sees *them* all right. I've

never seen him jump before, but he leaps right up in the air like a frog poked with a stick. The roar of the copter is all anybody can hear now, and it's not just JB caught by its noisy windstorm. Everyone else is looking up and pointing too. What's the point in my even trying? *Hello, everybody? Don't look at the chopper – look at the maniac. Over there!* I take my life in my hands and step towards the garage, still pointing and waving at JB, but not a soul is interested.

It's lucky for me that JB is focused on the chopper now too. He falls into a total panic station, the like of which the Digit has never seen. First thing, without taking his eyes off the sky, he makes a mad dash – and runs straight into a trucker eating a sandwich. Sandwich goes flying, but before the trucker can respond, Banks gives him such a look – like he's going to rip his head off – that the bloke backs off.

I hurtle back to his car, gesticulating at the boot where Alfi's locked in. Jumping up and down for the camera, making big arrow signs with my arms and hands. Could I make myself any clearer?

People are noticing Banks now though. They're backing away from him. And he's backing away from them. He looks worse than cornered. You can fight your corner. Here, he's exposed.

He punches himself in the face. Uh-ho. That's how he gathers his wits. He's refocusing himself – staring back at the car. Right where I'm stood.

I duck round the side. There's nowhere for me to go. If he sees me, I'm dead. I'm out of view, but that ain't going to last for long.

I hear JB coming. He's jibber-jabbering like a zombie giving a speech.

Under the car I slide, sandwiched between the tarmac and the frame. I see his boots, stampy-stompy, two feet from my face. He opens the door.

Alfi, I'm sorry.

Jackson laughs, or cries, and slams the door. He starts the engine, stalls it, smashes his fists – *bam! bam!* – against the roof of the car, starts the engine again and roars off.

For half a mo, I'm on a hot beach, lying on the tarmac staring up at the sky blue. Citizen Digit reckons he could stay like this for quite a while, in restfulness. Golden sands. Sky News up above, taking pics. Holiday snaps for the folks back home.

'Cept I ain't on holiday yet. Up I leap and wave my arms to all my adoring fans. If I'm going to be Hi-Vis, I might as well be Maxi-Hi Vis. Being in the company of Alfi Spar-Face has finally made me surrender the last of my power of invisibility. Thanks, pal; the whole world is Googling me now.

So I do the Digit Dance across the forecourt –let's be worth seeing. Lookie here, viewers! See the Good Citizen dance!

Ten spins, a shuffle and a bow-wow later, I look

up to see Sky News is joined by passing friends. Heli-Cops. Two of them. Circling overhead like vultures over roadkill.

Peeps pointing, and I see a Traffic Sherlock gawping my way, chinwagging his radio.

I make straight for my own wheels. I leap in, hotwire the engine and I'm away. Two Sherlockmobiles pull into the forecourt behind me. As I whizz away, their lights start to flash. I accelerate, and they accelerate, and JB on the motoroad ahead accelerates, and the Heli-Cops buzz down low, tracking the both of us. The game has reached the Highest Level.

Now the Digit has to really put his foot down. One hundred and twenty mph and rising, rising, rising. I could smash right into the back of Jackson's boot, if it wasn't filled with a skinny, all-too-snappable Spar-Boy.

And one of the Sherlocks is on my own tail, threatening my very own booty. Oh, you want a race, do you? Formula 140. Second Sherlockmobile drawing up alongside, and passenger Sherlock actually pointing a camera my way. Smile, please! I give 'em my cheesiest.

Two more Sherlocks revving up behind us. The speed dial goes where it's never gone before, and the steering wheel starts to vibrate like the ferocity is threatening to make the whole car go BANG!

The Sky copter is so low it looks like it's trying to land on JB's roof rack. The other side of the motoroad is suddenly empty, like the Sherlocks have blocked all the traffic, and sure enough our own three lanes are filled with nothing but flashing cop cars.

All of a sud, Jackson swerves left, ramming the Sherlocks, sending their wheels skidoodling over the hard shoulder and whizzbanging onto the soft verge.

But then another Sherlockmobile comes up and rams Jackson's car, and he rams it back and it all goes a bit *biff baff boom*. I wish they'd have a care, on account of the flesh-and-blood luggage in the boot. Best I can do is tail close as I can, so the Sherlocks can't squeeze in behind JB and give Alfi an ugly shunting.

Ooof! Now it's *me* who's getting rammed. Not having that, am I? So I ram 'em straight back.

Jackson Banks knows he can't escape. He can torch his own HQ, try and cremate Grace out of evidence's way. He can give Virus the kind of sending-off he don't actually deserve. And he thinks he can bundle Alfi back to Tenderness House, where he'll be locked up and Jimmyfied. But none of this is of any use when he's surrounded by Traffic Sherlocks with a Heli-Cop – *two* Heli-Cops now – dropping on his bonce.

I pull up alongside. I toot my horn and turn my head. Jackson looks at me and his jaw drops. I am dead. I am the Avenger Angel. *You thought you killed me?* I am back, for my sisters, and for Grace.

The colour fades from his face as he sees me, his unholy ghost. He frowns, puzzling it. He puts his head back, and opens his mouth and lets loose his terror.

He is finished.

So what does he do? He floors it. He zooms forward, swerves the Bentley left, edging tight into the hard shoulder, notches up the speed, and swerves back right. He's heading straight for the central crash barrier. He's planning to break through into Southbound.

And just like that, the chase stops.

I didn't think it through.

Jackson's car smashes up off the barrier, rolls, over and over, crumples and smokes. He has a tank full of fuel. Two hundred metres down the other side of the road, it comes to a wrecked, awful, stop. For a second, it sits there.

Then, it explodes.

25. NAMED

Ain't nobody surviving a fireball like that.

I pull up. I get out. All the Sherlocks in their cars do the same. The Heli-Cops land on the other carriageway. We all stand there and stare at the flames.

The car and everything in it, incinerating up into the blue sky. It's a media free-for-all. Cameramen crawling out of the roadworks. It's time for the Citizen to disappear again.

I zombie-walk over to the hard shoulder, clamber the barrier and slip down the embankment. Out of Sherlock view, I walk on for twenty minutes or so, then I make my way west, through a farmer's field. This territory is beginning to feel familiar. I ghost onwards, and after a while I come to a village. Villages are quiet, peaceful. I always used to wonder what people did all day. Now I get it. They don't do nothing. They just *be*. I suppose, right now, there's a certain appeal. I'm so tired all of a sud.

Alfi lived in a village, once. He had a happy foster family, and he used to do nothing as well. He liked that, just being. He told me he used to bake cakes.

So very, very tired. But Citizen Digit is not finished yet. Not quite. There's a bike leaning outside the village shop. It's chained, but it's the sort of lock the Digit can open just by staring at it. Thirty seconds later I'm pedalling away up the road.

I never thought I'd find myself voluntarily going back to Tenderness House. But this time, before he does a stretch in a Relaxation Room of his own, I want to give Norman Newton a *talking to*. Let my fingers do the talking. I'm normally a passive-fist, but my fingers are itching, just this once, to have a pop at his nosebone, knowing I've got Long Arms a stretch or two behind me. I'm all a-clench, thinking of the *crack* as his hooter snaps out of shape.

I stop at the perimeter fence and let the bike fall to the ground. I glance at the driveway. No police cars, so I guess they're yet to arrive. Suits me. Once I find my way in, I'm heading straight for Call-Me's office. Going to shove his face full of Bourbons.

Rest of Tenderness House is in afternoon lessons, which is just how I like it. I'm planning to surprise him. Go round the back, slip through his Party Lounge, sneak up through the adjoining corridor, pounce like a cat on a rat.

Alfi told me about the escape hole he made in the fence when he liberated himself. I hunt around, find it. I squeeze through. It's a tight fit. I guess I must be growing big.

Growing. Something that Alfi Spar is never going to do.

My trouser pocket snags on a loose wire, and I'm having to wiggle to get myself free.

"Citizen Digit," says a voice, up above me. "I should have guessed."

I feel the car slowing to a halt and then the engine stop. Where are we? Door opens and I hear the petrol cap pop. He's filling up – it's a petrol station. Yes! He'll have to go and pay. It's now or never. Digit reckoned I'm totally useless in any kind o' dangerous situation, but what he never knew is that Alfi Spar's got some skills of his own. What'd he think I did wi' me life when he wan't around to muck it up for us?

Digit, you'd be impressed wi' this, you would. This Great Escape is for you. First up, unzipping the gym bag is a doddle. You just need that little gap where it zips up, waggle your finger in, then, slowly slowly, tooth by tooth, ease it open. Once you can get a hand out it's just a case o' feeling round and finding the outside zipper, and then you're free.

Did you know, Didge, that the bit between a boot and the back seat of a car is – with a bit of elbow grease – completely removable?

Ladles and Gentlespoons, applause, please.

Obnob's been snuffling and whining in the back seat, and Jackson Banks probably reckons he'd have me nose off as soon as I stick me head through.

But it's Banks who'd bite a chunk out o' me face if he found us.

Don't care. Stick me head out o' the bag anyway.

Free.

Straight away the dog starts yapping with excitement. It's a giveaway. Me legs go rubber and I'm gonna mess me pants. Clamber back. Faint. Go under. Shut your eyes. Curl up.

Digit 'ud be rolling his eyes. He never had no fear. I've got to. I've got to do it, for him, and for Grace.

So I stick me head through to the seats. Instead o' biting me ears off like Jackson planned, Obnob starts licking me face.

I look through the window and see Jackson Banks walking towards the service-station shop. I slump again, wi' relief.

Rouse yourself, Blabber-Boy!

Split-second decision. Take Obnob with us. He shun't be with an animal like Jackson Banks. I put the seat back, open the door and the two of us go for it.

We run, fast as we can, to the back part o' the services. Push on. Sorry, Didge, I en't stopping for no bragging about me skills or displays of invisibility. I en't an entertainer like you was. I'm running for me life. Me and Obnob, straight round the back, away from that killer before he gets back and finds me and his dog gone.

Back road at the services turns into a country lane,

dunno where to, dunno how long, but we run and we run, as fast and as far away as possible. Lane is going up a hill, and it's good, is that. Me and Obnob stretch our legs, fill our lungs, leaving the car fumes behind. We run and we puff and our blood pumps. Up and up, and when we get to the top, we stop, and I turn round and I look back down.

No one after us. Obnob lies down, getting back his breath. Me too, great lungfuls of it. I can taste the countryside.

Obnob spots summat and gives a bark. A humming noise gets louder and I see it's a helicopter, and another helicopter, and they're hovering low, over the services. Were they there all the time? Squinting me eyes, I think I can spot Jackson Banks's car, speeding off, and I watch as it all unfolds.

It en't real. It's a proper high-speed chase, wi' the motorway shut down and flashing lights and sirens blaring. Somehow or other, they've cottoned on to the psycho-man, and they're after him, a zillion police cars. Me and Obnob have a bird's-eye view.

It should be peaceful up here, but there's nowt but sirens and helicopters and beeping horns, and all of a sudden there's a giant bang, and a great fireball and a whole load o' smoke. It's Jackson Banks's car, flipped, exploded.

Everything stops still and it's quiet again, just smoke rising up into the clouds, and a load o' police, standing and watching.

He can't hurt us any more, can he? He can't, can he?

It's all so dumb.

But I'm glad me and Obnob got out o' that car. We've got stuff to do with our lives. I have, leastways. I put me hand down, tickle the back o' the dog's neck. He were watching the fireball down below, like he were trying to figure out what it meant to him. When me fingers touch his fur, it's like me fingertips are passing on the understanding to him. He knows. His old master is dead. He's a free dog.

Listen. Birdsong. A cow mooing somewhere near by. A breeze rustling through the trees. It's the countryside, in't it? So we turn our backs on the deadly motorway, me and me dog, and we start walking.

Walking. Away from the cars and the people and the buildings and the noise and the nastiness. Walking, into the lanes wi' the hedges and trees and sheep and birds and the good times.

It's grand, strolling round, just me and the dog, all peaceful and free, till I realize where I am. I know these roads. I were right, weren't I? Banks were taking me back to Tenderness House.

What should I do?

Before I can figure it out, a bloke in a milk float stops and offers us a lift. He says he shouldn't really give a lift to a dog, 'cos o' food regulations, but he's on his way home for the afternoon, and he's got a dog just like Obnob, so he can't drive by and leave us hiking.

"It's a lovely dog you've got there, lad," he says. "You're dead lucky."

Is he a Jimmy?

He surprises the life out o' me, wi' what he says next.

"It en't safe for lads like you round here, anyway."

He sees the look on me face, and goes on. "Have you not heard the news? Never known owt like it. Pervert central. It'll not be long before these little roads'll be jammed wi' police and TV folk. It's all over t'internet."

I dunno what me face must look like. Amazed, I suppose.

"They're going mad over it on Twitter." He looks at me, wide-eyed. "Ee lad, you need to keep up."

I can't believe it. Did Citizen Digit do it? Did he really beat them? Beat the Jimmys, just like he promised? I wish he were around to enjoy it.

He said Mr Virus thought I should go back, din't he, to Tenderness? Banks were taking me back there too, like Tenderness House is where I really belong. I were running as far from that place as I could get. But wi' Digit and Mr Virus exploding the evidence in all sorts of places on the internet, Call-Me Norman's got nowhere to hide now.

So I know what I've got to do. I'm dead close; it en't far. I'm going to get back to Tenderness. Now. Before the police take Norman Newton away. I'm going to get to him first.

It's time I had some answers.

The milkman drops us off at the village nearest to Tenderness, so we walk it from here, me and me dog. It's so different to London. Instead of the roar of traffic and the stink of rot from all the rubbish, there's the sound of silence – just a twittering o' birdsong in the background – and the smell o' good, honest, fresh air. It reminds me o' when I used to go walking wi' Doug. He had a pair o' binoculars and one day he bought me a pair an' all. In the springtime we used to go birdwatching. We'd spot the nests up in the trees, and see if we could see the chicks, their heads poking up when the mummy birds returned wi' worms. They had fluffy hair and great big mouths. Doug said they reminded him o' me. We'd walk for hours, just like now. Obnob's zigging and zagging all along the little roads, catching a million scents and making mad dashes at the sparrows and bluetits. I bet he's never seen the countryside before.

The air is crisper here, fresh and clean. I could spend all day wandering through the fields. Me and Doug saw a dead mole once. It must have had a little heart attack or summat, 'cos there wan't a mark on it, and its fur were all shiny like velvet. It had little legs wi' huge claws for digging, and a long snout for snuffling worms. I seen an owl once an' all; flew right past me head. And bats, fluttering after midges at dusk. I love animals; they just get on with it, don't have to go making a mess o' things like folk do.

Funny, in't it, the way they stuck Tenderness House smack bang in the middle of all this peace and quiet?

At the perimeter fence I find the old escape hole, and squeeze meself through it. It's a tight fit. I'm growing.

I'm going to confront Call-Me Norman. He knows who me mam was. He knows, but he never told.

I'm going to have the truth.

Obnob gives a bark and I stop. Dog is looking back behind us, gives another bark. I turn round, look back towards the fence.

Citizen Digit!

Alfi Spar!

"Blabber-Boy! You're supposed to be dead!"

He looks as gobsmacked as I feel, but he gives a little shrug, trying to pretend escaping from fiery doom is as piffly a deal as it would have been for the Citizen.

I unhook the wire from my trousers and scramble up onto my dignity.

Alfi Spar. It ain't usually in the Digit's Comfy Zone, but I find myself in a hug. He smells of dog fur and petrol cans. The dog is dancing round our legs. And the two of us are laughing, giggling, shoulder-punching, trying to lift each other off our feet.

"How did you...?" he says.

"I was feigning, wasn't I? Give the boy an Oscar!"

He rolls his eyes at that and points at my face. "You've still got a proper black eye, though."

"Yeah, well –" full of humbliness "– I suppose his fist was real enough." Then I'm throwing Alfi over-excited *how-did-you*? hands.

He tries that casual shrug again and says, "Harry Houdini, Escapologist Extraordinaire."

What a dingbat.

Then his eyes brighten even more and he throws me a look, of sparkle and hope. But the bright blue hope darkens half a mo later, and he looks down at his feet.

I know what he was going to ask. If I'm alive, if he's alive, maybe Grace is good too? What a ridiculous hope.

I put my hands on his shoulders. "We're all good," I say. "All of us."

I thought I'd lost them all. After losing me mam, and Doug and Jenny, and Scarlett and Danny – Citizen Digit and Grace were the only family I had left.

All of a sudden I've got me life back. Digit tells me everything, all in mad, scatter-dash Digit speak. Me ears are taking it in, but all I really know is that he's in front o' me, throwing his silly poses as he tells us his story.

We look like a couple o' loonies, leaping about like we've escaped from a prisoner of war camp, when we've actually broken back in. We're cut and bruised and half killed and we stink of Jackson Banks's hands. It's so horrible, we can't stop laughing.

But we do stop. There's a silence. An eerie stillness. We turn and stare at the back of Norman Newton's block, the room where they have their parties, and our eyes meet, and he puts his hand on me shoulder again, and it's time.

I force the window and we climb into the Jimmys' stinking den. It's empty, but the door leading to Call-Me's office is ajar. The widescreen TV is switched on.

But it's not screening filth, like before. It's me, Visible Didge, and the fireball on the motorway. It's News24. It's Primrose's face, and Wedderburn, and the rest of the Jimmymen. We're all famous now. We stand for a moment, watching, as the reports shift to the earlier scene at the service station. JB's pimpmobile, the car door opening and a boy and a dog emerging and running off over the verge. The bird's-eye view, tracking Jackson, me making road angels on the forecourt, and the chase, and the fireball...

And there's Call-Me's face. In all its widescreen gory.

Alfi's face twists into an ugly sneer. He ain't an Angel-Face no more.

Through the end of the corridor we can hear shuffling and slamming, like somebody's opening drawers and cabinets and dropping boxes and rummaging, insaniac rummaging.

Obnob starts growling like a disgruntled lion. Alfi is stomping forwards into the corridor. The Citizen marches after them.

We stop outside Call-Me's door, take our breath, and then I kick that door wide open.

Door bursts open with a loud *crack*, slamming against its hinges and bouncing back at us. Alfi gives it a final shove, punching at it with his fist, and Obnob pounces in, blood-hungry. Me and Alfi lock eyes, and follow.

Call-Me cowers against his desk.

Obnob's ripping and tearing at his trouser leg.

Alfi Spar jabs his finger at Norman Newton's face, as self-righteous as ever. Call-Me whimpers and pleads with us to call off the dog.

Alfi roars over the top of him. "Who's my mother? Who is she? You tell us. You tell us, or I'll set the dog on you good and proper!"

Oooh. The Digit's going to enjoy this.

"All right! All right! Call off the dog. Call it off!" Not taking his eyes off the crazy canine making rags of his strides.

I glance around. There's paperwork everywhere. The shredder's gone into overdrive. And it looks like he's taken a hammer to his Mac and his laptop. There's burning paper in the waste bin. The man's been busy.

Alfi clicks his fingers. "Heel, boy."

Obnob only goes and sits a-peaceful next to Alfi's leg. It's a doggie miracle.

"Hello, Byron," says Newton, trying to gather himself together. "Hello, Alfi. You know that entering without knocking is a breach of the rules." He shakes his leg. "As is keeping pets on the premises."

He's sweating it, ain't he? Struggling to appear calm, trying to regain control. "Can't say it's a pleasure to see you again, Byron."

Citizen Digit takes a seat, trying to figure out the situation. Alfi stays standing, watching as Obnob growls and drools at Call-Me's tasty limbs.

"The Sherlocks are on their way," I comment, endeavouring to be all nonshalonse.

"Well, I think that's pretty obvious," says Call-Me, "following your and Mr Virus's media news storm bursting overhead. You wouldn't be here if you didn't have a good deal more back-up than that bloody animal. But do you know what?"

"What?"

"Alfi wouldn't order it to attack. Would you, Alfi?"

Alfi says nothing. I'm of the personal belief that, yes, indeedly, he would.

Newton snarls. "And do you know why?"

I think he's off his rocker.

"Alfi." He turns to my friend. "Do you know why? Why you wouldn't hurt poor old Norman?"

For once, Alfi Spar's keeping his squealer-slot zipped. Call-Me looks back in my direction. "You came storming in here like you own the place." Then he snaps his eyes back to Alfi. "Look at me, boy. You see, Alfi, in a way, you *do* own the place, don't you?"

Alfi's got a look on his fizzog like I never seen before. His baby blues have a steely glint.

Call-Me gestures around the ruin of a room. "Go on. Feel free. Explore. Consider it all yours."

I'm at a bit of an oddness as to what to do. How come Newton is suddenly so calm? How come he's making like he still holds the final cardie? Alfi looks livid, like he'd give Obnob the "kill" instruction at the drop of a hat.

"We've got files on Tenderness that go all the way back to its early days," Call-Me continues. He points to a filing cabinet tucked in the corner of the office. "Files on all the residents, going way back. We've even got the details of kids that were with us, say, fifteen years ago, when we were based down south. In London."

"What's this got to do with Alfi?" The Good Citizen has lost his fine articularity.

"Everything. So, Alfi, you want to find your mama. Go on, boy. Open that bottom drawer."

I get it. The answer was here all along. "Her file," I say. "Katariina."

I look over. The bottom drawer of the cabinet is the only bit of office that hasn't been ransacked. Like Call-Me was keeping it, just for us. Or for himself.

"Katariina," repeats Norman Newton, with a sigh, like he's remembering a particularly fine meal. "Look under *K*, for Kasparek. You always wanted to know your mother's last name, didn't you, Alfi?"

Alfi looks like he's been zapped to the max.

"Alfi," he says. "Alfi … Kasparek."

He's frozen in time. The Digit coughs sharply, brings him back to the here and now. "Go on," I prompt him. "Go look."

But Alfi won't take his peepers off Norman Newton.

Obnob is on constant snarl. Besides that, no one moves, or speaks.

There they both are, eyeballing at each other like

cats building up to a fight. I feel like I'm an intruder.

"All right," says I, "I'll go look, shall I?"

So I go to the filing cabinet, and I find the file – well, it's more of a single sheet, really, and I put it on top of the desk in front of Alfi. There's a photo of her. It's uncanny. Alfi looks just like her, except for the eyes.

"Katariina Kasparek," mutters Alfi, still trapped in his trance.

In the distance, I can hear the sound of approaching choppers. Call-Me is almost out of time.

"You kept it from us. All these years." Alfi's trembling now, as he picks up his mother's photo.

"Well," says Call-Me, "if you'd used the brains you were born with, maybe you'd have figured it all out. She did tell you, after all. *Alfi*."

Call-Me's eyes shift down to the point on his desk where his brass nameplate sits so proudly.

Governor Norman *A.* Newton.

I don't understand.

"Ever wondered what the *A* stood for? Your mother always intended you to know who your father was. *Alfi*."

"You?" says Alfi.

"Me," he whispers.

I think it's what you call a *dawning horror*. It's been a woeful week for Citizen Digit and I'm fumbling with the last pieces of the puzzle. Of course. Norman Newton hasn't just set up the Jimmy ring in recent times. He's always been at it. And Virus knew – from the moment

I first dragged Alfi, pongy and famished, up the *Cash Counters* stairs.

In my head, I'm putting it all together.

Norman Newton abused Alfi's mother, like he did with all his *favourites*.

That explains why he was always so creepy towards Alfi. Because Call-Me knew all along. That Alfi is his son. It makes you wonder what she was feeling, when she underlined his name and dotted the *i*...

"You'll understand why the baby – you – had to be taken straight into care. Katie – your mum – she was very unwell. Some colleagues took her away, as far as was sensible. There were problems then with ... some administrative staff, and I had to move, up to the north. I – I don't know if she survived." Alfi's hand holding the photo is trembling all the more. I look at his eyes. A rage is building. Call-Me goes on. "She was a lovely girl, your mum."

I'm sick. Alfi's mum was never a prostitute at all. She was just another kid, like us.

"So now you know," he continues. "I hope you're happy." He shoots a look at me. "You've ruined me. The pair of you."

The choppers, louder now, and sirens. Alfi's face, twisting in pain.

"You had to know it all, Alfi, didn't you? Well, now you do. Son."

*

I look like her. In the picture, she's the same age as I am now. She's got long blonde hair, round clear eyes. She looks dead young and scared. A kid. They must o' taken this photo when she arrived at the care home. Before Norman Newton...

All this time, he hid her from us.

I look at him. Me father. I see it now. It's his eyes. My eyes.

I don't get it. Me mam were just another kid. Just like all them other kids, lads and lasses, in the film Digit made. That lad Sniper, all of 'em. And me mam. Just nowt. Worthless. Nothing to him. All these years, and he's still doing it.

"Why?"

What a stupid question.

"Why?" *I yell it again. What else can I say? Why? Why?*

"It's just..." *He dun't know what to say, does he?* "When you're grown-up, you'll understand. Sex. It's – it's what grown-ups do. It's how it is."

"Not with kids!" *Byron snaps.* "Not with us!"

"Doug never!" *I say.*

"Doug?"

"And Danny wun't. You're a liar." *I look at Byron.* "Tell him, Byron."

"Virus never." *It's all he says. But he's right.*

"Virus is a freak," *says Newton.* "In the real world, there's sex everywhere. Don't tell me you've not seen it. On the internet. Porn sites. Sex clubs—"

"Not with kids," *I say.* "Not with kids!"

This is my dad. He takes a step forward. "Not you, Alfi." He'd reach out towards us, but Obnob gives a warning snarl and he steps back. "I'd never have let any of them touch you."

I feel sick. "Just all the others," I say. "Sniper and the rest of 'em."

Newton's sweating. He dun't look at us no more, glancing from side to side.

"You're my son," he says to me. "I love you."

I can't hardly stand to hear it. But I say, "I'm only your son because—" I have to swallow hard. I en't sure I can get the words out, but I have to. I have to say it. "Because, when she was the same age I am now, you forced my mother. You raped her."

It hangs in the air. The shame. He says, feebly, "I am your father."

I think of Doug. How much I miss him. And all the time, I've got this man in front of us. He gave me nowt apart from his eyes, and this: this horrible knowledge.

"You're nobody's father," I say.

Then the door crashes wide open, and Barry is there, and he's got a great big baseball bat, and he's swinging it right at me head.

I reckon Barry's been waiting for this moment for years. But he ain't going to have satisfaction, because Obnob's been waiting for his moment too.

It's uglification. Beast gets his gnashers into Barry's

wrist and I swear he's going to bite his hand right off, shaking and snarfling worse than I ever heard before. Baseball bat drops to the ground and Barry starts screaming like the cowardyguts he really is. That ain't enough for Obnob though, is it? He lets go of Barry's wrist and leaps at his face.

His ugly mug's about to get a lot uglier. I turn away.

Through the window I see the blue sirens of the first police car pulling up.

"Obnob," says Alfi.

The dog heeds his master, stops short of removing Barry's nose. Sits over him, lips curled, fangs glistening.

I clock Newton doing a swift about-turn, towards the corridor leading to his Jimmy den. The back exit.

Citizen Digit ain't a one for violence himself, but I break the habit of a lifetime and orchestrate a physical intervention. That is, I stick out my foot.

It's a wonderful sight to behold, Governor Newton flying flat out, buffing his head against his desk as he falls, sending his ashtray flying, all the stubs and ash puffing up like it's his own funeral pyre, his pack of Bourbons crunching to crumbs beneath him.

Behind me, Obnob sits guard on Barry's chest, growling and drooling.

A gang of Sherlocks bursts in through the door.

We've won.

*

What I'm really looking at, what's really in front of us, is what I've been searching for, for as long as I can remember.

Me mam.

Her face. Her face in her picture, not really any older than me. That's all that counts. There's nowt else in the room.

Me eyes are poring over her file. Her date o' birth. I know her birthday. It has her height and her weight, and her face. I can't stop looking at her face.

The police pile in through the entrance, and I fold up me mam's file, and I tuck it away, next to me birth certificate. No one's taking this away from us.

I look around for Citizen Digit, but he's nowhere to be seen. He's gone. First sign o' the law, and he's vanished.

26. HOME

Egg, bacon, sausage, mushroom and chips, wi' beans on toast (done proper, as described previously). It's the only meal that Danny knows how to cook, but if you can make this you don't really need owt else, do you?

Iggy has his own fried egg. I've never known a dog that only eats people food, whether it's toast or vindaloo.

This is me fifth week wi' Scarlett and Danny. And I en't an Emergency any more. I'd thought it were another good home I'd messed up. When I went back to 'em it were a right state. I used all me best woodworking skills to help wi' fixing stuff, even if I weren't much cop at it, but I needn't have worried. Summat changed. Maybe it were 'cos of all the stuff on the TV about what happened, but they din't want to let me go back either. Scarlett has had a million meetings wi' Social Services, and they've sorted out having us stay here for good. Permanent. I've never been permanent before.

Scarlett and Danny play loads o' weird music and you have to yell when you're chatting. It's noisier than I'm used to, but Iggy sleeps on me lap any chance he gets. We're always having a laugh.

We went to a print shop and we got the old photo o' me mam blown up into giant size, and then we got it laminated, so it'll never get torn or stained, and I've got it pinned up on the wall o' me room.

Scarlett and Danny even bought us a laptop, and we've been using it to try and find out if me mam is still alive or not. She might be. Which means she could be out there, anywhere. With a laptop you can find owt, anyone – just like Citizen Digit allus reckoned.

Plus, I've got Grand Theft Auto.

Course, I know where me father is. He's in prison, along wi' all them others. The copper and the MP and all the rest o' that mob. It kept coming up on the news all the time, until Scarlett and Danny stopped us watching any more. I could visit him anytime I like. But why would I?

Danny makes a much better dad than Norman Newton. And Scarlett is a pretty good mam. If we ever find me real mam, I reckon I'll be dead lucky because then I'll have two mams. After all this time.

Grace comes and visits every week as well. She were in hospital for a while, but she's all right now. She's started making dresses, to sell on the market – Scarlett bought one, says it's just her style.

Grace is sitting across the table from us right now, waiting for Danny to dish up that perfect scran. She's showing us how you can balance a spoon off the end of your nose. She's got all sorts o' tricks up her sleeve, has Grace.

I even miss Mr Virus, a little bit. I'm sorry that he

were killed. He'd have made a horrible dad though. Can you imagine, worrying about getting zapped all the time? I reckon he needed a pet dog, to help bring out his nicer side.

Obnob gets looked after by Grace, but he dun't come to visit with her, 'cos of what he did to Patti. Grace says he goes to doggie training class. He's getting rehabilitated.

Grace tells me that Social Services have been doing their best to try and farm out all t'other Tenderness lads and lasses to good homes too, like Scarlett and Danny's.

But I en't seen or heard a whisper o' Citizen Digit, not from the moment the cops turned up at Tenderness House. Course, the footage of him doing the Digit Dance across the sevice station forecourt has gone viral. When the Jimmys got broken up, he was the hero of the hour, on all the news reports.

Who Is This Mystery Boy?

But no one knew. Or no one 'ud say. Of them that did know him, Virus were dead, Banks were dead, me father weren't in any position to go talking, locked up as an evil Jimmy ringleader, and Grace were as solid as a rock. As for me? I kept me mouth shut.

Only Barry blabbed about Digit really being Byron. So Social Services checked the Tenderness House records, and all they found were

Blank Space.

Turns out you can't find Byron Blank Space *anywhere online either. Mr Virus helped wi' that, I reckon.*

So the Citizen achieved his Total Disappearing Act, exactly as he'd always planned.

Even so, I keep checking me Facebook page 'cos I'm sure that when he's ready, one way or another, he'll be in touch. No doubt bringing all kinds o' trouble with him.

It's funny, in't it? It turned out that Citizen Digit – Byron – was me best mate after all.

And so the Good Citizen must take his final bow-wow, and leave you with clap-happy memories of the villainous getting force-fed their just desserts and the pure of heart getting their beans on toast.

Not a search engine in the world can find Byron now. All you'll get is YouTube footage of Visible Digit dancing on a service station forecourt, before vanishing into the ether.

It was a wrench, naturellement, leaving behind the gorgeous Grace, but as the good books say: things to do, places to go. It may well be satisfaction for Alfi Kasparek to get his clod-hoppers under the table, and the family he always yearned for. But such a life ain't for Lone Strangers such as myself. Not for Citizen Digit enforced schooldays five times a week, evening curfews, followed by student loans and a suit and tie-me-up desk job.

After all, ain't there new scams to be pulled and fresh purses to be lifted?

And is it not the case that the Great Manager Virus kept his treasure trove of savings in a safebox of genuine inflammability? And when the evil monsterosity Jackson Banks met his Guy Fawkes on the road, that said life-savings remained unsinged on the flaming passenger seat next to him? And that, wrapping himself in his well-worn cloak of invisibility, the Master Storyteller and Rescuer of Young Awfuns returned to the cordoned off crime scene, and with all media eyes and Sherlock noses pointed in the direction of Tenderness House, his heart a-pounding to its own drumbeat, performed his Greatest, Most Stealthy Feat of Derring-Do since lifting that TV in Oxford Street's broad, busy daylight?

Surfing the heart-stomp. Wotta buzz.

Yes, indeedly. For my story – spectacular marvellosity as it was – does not end here. Citizen Digit is back on the road. Where? That's for you to guesstimate. To do what? You're just going to have to wait and see.

But believe this: when I do reappear, dearest reader, you will not see me coming.

Enjoyed this book? Tweet us your thoughts:

#NobodySaw @WalkerBooksUK @stevetasane

ACKNOWLEDGEMENTS

Thanks are due – overdue – to my agent, James Catchpole. I feel like the luckiest writer in the land to have him as a creative partner and Man of Great Wisdom. I'm additionally lucky to have such a great team at Walker Books, in particular my editors Lucy Earley and Emily Lamm.

Nobody Saw No One was inspired by my time as writer-in-residence for Dickens 2012, and I'd like to thank the Dickens 2012 team, especially Portsmouth's then Head of Literature, Dom Kippin.

I would like to warmly thank Arts Council South East and the National Lottery for a generous Grant for the Arts, which enabled me to complete this book, and *get it right*.

STEVE TASANE is a writer and performance poet. He has been writer-in-residence at the V&A Museum of Childhood, the Dickens Bicentennial Celebrations and Maidstone United Football Club, as well as performing at Glastonbury, and on TV and radio.

His debut novel for young adults, *Blood Donors*, was included in Seven Stories' Diverse Voices list of the best children's books celebrating cultural diversity from 1950 to the present day.

Steve's poetry and stories have been widely published in anthologies, including *How To Be A Boy* and the solo collection *Bleeding Heart*. He says, "Everything I've learnt in life – about People and Animals and Love and Hate – goes into what I write."

For more about Steve's writing, including links to poems on YouTube, visit stevetasane.wordpress.com

PEOPLES KEEP DYIN' IN THE FINGER,

the scuzzie old tower block where they put us antisociable families. Authorities say it dirty smack goin' round, but them bodies ain't all users ... an' they look like they die screamin'.

Marshall O'Connor the First lives in the Finger with his mum and li'l bro. His dad's in prison, school kicked him out, and the bedbugs are drivin' him <u>crazy</u>.

True, Marsh got himself some issues. But it ain't the drugs that peoples should be worryin' about, 'cos them bloodsuckin' bugs have grown some, and they ready for a bigger feed...

"DISTINCTIVE, FRESH AND DECIDEDLY CREEPY"
— *GUARDIAN*

"NIGHTMARISH AND UTTERLY CONVINCING"
— *ANTHONY McGOWAN*

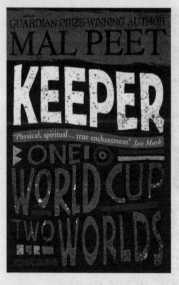

**WINNER OF THE
BRANFORD BOASE AWARD**

In a newspaper office, Paul Faustino, South America's top sports journalist, sits opposite the man they call El Gato – the Cat – the world's greatest goalkeeper. On the table between them stands the World Cup…

In the hours that follow, El Gato tells his incredible life story – how he, a poor logger's son, learns to become a World Cup-winning goalkeeper. And the most remarkable part of this story is the man who teaches him – the mysterious Keeper, who haunts a football pitch at the heart of the claustrophobic forest.

"Mal Peet [takes] the football novel into a new league."

Guardian

"A remarkable and absorbing story with football at its heart, but superb storytelling in its soul."

Branford Boase Award panel

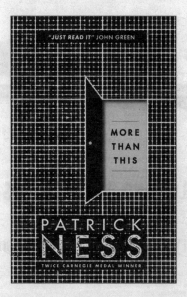

**A boy drowns, desperate and alone
in his final moments. He *dies*.**

**Then he wakes, naked and bruised
and thirsty, but *alive*.**

**How can this be? And what is this strange,
deserted place?**

**As he struggles to understand what is happening,
the boy dares to hope. Might this not be the end?
Might there be more to this life,
or perhaps this afterlife?**

From the multi-award-winning Patrick Ness comes one
of the most provocative and moving novels of our time.

"Patrick Ness is an insanely beautiful writer"
John Green

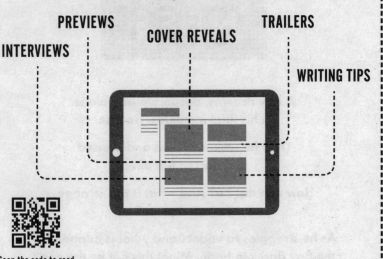